HE TRIED TO EXPLAIN IT. TO HER, AND TO HIMSELF.

"If you'll accept the possibility of a man loving two women, then I love you. I wanted you—and what you represent. For a long while I've had the awful feeling that time was passing me by, that life was becoming so damned predictable. But I would never have deliberately created this situation—by myself."

He reached out for her. "We're both, in our separate ways, going to regret this, I suppose. But in many other ways, I hope we'll be glad."

She nodded with a jerky abruptness, not looking at him. "Stay with me now," she half whispered, her voice raw with tears, "and we'll both know it's the last time. Then leave me without saying anything. Just don't let me think this was cheap."

He shook his head. "It hasn't been."

And at that moment, they both believed that what they were saying would always be true. . . .

Fawcett Books
by *John D. MacDonald:*

JOHN D.
MacDONALD

THE
DECEIVERS

FAWCETT GOLD MEDAL • NEW YORK

THE
DECEIVERS

The new County Memorial Hospital was just beyond the eastern edge of the city of Hillton. It had been opened less than a year ago, a four story, U shaped structure of pale tan stone with aluminum trim, curving walks, plantings, a large asphalted parking area. It was in pleasant country of rolling hills, spangled with the bright colors of the ranch types and split levels of the middle income housing developments that had grown up since the war. The hospital itself was a half mile from a long climbing curve of the six lane turnpike that had been opened in 1955.

Carl Garrett had told himself, and told Joan—possibly too many times—that it certainly would be a lot more pleasant for her in the new hospital than down in the dingy old red brick structure on Gollmer Street in the middle of the city. At County Memorial she would only be a little over a mile and a half from home.

Sunday, the fourteenth day of July, was a most peculiar day for them. Dr. Bernie Madden, family doctor and family friend, had confirmed the presence of ovarian tumors large enough to merit removal back in April, and he had agreed that July would be soon enough, when both Kip and Nancy would be away at summer camp for six weeks.

On the first of July they had driven the kids sixty miles into the mountains to Lake Muriel, depositing Kip at Wayna-ko on one side of the lake, and Nancy at Sar-ay-na on the other side, both camps under the same ownership and general management.

Kip, at fifteen, was returning to Way-na-ko for his third summer, and was consequently very blasé about the whole thing, yet barely able to conceal his eagerness to meet the choice friends of previous summers. It was Nancy's first summer away from home. She was thirteen. Kip, as the deadline for departure came closer, had alternated between a patronizing and superior attitude, and filling her with horrendous and disturbing lies about the treatment and facilities at Sar-ay-na. Nancy was both enormously excited and nervously apprehensive about the whole situation. She had packed and repacked an astonishing number of times, vacillating between the bare minimum required, and an inclination to take along every valued possession.

A week before they were due to take the kids to camp, Carl had informed the kids of the operation. He had caught them on the fly, so to speak, and told them in the back yard on a hot Sunday afternoon.

"While you tykes are up cavorting in the hills, your female parent is going into the hospital for a general overhaul." Even as he said it, he wondered why it had become so habitual, and even necessary, to use a light touch when talking of serious things with the kids. It was, he supposed, essential not to alarm them, but it did make for communication on a rather grotesque level.

Kip was in blue knitted swim trunks that made him look very rangy and very brown. He had a towel over his shoulder and he was anxious to go jump on his bike and pedal down to the Crescent Ridge Community Pool. He had inherited his mother's round and rather placid face, and her dark brown hair, which he wore in what was, to Carl, a distressing variation of the crew cut called a flat-top.

His impatience to be away evaporated very suddenly. Joan, who had been weeding by the rose bushes, sat back on her heels and looked toward them and said, with a thin note of strain that Carl hoped was too subtle for the kids to catch, "My million mile overhaul."

Kip sat down abruptly on an aluminum and plastic lawn chair and said, his eyes grave and very direct, "Is this anything . . . bad, Dad?"

"No," he said, rather irritably. And suspected that his own irritation might be an index to his own fears. "It's just one of those things, Kipper. No cause for flap. She goes in on the weekend of the fourteenth for an operation, and you kids will be completely informed, and we'll set up a deal where you can be near phones so I can call you and tell you all is well. Which it will be, according to Bernie."

"He took out my appendix very nicely," Nancy said in a rather defensive manner, and she went directly to her mother. Joan stood up and Nancy hugged her, and held onto her longer than was usual. Nancy, at thirteen, showed much promise of growing into a vivid and striking woman. She had Carl's dark coloring, his lean face, his long legs. At thirteen her body had begun to blossom at hip and breast—the merest hint of what was to come—and she was perhaps a fractional part of an inch taller than Joan.

"You kids run along now and don't fret," Joan said when Nancy released her. "I'm not nervous, so there's no reason for you to be."

They left with an air of reluctance. When they were in sight again, beyond the house, going down the hill, Kip was walking his bike and Nancy was beside him and they were talking intently. Joan stood by Carl's chair and they watched them disappear behind the Cables' tall hedge.

"A good group of offspring," Carl said, his tone casual, his voice slightly husky.

A week later, after they had left the kids at camp, they drove back to the house, and it seemed very empty. Joan said, "Honey, do you realize this is the first time in . . . fifteen years they've both been away?"

"Good practice for a pair of old floofs," he said. "College coming up before you know it."

"But it's so awfully quiet," she said.

"Restful, you mean," he said, grinning at her.

The hospital seemed a long way off, but the time went by too quickly. Joan had the house gleaming by the end of the two weeks. They had bought it in 1952, the year after the Ballinger Corporation had transferred Carl from the plant in Camden to the Hillton Metal Products Division. They had spent the first year in Hillton in an ugly and inconvenient rented house in the city. They had purchased the Crescent Ridge home on the basis of the architectural drawings and the promoter's promises at a time when the cellars were being dug for the first block of fifty homes.

It was more house than he had felt they could legitimately afford, but he had never regretted making the decision. It was on a one-acre plot at the highest point on Barrow Lane, the first paved road in the development. It was a ranch type, with three bedrooms and two baths, a double car port, a twenty-six by twenty foot living room, complete, on occupancy, with oil heat, dishwasher, garbage disposal, electric range, washer and dryer.

He remembered the excitement of driving out in the evening to see how much more had been done each day. Joan would go out during the day and she somehow managed to get the workmen to make small improvements for her as they went along. When at last it was ready, they drove out on a day in May, following the moving van. Nancy, at eight, was tearful about leaving behind her very dear friends on the block. The lot was raw dirt and the road was being paved, but the new house had a wonderful smell of paint and newness. Joan supervised the placement of the furniture. After the van left they all wandered around, turning on hot water, flushing toilets, clicking the light switches. Carl went into the living room and found Joan sitting on the couch with the hopeless tears running down her face. When he sat beside her and took her in his arms and asked her what the trouble was, she began to sob in earnest. It seemed that she had thought everything would look so wonderful, but now the house made the furniture look horrid. He could see what she meant. The inevitable scars and abrasions inflicted by small children had not been very noticeable in the gloom of the rented house. But in this light and airy home they were all too evident.

Nancy came and stood by the couch for a few moments, and then with a wail of heartbreak she flung herself onto Joan's lap. Kip came and expressed silent contempt at such female goings-on, but his lips were tightly compressed and his eyes were suspiciously shiny.

When Joan pulled herself together, she had a hundred ideas about how they could make the furniture look right "without really spending any money hardly."

Carl Garrett, in spite of the fact that his father had been a building contractor, had always been unhandy with tools. But during the five years they had lived at 10 Barrow Lane, he had pleased himself and astonished Joan by turning into a reasonably competent carpenter, a dogged stone mason, a timid electrician and a strikingly inept plumber. During leisure hours he had paneled the cellar, dividing it into play room and workshop. He had put in a fifteen by thirty foot flagstone terrace behind the house, and surrounded it with a low wall. He had installed a whole storage wall in the car port, built a fieldstone barbecue fireplace in the rear yard, built an insulated study in the attic, assembled the components of a high fidelity system, built low bookshelves and coffee tables. The house was comfortable, livable, and quite handsome in barn red with white trim. The plantings had thrived and the lawn was healthy. Most of his projects had been accomplished with a great deal of advice and a certain amount of help from his neighbors on Barrow Lane. In turn he passed along the hard-earned results of his experience.

After five years the original mortgage of $15,500 had been

reduced to $12,000 and he knew that if he were transferred he could get five thousand over the twenty he had paid for the house. At least five thousand.

During the two weeks after the kids had been put in camp, Joan was endlessly busy. She had him bring boxes down out of the attic, and she sorted and discarded. She emptied drawers all over the house. She made lists for him, and tore them up and made other lists. He was tempted to tell her to take it easy, but he sensed that she had a need to keep herself busy.

Sunday, the fourteenth, finally came. It was a sticky day with far off thunder. They had breakfast at ten-thirty, and then she packed what she would need at the hospital. Bernie wanted her delivered there at four o'clock.

At one o'clock they locked the house and drove down into Hillton, nine miles away in the red and white Ford wagon, with Joan's small suitcase on the rear seat.

"Good-by, house," Joan said.

"By the time you get back I'll have turned it into a shambles," he said. "Dishes piled all over. Empty bottles in the yard. Grass up to your knees."

"I'm not going to be gone that long, and anyway, Marie is coming on Thursday to clean, and Bernie says I'll be out probably a week from Tuesday."

"That seems awfully quick to me. I mean, it's abdominal surgery and . . ."

"You heard Bernie, dear. They used to keep them in for weeks, but now they have them walking around in a day or two."

They were heading down the turnpike into Hillton, and they both looked at the hospital off to the left. Chrome twinkled in the parking area, and the flower beds were bright patches of color.

"Better than Gollmer Street," he said.

"Oh, much much better!"

They had had experience with the dingy hospital on Gollmer Street, when Nancy had had her appendix removed, and when Kip had broken his left wrist in a fall from the railing of the porch of the rented house a month after they had arrived in Hillton.

On the eastern outskirts of Hillton, the new turnpike made a long curve to the north and crossed the Silver River on the big sweep of the Governor Carson Bridge, bypassing the congestion of the city. When they had first bought the

Crescent Ridge house, the commuting problem had been severe. Carl had had to drive nine miles to Hillton on a winding two-lane highway in fast traffic, find his way through the city, cross the inadequate Prince Street Bridge, and drive three more miles to the parking lot of the Hillton Metal Products Division of Ballinger. Though only a little over twelve miles, he could never make it in less than forty minutes, and when there was sleet or snow or heavy rains, it would often take over an hour.

When the limited-access turnpike was opened, it cut the trip to a comfortable fifteen minutes. He could bypass the city and exit from the turnpike just three blocks from the plant. Now, however, he turned off at the eastern edge of the city and drove down through the quiet streets of a Sunday summer afternoon and parked in a metered space almost in front of Steuben's, the best restaurant in the city. They took a small table in the air-conditioned, dimly lighted cocktail lounge and had two rounds of martinis.

Their conversation had a strange tempo. There would be times of being very gay and amusing—and being too amused by what they said. And then she would give him earnest instructions about all manner of household trivia. And then would come a silence that would begin to be uncomfortable.

"It's like a funny kind of celebration," she said.

"I know what you mean."

"You've gone away, but this is the first time I've gone away."

"Don't stay as long as I did," he said, knowing that she was thinking of his two years overseas in the war.

"Darling, don't try to come out for the afternoon visiting hours tomorrow. Tomorrow they're just going to be doing tests and things. Tomorrow evening will be soon enough. Seven to eight-thirty."

"That isn't very long."

"To sit and look at somebody in bed? It's long enough. And please don't think you have to come in and sit for the whole hour and a half. I know how restless you get."

"I'm paying for the accommodations. I guess I can sit as long as I want to."

"God knows I'm going to have enough company," she said. "Every one of the girls will come piling in, dragging their reluctant husbands whenever they can."

"Time to eat," he said, glancing at his watch. He paid the bar check and they found a corner table in one of the smaller dining rooms. They ordered abundantly and told each other how good the food was at Steuben's, but neither of them finished the dinner. As they were having coffee, Carl looked across the room and saw their reflections in a mirrored wall. He tried to look at the two of them as a curious stranger might. After seventeen years of marriage, it was as difficult for him to be objective about Joan's appearance as about his own. He thought that it would have to be a most inquisitive stranger to waste more than the single glance required to ascertain that this was a married couple, the man about forty-two, tall and quite spare, with black hair thinning on top, rather swarthy complexion, two deep lines bracketing the mouth, the habitual expression rather morose and withdrawn. The woman was a year or two younger, not over five feet six inches tall, a round, brown-haired woman, with an open face, a woman probably merry and competent. She would weigh about a hundred and forty pounds, and she would be forever attempting miracle diets. The man wears a pale gray sports jacket, a white dress shirt with a blue necktie. The wife wears a gray skirt, a white blouse, with a dark red cashmere cardigan around her shoulders.

Nothing startling about this pair. Perhaps there is a detectable flavor of contentment, the aura of a marriage that is good and has lasted, and will continue to last.

But the stranger would not see what happened when Carl looked at his watch and said, "Time to saddle up."

Then Joan found his hand under the table and squeezed it very hard, and he looked into her eyes and saw the shadows.

"I guess I've got a right to be a little scared," she said.

"I would be completely terrified. So go ahead. Be scared a little."

She smiled at him. "I'm okay now." And they left. As he followed her out, he thought, You look at your woman from the time she is twenty-three until she is forty, and somewhere along the line you stop being able to see her. You see a face that is dear to you, and a body you love, and you have no idea how she looks to anyone else. I like her tidiness and her gift of laughter. Her face is round and her eyes are gray and her hair is brown and silky. Her waist is slim and her legs are good, and her body is firm and solid. I feel good when I see her across a room. In the beginning it was magical, full of electric excitements, quivering emotional scenes. Now it is all warmth and custom and habit and content. But in the beginning she was a stranger. And now, when I think of the scalpels and the wound they will make, I feel a horror and a sickness as though it were my own belly they will cut.

She stood by the car while he unlocked the door for her, and then they drove to the hospital and parked in the big lot as the afternoon visitors were leaving at the end of the two-thirty to four visiting hours. He carried her small bag and they went to the admissions office. They gave the information required and he turned over the hospitalization policy. Bernie had reserved a bed in a semi-private room on the third floor, Room 314.

The visitors had left by the time he took her up to her room. The bed was freshly made and turned down. A floor nurse came in and explained the call system. The other bed was rumpled but empty. Just as he was about to leave, a small sallow brunette on aluminum crutches came hobbling in and went over to the bed by the windows. "Welcome to good old 314," she said. "I'm Rosa Myers and a jerk kid ran a stop sign and busted my hip and cracked my pelvis and I've been here nine and a half weeks and you're my sixth room buddy."

"I'm Joan Garrett and this is my husband."

The girl worked herself onto the bed. "Honey, I'm pleased to meet you because I'm happy to have a change. The little old lady who was in that bed was released at noon. She snored ten hours a day and groaned the other ten. By the way, the room service stinks and the food is inedible. Otherwise, you'll have a ball. What are you in for?"

Carl said, "I better go before I get thrown out. See you at seven, honey." He kissed her. She seemed distracted, as though already she had gone a little bit apart from him.

He went down the corridor to the self-service elevators. When the elevator door opened, two nurses rolled a bed off the elevator. It contained an unconscious girl of about ten or eleven. There was a flask fastened to a post and a tube taped to her arm. The child's face was gray and sweaty, and there was a lingering sick-sweet smell of anesthetic.

He rode down on the elevator and when he got off he was facing a panel board of the names of doctors, and a light was blinking beside two of the names. The hospital seemed full of a silent bustling impersonal efficiency. He felt as if there were more things he should have done. Just as he was about to leave, he saw Bernie Madden hurrying down the first floor corridor.

"Bernie!"

"Oh, hi, Carl. Just bring her in?"

"A few minutes ago. She's a little scared."

Bernie took him into a small waiting room near the front desk. He was a small man with wide shoulders, cropped black hair, horn-rimmed glasses, a pale face with dark shadow of beard, a look of vitality and controlled energy. "They're all scared. Perfectly natural. And so are you. And right now you're hoping I know my business as well as you think I do. Relax, boy. I don't tell this to my associates, but I'm a pretty sharp operator. And that's a sort of a pun. We'll fool around with some tests and I've got her scheduled for ten o'clock Tuesday morning. I'll give her a spinal."

Carl frowned. "You mean she'll be conscious?"

"Listen, she'll be so full of joy juice, she won't mind a thing. I wish they were all as easy as this one is going to be. Joanie is as healthy as a horse." Bernie punched him lightly on the shoulder. "You run along and leave everything to Uncle Bernie Madden."

He went out and got into the car and drove back to the house, pulling into the car port to park beside Joan's elderly and moody Hillman. It was five o'clock when he let himself into the house. He stood in the kitchen and listened to the silence. The refrigerator made a subdued whirring. The electric clock on the kitchen wall had started the habit of whining a few months back. When you rapped it briskly, the whining stopped. He rapped it.

And he said aloud, "Welcome home, ole Carl."

His voice had a hollow sound in the house, and his footsteps seemed loud, and he heard creaks in the hardwood boards of the floor that he had not noticed before.

In less than two hours he could head back to the hospital, and he would see her again tomorrow evening, and then there would be the longest wait of all, until he could talk to Bernie after the operation.

TWO

He left the hospital for the second time that Sunday at eight-thirty when the visiting hours ended. When he had arrived at a few minutes after seven, the Gray Lady at the temporary desk in the lobby had told him Mrs. Garrett already had two visitors, and patients were only allowed two at a time. He told her that he was Mr. Garrett and she told him somewhat dubiously that he could go up provided he sent one of the other visitors out into the hall.

He heard and recognized Al Washburn's hearty and appalling laugh the moment he stepped off the elevator. Joan's room was only a few doors from the elevator foyer. Al and Jen Washburn were there, and Jen had brought a vase of cut flowers from their garden. Al was the general agent for a large insurance company and the Washburns had moved onto Barrow Lane at Crescent Ridge just a few weeks after the Garretts. The two couples had been reasonably friendly during the five years, drawn together by the bond of being "early settlers." And Carl had served with Al on the board of the Crescent Ridge Association when it was first formed.

The bed of Rosa Myers was crumpled and empty. Jen sat on the foot of Joan's bed. Jen was an arid looking, withered blonde with a great deal of spurious animation in her face, a shrill voice, a great many large dead-white teeth. Carl had never before realized quite how much noise the Washburns created. He hoped they'd have the sense to stay away when Joan was feeling wretched.

Joan's bed was cranked up at the head and she was wearing a bed jacket with small blue flowers embroidered on it. She was smiling, but she looked pale under her summer tan, and rather worn. He greeted the Washburns and bent over and kissed Joan, and admired the flowers. After some of the casual and pointless conversation that occurs in all hospital rooms, Al Washburn tugged Carl out into the hall and said, "Fella, we're going to run into some trouble with the town supervisors again. Now I know you're not on the board any longer, but we're going to need the benefit of your advice."

16

"What now?" Carl asked, feeling curiously weary. "The school thing again?"

The year after they had moved to Crescent Ridge, Carl had put in a great deal of discouraging time as chairman of the committee empowered to work out some sort of agreement with the near-by village of Scottsville. He had shown, through projected tax tables, that it would be of benefit to both Scottsville and Crescent Ridge to enlarge the town boundaries to include the entire development. But the village residents were afraid of being gobbled up by the large housing development, and the people of Crescent Ridge were afraid of town taxes. So he had worked out a compromise scheme whereby the children of Crescent Ridge could attend the town school a mile away by paying fifty dollars a school year, or, if the parents preferred, the kids could attend, free of charge, the large County Central School, ten miles away.

"The school thing again," Al said dolefully. "Now the fifty bucks isn't enough. It should be a hundred, they say. They got to enlarge the town schools. They want to pay the teachers more. By count, two hundred and twenty-one of our kids went to the town schools last year."

"Including yours and mine."

"Will you do some thinking on it and come and talk to the board a week from tomorrow night?"

"You already know what I'll come up with."

"Do I?"

"Yes you do, Al, and you know it's an unpopular point of view so you'd rather have Carl Garrett do it than Al Washburn, everybody's buddy." He had spoken more sharply than he intended.

Washburn's large red face turned slightly darker. "Don't get so hot, boy."

"We've got over fifteen hundred population. We've got the land set aside for our own school. We get inadequate police protection from the state and the county. Running the water and sewer system on an assessment basis is clumsy. Snow removal on a volunteer basis just doesn't work. And it's damn well time we petitioned the state legislature and became an incorporated municipality, Al, and you know it."

"But Jesus, Carl, the people came out here to avoid city taxes."

"And they want just as many services as they got in the city, and nothing comes for free. Scottsville won't play, and that's a stupid reaction on their part. If you want me to come and be unpopular, okay. I'll do it."

Al beamed at him. "Wonderful! And look, put it in writing so you can read it and then leave a copy with the secretary."

"When we become an incorporated municipality, you'll be mayor, Al."

"If elected, I will serve. Say, Joanie seems in pretty good spirits. Jen says this is a female type operation. Bernie Madden is tops. You haven't got a thing to worry about."

After the Washburns left, Carl had a few minutes with Joan alone. "What are they doing to you, honey?"

"Castor oil is what they're doing to me, dammit. Hand me my robe, please, dear. I'll be right back."

While he sat in the chair by the bed, waiting, Rosa Myers came back in on her crutches and gave him a wry grin and hitched herself into bed. "You got a good gal there, Mr. Garrett."

"Thanks."

"In between her little jaunts down the hall, we've been trading life histories. I've seen her in the store a couple of times. I'm an assistant buyer at Gliddens. Sportswear. At least I was before that yuk bounced me into the air."

Joan came back and got into bed and Carl hung up her robe. She looked slightly wan. "Rosa calls this the Memorial two-step," she said, and she looked beyond him toward the door and smiled widely and he turned and saw Cindy Cable come in.

Bucky and Cindy Cable were the younger couple who lived next door to them on Barrow Lane. Bucky, christened Gilbert, was an energetic and successful salesman of industrial abrasives and solvents, covering five states with the aid of a private Beechcraft he kept at the Hillton Airport. Cindy, christened Cynthia, was a tall girl of about twenty-six with dark blond hair, long hair that she wore alternately in a pony tail, or a bun at the nape of her neck, or piled high. Her cheekbones were high, cheeks delicately hollow, gray-blue eyes set wide, mouth wide and soft, with a not unattractive hint of petulance. She moved slowly, and held herself well. They had two small children, Bobby who was four and Bitsy who was two.

When the Garretts had first moved to Crescent Ridge, they had been most unhappy about the neighbors who moved into the new house next door. They were a couple in their middle years named Riker. He was a C.P.A. in Hillton. They had no children. In the beginning there was a period of superficial friendliness between the two families. But it ended with a bitter boundary dispute over the location of a small red maple Carl had brought home from Hillton and planted on the western border of his lot line. When it was proven, by a surveyor, that one half the slender trunk was on the Rikers' land, Mr. Riker said that unless it was transplanted, he would cut it down. The tree did not survive the second transplanting. Then the Garrett children were caught racing across the Riker lawn, and there was a full-scale scene about that.

They were still nodding coldly at each other when they met, but it ended with great finality on a Halloween night when Riker, ashen and trembling with an almost ungovernable rage, hammered on the Garrett front door at ten o'clock, demanding that "your brat kids be thrashed in my presence, or I will go to the law."

Someone had soundly plastered the Riker front door and picture window with elderly eggs. Carl had tried to retain some semblance of amicable relations up to that point. But both Kip and Nancy were at a party at the school and had been there the entire evening, and Joan had driven out a few minutes before to go pick them up.

Carl had rarely been as angry. He put his hand against Riker's gaunt chest and walked him backward out into the darkness and chill of the front yard. As Riker gasped in outrage, Carl said, "My kids have been away all evening at school. You can consider the rotten eggs as a gesture of opinion of the entire community here. You are ridiculous, petty, half-crazed people who don't belong here, and never will. I don't want any further contact with you in any way. Now get off my property." He walked trembling into the house and slammed the door.

A year later Riker was hospitalized for a serious ulcer condition and failed to survive the operation. The house went on the market. The Cables bought it. The Riker episode had made the Garretts gun shy, and so it was several months before they went beyond normal politeness. Cindy, to Carl, was the tall young woman next door who was as thoroughly pregnant as anyone he had ever seen. After the baby was born, the Garretts began to run into the Cables at neighborhood parties when Bucky was in town.

The new couple was measured in the eyes of the community. Bucky was a nice guy. His wife was a character. The reason for the designations was most simple. Bucky was intent, uncomplicated, friendly as any pup. But Cindy was quiet and watchful, and when she expressed an opinion, it was uniquely her own. She had an offbeat mind, a great deal of skepticism, and she could be appallingly frank.

Soon the four of them were warm friends, in spite of the difference in ages. It was one of those rare and pleasant situations where everybody in the foursome liked everybody else and enjoyed being with them. Cindy and Joan were forever wandering into each other's houses during the day. Bucky and Carl assisted each other on their do-it-yourself projects, trading monstrous insults.

Cindy had been an army brat and had lived at military posts all over the world. She had said to Carl and Joan once, "Just look at me now. I didn't want my kids to be rootless army brats, forever changing schools and friends. So I married this here industrial type because I had the childish idea we'd stay put. And I find the modern corporation has taken a leaf from the army manuals. Move the boys around. So it's the same deal, only this time without a PX and without free medical care."

Carl had, after a time, analyzed the reasons why the four of them got along so well. Bucky was, essentially, very like Joan in temperament, disposition and quality of mind. They were both cheerful optimists, both unfailingly energetic, both strong proponents of neatness and orderliness. Neither of them had the slightest appetite for any kind of philosophical conjecture. They were impatient with theory and intellectual speculation.

Cindy's mind was more like Carl's, yet more subtle, more oblique, more prone to dissect and be amused by the grotesqueries of life. And both he and Cindy were inclined to be pessimistic, frequently moody, frequently lethargic. And not particularly neat.

Sometimes when the four of them were talking, Cindy and Carl would go bounding off the beaten track into one of their conversational games, projecting the customs and practices of Crescent Ridge into exaggeration and absurdity, or making up new words to fit unique social situations, or establishing the platform of a new political party, a party which would outlaw cookouts, funny chef aprons, slacks on fat female picnickers, and meat which was charcoal on the outside and only slightly wounded in the middle.

And then Bucky would look at Joan and say, "There they go again." And Carl would sense in Bucky and in Joan a slight hurt at being left out, and perhaps a tingle of jealousy, but also a curious pride in them that they had married and they loved these two more intricate creatures. Sometimes Cindy was able to look at an accepted situation from such a wry angle that Carl would suddenly see the absurdities of his own behavior and laugh with pure delight and also with a feeling of discomfort, as though he had been mercilessly exposed to the world and to himself.

Also, in Cindy, Carl saw those emotional factors which, in himself, had kept him from attaining the success in the business world which he might otherwise have achieved. A skepticism, a reluctance to conform, an appreciation of the ludicrous, had kept him from being thoroughly sold on the necessity for an unthinking devotion to the mighty Ballinger Corporation. In too many conferences he had heard himself say things that affronted the gods of commerce. He knew he was considered something of a maverick, and he was aware of being passed over several times in the past so that more malleable, less skeptical, and less able men could be promoted.

Yet, as an assistant to the plant manager of the Hillton Metal Products Division of Ballinger, he drew eighteen thousand five hundred before taxes and other deductions. It was a respectable wage, and it enabled them to live in comfort. He was in charge of factory cost accounting and, in that position, was more directly answerable to the Comptroller of the corporation in the New York main offices than to the resident Plant Manager.

Ballinger had a paternalistic attitude toward the corporate executives on all levels, and he knew that it was likely that he would be left in Hillton until he reached the optional retirement age of sixty, or the mandatory retirement age of sixty-five. Were he to retire at sixty, he would have eighteen more years here. It was conceivable that by retirement time he would be making around twenty-five thousand. By 1975, after thirty years with Ballinger, the kids would be married, educated and have families of their own. He could count on eight or nine thousand retirement pay, and they would probably do the traditional thing of moving to Florida.

Unless he should suddenly become hopelessly inadequate in his job, there was little chance of being released by Ballinger. The work was just demanding enough to enable him to maintain a satisfying level of interest in it. So it was a good life. But at times he wondered where he would be had he been able to accept the adjustments and compromises and devotion that high level executive work demanded. He suspected that his mind was good enough to have enabled him to reach that chill climate above the corporate timberline where income becomes a matter of bonuses, stock options and capital gains. At times he felt wistful and half guilty about his inability to commit himself totally, but he justified and rationalized by telling himself that he had and was having a good life, that there were many family advantages in being a nine-to-five guy, that he did not like airplanes and slept poorly on trains, that he was out of that decision-making area where flourish the ulcer and the massive coronary, and that, in the long view of history, it mattered very little whether his split second of existence in eternity was spent as Chairman of the Board of the Ballinger Corporation and advisor to the head of government—or as a sweeper in C Building.

Yet, on those rare times when he was called to New York, it was not amusing to be called Garrett by some florid and flint-eyed man whose manner was imposing, whose income was fabulous and whose thinking was appallingly fuzzy. It was not enchanting to be summoned like a clever and somewhat mischievous child and be asked to present neatly typed and bound analyses of cost trends and remedies for the approval of men who had not the ability to have composed the reports.

He had told himself many times that it was very much like the kid game of king-on-the-hill. The kid who was strongest and most ruthless and desired with the greatest desperation to achieve and retain the summit would do so. And the others, weakened by their suspicion that perhaps the top of the hill was not so terribly important after all, could select places on the slope where it was not likely anyone would try to dislodge them. Or they might be weakened by doubt as to their ability to attain and defend the summit.

This was a philosophy he had once attempted to expound to Cindy Cable. She had caught on immediately, and had looked at him in a mocking way and said, "How wonderfully selfish, Carl. Not your attitude, but the way you've kept from relating it to the world around you. Don't you see that's one of the very crucial problems of our society? How far can a man justifiably go in search of security?"

"Or a well-rounded life."

"Isn't that a rationalization rather than a description? The thing that gnaws, dear Carl, is your nasty little suspicion that a man, to be a man, must involve himself with total commitment."

"Or be half a man?"

"Don't give me that abused and huffy look. I'm one of the uncommitted too. From twelve years old to twenty, I filled a great box with hundreds and thousands of words of ringing beauty. I burned with that good old hard gemlike flame, I did. But I couldn't face the complete involvement of sending my deathless works to publishers. So long as I did nothing, I was avoiding the horror of being told the stuff stinks. And so I can keep on half believing in my heart that I had a great talent."

Joan, who had been listening, said, with a slightly irritable expression, "Carl, I just do not understand why you say those things about yourself. You have a perfectly splendid job and you've been getting raises right along, and I don't see why you talk yourself down so. I'm very proud of you and so are the kids and . . . I just don't follow you at all when you talk about things like commitment and total involvement."

And he remembered that Cindy had done an odd and quite touching thing. She had gone over to Joan and kissed her quickly on the cheek and said, "Carl and I have to turn everything into vast problems, Joanie. It doesn't mean anything. It's a disease. Like Scrabble." And when she turned away from Joan, Carl saw a surprising glint of tears in her eyes.

"I read some of Cindy's stuff before we got married," Bucky said. "It was pretty damn good. I tried to get her to let me send it to an old buddy of mine from Ohio State who was in the advertising department of *Collier's*, but she wouldn't let me send it along. The way I figure it, if you want to get stuff published, you got to have contacts in the business end of the magazines."

"Bucky has got old buddies scattered all over hell and gone," Cindy said, not too kindly.

Bucky said, in a defensive way, "You got to keep up your contacts. You never know when you can help somebody or a guy can help you. That's what makes the world go round."

"It never hurts to have friends," Joan said.

"Except that sometimes it hurts to have friends," Cindy said.

"There they go again," Bucky said. "Why don't you pair of eggheads go on a quiz program some place?"

Now Cindy came slowly, with her smile that tilted higher

on one side than the other, into the hospital room, hair in a
pony tail, wearing a white tailored shirt with the sleeves
rolled up, gray walking shorts, red sandals, carrying a flat
package in red polka-dot paper under her arm.

She handed the package to Joan and said, deadpan, "This
is a hilarious book. It is excruciatingly funny. The clerk
laughed so hard while she was explaining it to me that I
haven't the faintest idea what it's about."

"Thank you, Cindy."

Carl gave Cindy the chair and sat on the end of the bed.
As Joan unwrapped the book, Cindy said, "This is my first
day of settling into the life of a slob."

"Oh, did the kids get away?" Joan asked. "Say, I heard
about this book! I read a wonderful review. Thanks so much,
dear."

"What's this about the kids?" Carl asked.

"Bucky's parents drove over yesterday from Battle Creek
and picked up the little monsters. I think they suspect I am
an unnatural parent and all that, because I did do a little
devious staff work to get them off my hands for a while. I
suspect I am called that strange girl Bucky married. Anyhow,
they are doting grandparents, and they have a lovely place
in the country not far from Fort Custer, and they did a decent job of raising five kids of their own, and they have the
devoted services of the irreplaceable Myra who has been
with them several centuries. They will be returned, spoiled
rotten no doubt, on the last day of August to their loving parents. I do love the little animals dearly, but I have had too
much time in the sole company of infants. The conversation
is not very stimulating or rewarding. I had to do something
before I ended up going around thrumming on my lips and
wolfing pablum."

"They can be an awful chore," Joan said.

"I just had to have a break. I hope it's going to turn into a
summer custom. I've always been the sort of a person who
needs privacy to sort of renew myself. And, boy, am I going
to have it now. I'm going to turn the television to the wall.
I'm going to read and loaf and toast in the sun and eat when
I feel like it, and drink beer when I feel like it, and let the
Cable manse go to rack and ruin. Bucky and I plan to take
our three weeks in August, and end up at the farm to pick
up the kids. And by the way, Carl, Bobby took along that
little microscope thing you gave him. I asked him why and he
said it was essential. That was the word he used, and you

can't argue with that. So I asked politely why it was essential and he said he planned to look at a chicken with it. I asked him if the chicken would stand still and he said if it wouldn't, he would run too. I get an odd mental image out of that. Old Bitsy, the butterball, was a gem. She cooed and danced and admired her new dress and babbled away about the wonderful farm. She is convinced from her personal research library of children's books that all the animals will, of course, talk. It will break her heart when they won't. She was terribly good until the car started to move and I waved. The last I saw of her was a bright red mask of anguish and a mouth you could have slipped a grapefruit into with no trouble at all."

"They grow so fast," Joan said wistfully.

"And this here unnatural mother hopes and prays that we'll wind up with a pair like the Garrett heirs."

"That's nice of you to say that, Cindy," Joan said.

"They are good kids. That Kip makes me wish I was fourteen again. He's turning into a handsome devil."

"When does Bucky get back?" Carl asked.

"He's on the deal he calls the Big Swing. He called last night to make sure the children got off all right. He's had the best trip ever, so far, and, on Friday, instead of coming home, he swings down to Memphis to some kind of a convention of industrial chemists. He made the usual wistful request for permission to do some night flying to save time and I gave the usual hearty No. I know what would happen. A lot of drinks with the customers, and then he'd decide to be an intrepid birdman and rack himself up on a mountain somewhere. You kids need some visiting time of your own, so I will now return to my new career of being the compleat slob. When do they excavate, Joanie?"

"Tuesday morning."

Cindy stood up. "I'll see you again before then, honey."

"Cindy, you keep an eye on our house and make sure Carl doesn't stay up until all hours. He gets his nose in a book and he loses all track of time. If you see the lights on late, call him up and give him hell for me."

"I'll sling rocks at his window. Be good, now." She strolled out and turned in the hall and smiled and waved.

"It will be good for her to have a little rest," Joan said. "But I didn't know the kids would be gone practically the whole summer. She's so odd about some things. If mine were gone that long when they were the age of Bobby and Bitsy, I'd have gotten lonesome for them by the second day."

"And gone and gotten them three days later."

"I suppose so. She's just like you used to be, Carl. She's good with them, like you were, but you used to get so impatient sometimes."

"I'll take them at the present ages, thank you."

The hall speakers softly announced the end of visiting hours in five minutes. He spent a few minutes looking at the book Cindy had brought and then kissed her good-by and she said, "Dear, please hand me my robe again. No rest for the wicked, I guess."

He left at eight-thirty, walking out into the long gray and golden dusk of summer, walking out of the medicinal aromas and electronic efficiencies of the hospital. A pretty nurse stood on the lawn under a tree, smoking a cigarette and talking to a young man in a T shirt and khakis. As he passed them, walking toward the station wagon, the man said something to her in a low voice, and she laughed in a teasing and flirtatious way that was as old as time.

He went to a drive-in and had a hamburger and a milkshake and listened on the car radio to the Yankees scoring heavily against the Red Sox. He felt restlessly alone in the world. He had gone away many times. He had gone to a war and he had gone on business trips, and once he had gone on a hunting trip to Canada as a guest of the Treasurer of Ballinger. But she had never gone away before. Not in seventeen years of marriage. She had never been in hospital since they were married with the two exceptions of the births of Kip and Nancy. And this time was not like those times. He had been scared then, but not in this way.

The car next to him was full of teen-age boys. They were kidding the car hop in a noisy and unfunny way, and she was not taking it well. When he blinked his lights she came and got the tray and the tip and said good night, mister.

He drove home, knowing how empty the house would be, and how empty her bed would be. Sunday evenings had always been a quiet and pleasant time for them. Perhaps the television set would fill the emptiness, or at least mask it.

When he turned off the turnpike he looked west and saw the nightglow of the city against the overcast. There was summer lightning in the hills a dozen miles beyond the Silver River. It would be hot down in the city tonight, and they would sleep on the roofs and fire escapes and in the parks and they would hope for rain. The neighborhood bars would stay full until late because it would be too hot to think of leaving the hum and frosty breath of the air-conditioner to go back to hall bedrooms. The young girls would walk arm in arm, giggling over their delicious mysteries, arching their backs slightly and whispering together when they passed the young men who stood outside the sundries store. And the young men would make casual appraisal of the young swaying abundance of hip, and the tilt of the nyloned breast, and spit toward the gunmetal trunk of the light post and, quite often, two of them would leave the others and saunter after the girls with enormous casualness.

And, he thought, down in the city tonight there will be episodes of an ugly and savage violence. The sweating cops who make the arrests will be irritable and brutal. In small stale rooms the sweet coppery stench of blood will float on the motionless air.

There were a lot of words for Hillton. Industrial complex. Lunch-bucket town. A forward-looking American city making a wise and valiant effort to solve its problems of traffic congestión, slum clearance, high taxes and high crime rate. Or, a vital clog in the industrial might of America. Or, a rather inviting target for an atomic warhead. Or, a foul and grubby place to live and try to bring up kids, for God's sake, and keep them from running wild.

It was, he suspected, like all of the other cities in the heartland of America. Or maybe all of the cities of all time. Dedication mated to venality. Energy and progress linked to idleness and sin. But in this time, louder than ever before, rang out the plea that was more than half command— AMUSE ME. Fill these sour hours of this, my own and only life, with the gut-buster joke, the rancid ranch-hand laments about love, the talcumed armpits and shaven crotch of commercial love, the flounderings and hootings and vomitings of the big bender. By God, I want the girlie shows and the sex books, and a big cigar is a sign of masculinity and success. I want to be slim without dieting, smart without half trying, rich without working. And I want to read all about it, read all about hell for the other guy—with pics of him strewn on the highway, or cleaved with an axe, or being carried out of the mine. So I can hug old precious, invaluable, unique and irreplaceable me. Amuse me. That keeps me rolling along, boy. So I can live without dying, and right at the end of my world, die without thinking. Then all the rest of you can go to hell because I won't be here, and by God, when I was here, I had it good. I had it sweet and hot and often.

THREE

After he had parked the wagon next to the little Hillman, known in the Garrett family as Lucinda May, he went into the house and hung up the gray sports jacket, took off his tie, rolled his sleeves up, pried holes in a can of beer. He turned lights on all over the house, opened windows to let a frail west breeze through, and turned on television. He checked the five available channels and found nothing that he felt like watching. He looked through his records and could find nothing he wanted to play. He leafed through the current copy of *Life*, glancing at the pictures, skipping the text. He threw the magazine aside and went into the kitchen and opened another can of beer. It was a little after ten, and he knew he could get a good night's sleep, and it would be a sensible thing to do, and there were some pills that would push him over the edge into sleep in a gentle but convincing way, but he did not feel like sleep.

He carried his beer out through the screen doors onto the patio. (Item: 1955 project. Removed big picture window with flanking dormer windows from south wall of living room. Enlarged opening. Replaced with folding glass doors and screen doors opening onto the patio that had been 1954's major project. Managed to conceal all evidences of unskilled labor. Left hand folding door has never worked right. Much experimentation with weather stripping still does not eliminate wintry blast when winter wind is from south.)

He sat on the low wide wall and sipped his beer. At infrequent intervals he could hear a distant grumble of thunder to accompany the summer lightning in the west. The west breeze had turned gusty. He looked into the house, and decided that when Joan was well they should go through the living room and mark some items for disposal. Somehow, without being aware of it, they had acquired too much stuff. The room was looking cluttered. The clean lines of the low furniture were being destroyed.

He got up and stepped over the wall and strolled to the west boundary of his land. The Cables' house was set about five feet lower than his. Barrow Lane sloped down from his corner lot at what they had told him was a seven percent grade. He was above the roof level of the houses farther down the street. He walked to the red maple that had replaced the one assassinated by the Rikers and hooked his arm in the crotch of it and looked at Cindy Cable.

The kitchen window was about thirty-five feet away, and five feet below him. The fluorescent lights made the kitchen glaringly bright. She sat in the breakfast booth on the far side of the kitchen, elbows on the table, a book open in front of her. She sat there, dressed as he had seen her in the hospital, with cigarettes, lighter, opened beer bottle and a third of a glass of beer. It made him feel guilty to look in at her. Due to the screen of plantings, you could not look from one house into the other. But from this place on the lot he could see into the kitchen perfectly. She had pulled a strand of her dark blond hair forward and she wound it around a finger. He watched her sip the beer, turn pages, light a cigarette.

There was, for him, an inexplicable quality of tension in the scene. It was as though he looked into a stage set. Girl sits reading. Somebody enters. Or something. He felt an odd compassion for her vulnerability, something that he had previously felt only about Nancy. She was alone on a summer night, and the dark world was full of dark motives. Her slim attractiveness was a provocation to the things of the night. But, of course, nothing happened and nothing would. The night bugs would bang their hypnoid heads into the screening, and she would read her book until she finished it, or felt sleepy and went to bed.

On impulse, and because he was both lonely and restless, he walked cautiously down the abrupt slope and then across the flatness of their rear yard to the kitchen door. He stamped on the two concrete steps noisily and said, "You sell beer, lady?"

"Come on in, Carl," she called. She got up from the booth as he walked into the kitchen. "Hey, you've already got a beer."

"One tenth of an inch left in the can. And, to be perfectly truthful, a full six pack in the refrigerator. If you're short I can . . ."

"Got scads," she said. She took a bottle out of the icebox and jacked it open on the wall opener in the corner. The cap came off but the magnet failed to catch it and it fell behind the waste basket. "Damn!" she said. "Last week I would have dived after it. Now it can stay right where it is."

"No glass. I'm a bottle man."

They sat in the booth, facing each other. "What are you reading?"

She turned it so he could see the jacket. "A modrun novel. All full of hangovers, remorses and fornication. It's supposed to be a tragedy, sort of, and see it says here that it ranks right up there with *Appointment in Samarra*. But I find it faintly queasy and mostly dull. I'm a classicist, I guess, when it comes to tragedy."

"How do you mean?"

"I haven't tried to put it into words before. I mean that if you take a lot of mealy little people who have already sort of sold their souls down the river before the book even starts, then you can't really give a very large damn about what happens to them. The author can put them into perfectly frightful situations, and the poor little things can run back and forth, bleating like anything, but you sort of say so what."

"But isn't it a tragedy to them?"

"Hell's bells, boy! Isn't life itself a sort of experiment in tragedy? That sounds a little too good to be me. I must have read it some place. I've got a ragbag mind, full of snipped ends and bits. Tonight Mr. Walter Upshot and his wife Delicious Upshot and their three little Upshots are killed when their Super Rapier tries to uproot a hundred year old elm tree in West Armpit, Wisconsin. And that's too damn bad, and I can feel empathy and a sort of remote grief for the Upshots. But it isn't my kind of tragedy."

"What's your kind?"

"Before something can fall in a dramatic and glorious way, it has to be way the hell up in the air. There has to be a greatness and grandeur about it. And then it falls, and it's a long time falling, and it makes a glorious and tragic noise when it hits bottom. Hamlet. Richard the Third. You see, life never let the little worms in this book get off the ground. Or the author didn't."

"I don't know."

"You look pretty dubious, old antagonist. Let's cook up an argument here."

"Well, Cindy, it's just that you sound pretty damn arrogant. As if you're looking down on all us poor little worms. Suppose, and this is a hell of a poor example to use, I guess, but just suppose that Bernie should find that Joan has got something . . . malignant and incurable. Your way of thinking makes it impossible for me, under those circumstances, to experience legitimate tragedy. You leave me with just a sort of sniveling grief. Because I'm one of the little guys. Whoever authored me never let me get off the ground."

"Well, that *does* require an answer, lad. I better take it in segments. First off, I am not being arrogant and patronizing. I don't think my soul is so grand and its texture so fine that I can participate in any grand tragedy."

"And I can't either, then."

"Don't jump so fast. Give a girl breathing room. I have been talking about classic literature. Not about life."

"Shouldn't they be the same?"

"Not in the dramatic sense. Look, you are a good man, Carl. There aren't too many around who have that quality of gentleness and goodness that you have. Take your mind and add selfishness and arrogance and a quality of greed and you could have been a very powerful man. But that doesn't alter the fact that there are a lot of good men in the world and a lot of good women who have had to hear the kind of sorry news that you used as an example. Illness is a condition of living. You can't make dramatic material for the novelist out of a statistic."

He drank from the bottle and put it down. "Okay. Statistic. I guess a lot of ambitious young men have killed young women who stood in their way. Rather ordinary young men. Selfish and greedy. So a guy like Dreiser makes a novel of it that not only stands up, but I would consider a legitimate tragedy, even though the fallen could not be considered grand and mighty."

"Hmmm," she said. "That rocks my little boat, but I don't quite founder. Take good old Crescent Ridge, this sterling experiment in planned community living. Make me a tragedy in this locale, sir. I mean a dramatic tragedy. Take that Crosby thing over on Shattuck Road last year. She was sleeping around and he was the traditional last to know, and when he found out, he cut his wrists but they found him in time and now they're divorced. But you know and I know that her pseudo-nymphomania was based on alcohol, and she drank too much because living sober with that petty little self-important tyrant was too much to take. And we both know that the wrist cutting was so superficial he could have been found twenty-four hours later without any special damage done."

"No, Cindy. We're just too close to Crescent Ridge. And we

both despise certain aspects of it for too many of the same reasons. If we could be objective, we could see legitimate tragedy, maybe not in the case of the Crosbys, but certainly in some other episode."

"Dear Carl, I didn't mean to imply that your example would make you something weak and sniveling. It won't happen, of course, but were it to happen, you would take it in a gutsy way. But the guy who wrote this book wasn't dealing in that area. He is in an area where I seem to be currently functioning."

"What do you mean by that?"

"Forget it. I shouldn't have said it. Refill?"

"If you're having one."

"I certainly am. A true slob goes all the way. I am going to put on pounds of suet." She brought the beers back to the booth and slid in and sat with her cheekbone propped against her fist in a way that tilted her left eye up. "But I am not going to stick with books of this ilk. I wonder what language ilk comes from? No, I am moving from this into the hard stuff. Stuff I've neglected too long. I want to flex some of the sagging muscles between my ears. You should too, Carl. It will give us some fertile new areas for argumentation."

"I know I should. I used to read a lot. I'd program my reading to pick up the stuff other kids learned in liberal arts colleges while I was taking banking and insurance and accounting in the Wharton School at Pennsylvania. Big programs. Anthropology one winter. Then geology. Then archeology. I started to goof when we moved out here. There didn't seem to be any time. Too much do-it-yourself. And then the Crescent Ridge Association and so on. Now my reading is pretty superficial stuff. Escape, I guess. No work involved. Who killed whom, and who rose to the rescue of the beleaguered wagon train. I should start again, I guess."

"Sometimes it gets to be too easy not to do any of the hard stuff. My God, I'm not after information, stowing away definitive little facts like a squirrel in September. I just want to use some of these muscles up here that God gave me before they wither away entirely. I want to read some of the boys who make me have to strain to stay up with them."

"I know what you mean."

She looked down and drew a fingertip through the wet ring her glass had left. "About what I said before."

"I didn't understand what you meant."

"I know you didn't. I shouldn't talk about it. I don't want

advice or guidance or anything. I don't want you to think I'm putting you in the position of being a marriage clinic. But, dammit, there isn't anybody else to talk to. And you can always get things in more perspective in your mind if you talk to somebody. You and I . . . we sort of think alike. I guess I have a masculine turn of mind. That's what they told me in school. It made me nervous at the time, I remember." She kept looking down at the table.

"Troubles?" he said.

"Now try to tell me you didn't know," she said, defiantly.

"Just a little suspicion here and there. A sort of strain between the two of you. But, believe me, nothing very apparent. At least nothing so apparent that Joan has noticed anything. If she had, she would have spoken to me about it."

"I'm glad we've hidden it that well. It's the main reason I had to get the kids out of here this summer. To do some heavy thinking, Carl. To make up my mind once and for all whether to accept the situation and make the best of it, or get out while the kids are young enough so it won't mark them too badly."

"I'm very sorry, Cindy."

"I know you mean that sincerely, and I thank you. It's no grand tragedy. I guess it happens all the time. But I didn't expect it to happen to me. I've fallen out of love with Bucky, if I ever was in love with him. Believe me, I know how sappy that sounds. I have a certain amount of tolerant affection for him. I didn't expect marriage to be magical forever, but I did expect to stay in love. Damn it, I wish it didn't make me feel so creepy and disloyal to be spouting off about my marriage to a third party."

"Sometimes you have to talk. I'm glad you picked me."

"I was terribly sophisticated when I met Bucky, I'd just terminated my only affair. It was very intense and very dramatic and it had lasted nearly a year. I was a woman of twenty-one, by gad, and I'd lived, lived, lived. I had the sense to get out when the pink clouds parted and I found out I'd given my all to a very selfish and talented and neurotic man who didn't give a ghost of a damn about me, just so long as I kept playing my part of Camille. After that somewhat humiliating revelation, our Bucky was as refreshing as an April sun. That good All-American grin of his and those lovely bulgy shoulder muscles and that restful conversation that didn't require much of me but a nod in the right places."

She paused and poured beer into her glass. "I didn't realize that it was a rebound situation. The affair had made me emotionally sick, and Bucky was my rest camp. Now I know full well that I am not the wife for him. I'm not what he wants. He wants blind and utter adoration and respect, and he needs to be told quite often how wonderful he is and how well he's doing. I recognize that need, and I try to give him what he wants, but I can't keep the act consistent. Every once in a while I come out with a tart little wise-guy comment that cuts him down to size. He resents the fact, and won't admit it completely to himself, that I am more intelligent and more mature than he is. He would be happy with a ball of fluff who could keep his house, take care of his clothes, feed him well, grace his bed and bear all his kids. He wants six kids. We have had some mighty hassles about my reluctance to start the next one. I could have cheated him without his knowing it, but I thought it best to be frank.

"You read about a man going up the ladder and the poor little woman unable to grow with him. This is the other side of the coin. I'm learning more as I grow older. Bucky is in complete mental stasis. What he believes now, he'll believe when he's sixty.

"I'm not the right wife for him, and he's not the right husband for me. God knows what I do want for a husband, but I don't want someone who . . . is so oppressively stagnant. When he's home I want to stick pins in him to see if he'll jump. I keep thinking that if he says the same trite things over and over one more time, I'll go screaming mad. And I can see his future all too clearly. Just as I can see the beginnings of what will be an impressive paunch. He'll be sales manager of the firm some day. With a whisky voice and a bloated red face and a clap on the back and a locker room personality. And I am not going to be the little woman to another Al Washburn, I swear. But you can't change him. The mold is set. He's sublimely confident that he, by God, has his feet on the ground, and I am being neurotic and petulant and dreamy and impossible. I am being practically un-American, or something."

"Bucky is not a complicated human being."

"I think he was faithful up until a year ago. But I can't blame him completely for the change. He wasn't getting the respect from me that he needs. So there has been a succession of cheap little affairs. That hasn't come out in the open yet. I'm afraid of what I'll say when it does. But there have been all the little clues. Too many of them, because Bucky is not really bright enough to be a good conspirator. He's sort of pathetic in the way he thinks I'm ignorant of his infidelities.

"Maybe it could all be patched up and I could endure it if the . . . bedroom department had not gone sour. Once I began to doubt the wisdom of this marriage, I found it more difficult to . . . respond to him. And, with Bucky, any slowing of response is fatal, because his technique is . . . pretty damn hasty. God, I shouldn't have brought that up."

Her face was pink and she avoided his eyes.

"When you talk, it ought to be the whole story."

"All right. This slowness of response has been turning into an actual physical revulsion. I try to conquer it, but it is getting worse. Carl, I don't know what to do or where to go from here. He's talking about our three weeks in August as a 'second honeymoon.' And he says I'll come to my senses. I *have* come to my senses. It is my senses, or my sensibilities, that are being . . . violated. It's a sour and sorry mess. I'm sorry to inflict it on you. But you see, it isn't grand tragedy. It's just a messy little marriage between people of no particular importance or interest to the reading public at large."

She said the last part lightly and tried to smile, but her mouth broke and she laid her forehead on her forearm on the top of the table in the booth. A few moments later he realized she was crying silently.

He had an impulse to touch her hair, but he suppressed it. He knew he should say something, but he had no idea what to say to her. He had suspected that all was not well with them, but he had no idea that it was this bad, that it had gone this far. She had showed him the true flavor of their marriage, and he did not see how it could be retrieved, made sound again—if indeed there had ever been any soundness or validity in it.

"Everybody has to make adjustments," he said, and was immediately ashamed of the stock phrase, empty and inane. He went on quickly: "I've made adjustments to Joan, and she has to me. Joan isn't the most . . . stimulating mental companion in the world." He felt the guilt of disloyalty as soon as he said it, but he sensed that the easiest way to soothe her guilt at her own confession was to answer in kind. "I can often feel a sort of impatience with her. There are a lot of little social goals that I think are pretty damn dubious. But Joan accepts all the truisms without question. Sometimes I envy her because it makes life so damn simple. If you accept everything you read and everything you're told, then you can be at home in the world and you don't waste time, as I do, trying to detect how society is kidding you. And trapping you into a lot of empty effort."

Cindy raised her head. Her eyes were reddened and slightly puffy. "But that isn't the same, Carl. It isn't the same."

"Why isn't it?"

"Joan accepts you. She's perfectly content to have you as you are, and when she doesn't understand you, she just says that Carl is kind of moody sometimes, and lets it go at that. But Bucky doesn't accept me the way I am. He wants to force me down into . . . into the shiny little neoprene and plastic world where he lives. He's so bloody damn sure he's absolutely right about everything and that I'm the weird one who has to come to her senses. Joan loves you the way you are. Bucky only loves—if he has the capacity to love—his private image of me the way he thinks I should be. It's as though I'm trying to live with another girl in the house, the one Bucky wishes he had married. That girl looks just like me. But she takes the ironing into the living room so she can watch the soap operas while she works. And the only things she reads are the fashion magazines and the home making magazines. And when he takes her to parties, she wears a pretty little simper and she never, never says anything that could possibly offend anybody."

"Conversely though, Cindy, I accept Joan. I don't want to stick pins in her. I don't resent her because there are certain stretches of back woods and jungle in my mind that she can't inhabit. I realize that there are a hell of a lot of other areas where we share."

"So I should accept Bucky. Is that what you're saying? I'll answer that by being terribly trite. A woman, due to her reproductive obligations and her responsibilities before and after the birth of a child, has a very primitive yen for total security. So that means that love—and by love I mean all aspects of the marital relationship—must occupy a much greater area of importance in her mind than in the mind of a man. The emotional-sexual relationship is just one area of interest in the male. He has many other areas. For a woman it is damn near everything. So do me the courtesy of reversing your own situation. Be Carla, the wife. And Joan can be John, the man who holds down your job. Then maybe you can better see the dimensions of my own special trap."

Carl thought it over. "I can see just what you mean."

"Anyway," she said, "we're making a silly damn parallel of this. You and Joan have a good marriage. And I have a rotten one, and I've got six weeks to come to a decision. It's up to me. I can make this marriage work, but I can make it work on such a limited basis that it means I'll spend a zombie life from here on in. I have to decide if it's worth it. Maybe I'm just a damn neurotic, and Bucky is right. Maybe I romanticized marriage too much. Maybe this is what all marriage is. But somehow, I doubt it. I doubt it very much. And because I've spilled all my soiled laundry out of the hamper and picked it over in front of you, I feel a silly resentment toward you, and I know I shouldn't."

"I suspect that's a very normal reaction."

"Thank God there's something normal about me. I keep thinking that you've got enough to think about without serving as an emergency wailing wall." She looked at her watch. "Do you happen to know it's damn near one o'clock in the morning? And Joanie told me to see that you get your sleep."

She walked with him out into the warm night. The thunder was closer.

"It's raining in Hillton," she said.

"It'll be here in another fifteen minutes."

"You are a patient man, Carl Garrett."

"One of my more noticeable virtues, I guess."

She held her hand out in the white light that slanted out into the yard. He took it. The pads of her long hand had a velvety warmth. "Thanks, Carl. I think it helped."

He released her hand. "Just don't resent me for listening. And I will listen some more, if you want."

He walked back to his house, climbing the abrupt slope, then pausing and, on an impulse that was not, he suspected, entirely without a strange flavor of guilt, went back to the red maple where he had stood before. He watched her in the kitchen. She took the bottles away, put her book on a counter top, wiped off the booth top. She moved in her slow and leggy way, but without waste motion. Her face, when he could see it, was quite still and thoughtful, her rather heavy lips set in a level and contemplative line. She stood quite still in the middle of the kitchen, elbows in her palms, head bent at an angle as though she were listening, standing hipshot and quiet. Then she so evidently sighed that he imagined he could hear her.

Thunder had eaten half the sky. Lightning stabbed into the black earth a mile away, and the thunder cracked and then rolled around the hills. She picked up the book and moved out of sight and the kitchen lights went out. He saw another light come on and shine pallidly through the windows of the room that he knew was their bedroom. Just as he reached his back door the first swollen drops began to fall, and one struck the back of his left arm, just above the wrist.

He turned out the lights and closed the windows against the rain. He took a long shower, and when he was in his bed the brief heavy rain had stopped, but the lightning continued, so that in its flashes he could see the sterile flatness of Joan's bed.

He thought of how it would be at night in the hospital, the hushed steps hurrying down the corridors, the starchy rustlings, the sighs and the moanings. He did not want to think of Cindy and her problems, but only of Joan.

And he remembered . . .

FOUR

He had graduated at twenty-two in the class of '37 from the Wharton School of Finance at the University of Pennsylvania. His kid sister, Marian, had just graduated from the same high school he had attended, back home in Youngstown, with grades almost as good as the ones he had made there.

The four years had been rough, financially, and would have been impossible had it not been for the partial scholarship he had won when he graduated from high school. He remembered that his father and mother and Marian had driven to Philadelphia in the old gray '31 Packard to attend the graduation ceremonies.

And after the ceremonies, when he had changed out of the cap and gown, he had the showdown with his father in the room at the Ben Franklin Hotel. Bill Garrett was a construction contractor. He had learned his trade working for other men, and in 1924 he had gone into business for himself. He was honest and energetic and likable, and he had built up a good business. Bill Garrett liked to live well, and he was about as provident as any grasshopper. In the fall of 1933, a month after Carl had entered Pennsylvania, Bill went bankrupt, and went back to working for other men. They lost their home and moved to a flat no better than the one where Carl had been born in 1915.

In 1937, two months before Carl graduated, Bill Garrett had gone back into business for himself, in a very small way.

Bill sat on the bed and packed his pipe and said, "Like I've been writing you, it looks like we can make this thing go. It won't take too damn long to get out of the business of building chicken coops and repairing roofs. I've got a good lease and a truck that will run, and I've got back some of the boys who worked for me before."

Carl had been standing at the window. "I . . . I don't want to take a chance on it, Dad."

"What the hell do you mean, son? Good God, I've got the know-how. You can take all the paper work off my back."

40

"I don't want to help build something up and lose it all over again." ·

"But don't you see, you're working for yourself. We own the business. We can spit in any man's eye. It'll be mighty lean going for a while. I won't deny that."

"How about Marian?"

"What about Marian?"

"It'll be so lean, Dad, that there won't be a prayer of sending her to college."

"It isn't so important for girls. She's a pretty kid, son. She'll be married before too long. She's eighteen."

"I just can't see it. I'm sorry. I don't want to hurt you."

"But I've been making these plans how we . . ."

"Dad, you can handle it yourself. You did before."

"I can damn well sure handle it myself! But I figured you'd be able to see . . ."

"Maybe I want something with more security. Maybe I *want* to be an employee. Maybe I don't have the temperament to have my neck stuck out."

"You sound like you don't have any guts, like you don't want to take a chance. The bigger the chance you take, the bigger the money when you win. Didn't you learn that much in this place?"

"Yes."

"I like the way the future looks, Carl. I can smell money ahead. The world's stirring again. I want to specialize in home construction. Build 'em fast and cheap and honest. There's a hell of a shortage, boy. Things have been at a standstill too long."

'I'm truly sorry, Dad, but I've given it a lot of thought. I'll just be another mouth for the business to feed. And if I do it my way, I can help Marian. She's willing I should help her."

"When did you talk to her about this?"

"We've been writing."

Bill Garrett crossed the room and knocked his pipe out into a tin waste basket, noisily. He sighed. "Well, I can't force you. If I'd been able to pay the freight on this fancy education, I guess I'd have some kind of a claim. But you got the scholarship, and you worked for the rest of it. Where are you going to try to get a job?"

"I've got one. I was interviewed here at the school six weeks ago. I got the firm offer ten days ago and I accepted it. I'm going with the Carrier Corporation in Syracuse, New

York. The pay is okay and I'll keep my expenses down."

Bill Garrett shook his head and smiled in a sad way. "The little frog in a great big puddle, boy. Punch the clock and draw your pay. But if you've got to have it that way, I better just shut up and go along with it. But I've got a hunch you're going to be mighty, mighty sorry one day."

So he had gone to work for Carrier in July. Marian worked all summer and entered Columbia in the fall. And Bill Garrett fought doggedly and well to keep the tiny new firm from foundering. Carl sensed that his mother approved of his decision, but such was the quality of loyalty of Betty Garrett that she would never give voice to her approval. She had accepted the loss of the company and their home with gallantry. She loved Bill Garrett. It was, perhaps, that simple.

Carl met Joan Browning at two o'clock in the morning of a January Sunday in 1940 when the thermometer was down to eight below zero.

By then he had worked for Carrier for over two years. As far as he could find out, he was doing well. He had received two raises in pay. He lived in a furnished room on West Addams Street not far from Syracuse University. Marian had ceased to be as much of a drain because she had found a job, and also because Bill Garrett, doing slightly better, insisted on helping out too. So, for fifty dollars down, Carl had bought a black 1936 Ford tudor in good condition.

During the past year he had become friendly with a young couple named Dick and Deedee Hightmann. Dick was an engineer at Brown-Lipe-Chapin. They owned a house out near Jamesville, southeast of the city, an old farmhouse. Carl went out often. They were comfortable to be with, and very much in love. They had decided that marriage was such a fine institution that it was a shame that Carl was not a participant. Deedee was tireless in her attempts at matchmaking.

On this occasion, the Hightmanns had thrown a party for a house guest, a girl named Miriam something who had been Deedee's roommate in school, and who, according to Deedee, was fabulously attractive. Three other couples were invited, and Carl was lined up to be the date of the fabulous Miriam.

She had turned out to be fabulously attractive, as advertised, and, within an hour of the time the party started, fabulously drunk. Her pretty mouth wandered all over her face and her pretty eyes were glazed. Not long after she had ceased being comprehensible, she attempted a rather distressing strip tease, and was bundled off to bed by the Hightmanns. Deedee said, sorrowfully, "She never used to be like that." From then on the party was fun.

Carl left a little before two to drive back to the city. It was an exceptionally clear night, crackling cold, with the stars high and a remote moon making the snow banks on either side of the road gleam. He felt slightly fuzzy from the drinks he had had, so he drove slowly and fixed the window so that the frigid air blew against his face.

As was his habit when driving back from the Hightmanns', he took a small county road from Jamesville over to DeWitt where he could turn left on Route 5 and head into the city.

He was not over a mile from Jamesville when he saw, far ahead, a figure walking on the right hand side of the road, next to snow banks half as high as she was. As he came closer he saw that the girl was bareheaded. She wore a pale formal dress and a small wrap. She carried an evening purse and her high-heeled slippers. She did not turn or make any gesture when he drove by her. He stopped forty feet beyond her and reached over and rolled the right window down.

When she was even with the car he said, "Hello!"

She walked on, chin high. He started up and drove slowly beside her. His tires creaked on the snow. He saw that she was a very pretty girl.

"Look, you'll freeze your feet."

No glance or answer.

"Miss, I assure you I am perfectly harmless. It's below zero. Do you want to lose your toes?"

The steady walk continued.

"My name is Carl Garrett and I work at Carrier and I'm on my way home after a party in Jamesville. I've got a heater in here I paid eleven dollars for and it throws off a lot of heat. I'll take you wherever you want to go."

The steady pace slowed. She stopped and turned and looked in at him. "A lot of heat?" she asked, and her teeth chattered.

"More than you can stand when you turn it on high."

She opened the door and slid in quickly and rolled the window up. He closed the window on his side. She hugged herself, teeth chattering, shuddering all over so that he could feel the vibration in the car. With the slender shoes and the evening purse she had erected a fragile barricade on the seat between them.

"S-S-Syracuse," she said.

By the time they reached DeWitt she had stopped shuddering and chattering, and the heat inside the car had released the frozen fragrance of her perfume.

"What happened?" he asked. "You don't have to tell me if you don't want to."

"Oh, I'll tell you, all right. I'll tell you."

Anger burned behind her words. He found out that her name was Joan Browning. She had graduated from Syracuse the previous June. She worked in an insurance office in the city. On this Saturday night she had gone back to a formal dance at her sorority on the campus with a boy she had been dating. They had left the dance and driven out into the country and parked and had quarreled bitterly and violently. She didn't say what about. She had gotten out into the cold, expecting him to plead with her to get back into the car. But instead he had driven off. That had made her so angry that when he came back five minutes later, looking for her, she had hidden. When he had given up, perhaps assuming she had been picked up, she had started walking. It was almost impossible to walk on the packed snow in high heels. She had soon taken them off. She was looking for a house where she could phone a cab to come out and get her. But the houses were dark. He was the second car that had come along. The first one had nearly run her down.

"But if you hid from him, it isn't his fault you're walking."

"He drove away, didn't he?" she said grimly.

"How are your feet?"

"They feel terrible. They hurt like fire."

"Good sign."

"You wouldn't say that if they were your feet."

"We should stop and rub snow on them."

"Thank you very much. No."

"Look, Miss Joan Browning, I'm not the guy who drove away. I'm the guy giving you a ride."

"I'm very grateful for the ride and I'll try not to be so cross. But I'm still mad. I'm . . . I'm damn mad."

She told him the address. She shared an apartment with two other girls in a big old frame house on Genesee Street. After he stopped in front, near a street light, she put her shoes on. As she was putting them on, he went around the car and opened the door for her. She got out and he could see that she wasn't tall, even in the high heels, and she was wonderfully pretty, and her smile was good.

"I'm getting over being mad now," she said. "Thanks an awful lot."

"I was glad I could help."

They said good night and she started up the walk. "Joan," he said. She stopped and turned. "Look, maybe I could stop by tomorrow afternoon, just to see if . . . you're all right. About three."

"I'm perfectly all right."

"But if I don't know, I'll worry."

"Well . . ."

"I can make it any time you say."

"Then . . . three will be okay . . . Carl."

By the end of the following week they were spending every possible moment together. She would wait for him after she got out of work, and he would be along fifteen minutes later. And there came to be a dozen of "their" places. Drugstores. Sandwich shops. They sat and talked for uncounted hours. Never before had he been as eloquent, or his mind as agile and perceptive. Never before had there been so many things to talk about, so many that it seemed they could never cover them, not even in a lifetime. Sometimes he was uncomfortably aware that he was doing most of the talking, but she seemed pleased to have him.

He did learn that she was the only daughter of a doctor, a widower and general practitioner who practiced in Watertown, New York. She was twenty-three and had a brother, Walt, ten years older, an Annapolis graduate then on sea duty on a light cruiser. The other child, a young son, had died as an infant.

Her eyes were brown, her nose snubbed, her mouth generous. Her brown hair was particularly fine and silky. She was five feet five and weighed a hundred and twenty pounds, and he could almost span her waist with his hands. She was ripely, glowingly, abundantly mature. They sat in small quiet places in the heart of the upstate winter, and they looked into each other's eyes until there was nothing at all in the world but their awareness of each other. And they talked. And talked. And talked.

She learned about Lois back in Youngstown, and Marie and Christy in Philadelphia, and immediately despised all of them as avidly as he hated the two boys she told him about.

After three weeks had passed they knew that it was love and they knew that it had never happened this way before to anybody else, and they knew that it was a miracle that would last forever, and they both accepted the inevitability that, had they not met on that January night, they would have met very soon in any case because it was inevitable, you see. But it was especially nice to meet the way they had. And how did you meet your wife, Mr. Garrett? Oh, I picked her up on the highway one night. It was very delicious.

In late February he drove up to Watertown with her and met Dr. Browning. He was a gruff and busy man who appeared to bully his housekeeper, his nurse, his dog and his daughter. But all of them seemed quite unaware of being bullied.

He said, "Wedding in June, eh? Rhymes with moon and spoon and very damn soon. Sure you kids know which end is up? I imagine I'll have to endure having it here. But why you want to go batting around Canada on a combination two-week vacation and honeymoon, I'll never know." He winked at Carl. "Me, I'd rent a cabin in a pine woods and stock it up with food and stay right there. Fewer distractions." And he slapped Joan's rounded rear with a gusto that made her yelp, then kissed her forehead gently and said, "Time you were married, Joanie. Time to put all that female equipment to work at its proper function. Life is function, and any man looking at you would know damn well you can't function at your best adding up insurance premiums."

"Father!" she said, red-faced.

"This one doesn't look as if he's ever had enough to eat, but from the way he looks at you, girl, your marriage might last a couple or three years. Too bad Walt can't come join the festivities."

And on a much more harrowing weekend in March, after having prepared them by letter, Carl drove Joan down to Youngstown, arriving at ten on Saturday night. His parents took to Joan immediately. Bill bragged about how much better things were going in the construction game. He had acquired a plot of land and he was mortgaging every resource to put up a half dozen speculative houses. He talked largely, but he looked worn and weary. They left at noon on Sunday and arrived in Syracuse late and exhausted.

Spring came on an April day and after that, whenever

they could, they drove out into the country. Later, after they started having picnics, they found a special place, a stream flowing through a narrow curving valley where there were grassy banks. The isolation and privacy of the little valley complicated the problem they had set for themselves. They had agreed, with a certain solemnity, to wait until they were married to consummate their love. They agreed, in a most sophisticated way, that it was actually only a symbol, but at least it was one way of proving to each other that they were people of character and restraint. But as the spring became more florid, the grasses more heated, the sun more languorous, the agreement became increasingly difficult. She was not a sensuous woman, but she was lusty and hearty and primitive in her needs, and her responses to his every touch were almost instantaneous. They took increasing liberties, aware of the tantalizingly narrow path they walked, but telling each other that so long as the ultimate was not accomplished, they were living up to their sacred agreement. When he would slide his hand under her clothing to cup her breast, large and warm and firm, the erectile nipple would rise to hardness against his palm and her breath would become bellows and furnace.

Time after time they would, in their quiet place, on the khaki blanket spread on the shady grass, go beyond the limits of control, but always one or the other, much more often Joan, would bring them back from that edge of danger to sit rigidly apart until breathing slowed and the high flush faded. And he began to depend on her to take the responsibility. And later drive back to the city with aching loins and feeling of tension.

He grew to depend on her so much that on one Sunday afternoon in May when she was carried beyond her ability to protest or object, he could not turn back. She was virgin, but after a single moan in the initial shock and pain, her passions returned undiminished, and the sun circled in a crazed sky, and the trees in the valley trembled, and the sound of the busy stream running over stones faded into an utter silence.

Afterward, with tears in their eyes, they each demanded to be given the responsibility and the blame. They did not think to blame it on Spring, or the softness of the grassy bank. And then she became very upset and nervous about the possibility of her being impregnated. It did not seem possible to them that such a fierce union could have oc-

curred without creating a child. He drove her back to the
apartment at reckless speed where, using the equipment of
one of her apartment mates, she performed the futile and
rather degrading ceremony of contraception, knowing full
well that it was much too late—while he waited down in the
car. They went to a movie that night and all through it she
clung tightly to his hand. Once when he looked at her he
saw tears on her cheek.

After ten suspenseful days she met him with guilty joy
to announce that her period had come precisely on schedule,
and then they told each other how lucky they were, and
then they began to worry if whether, after they were married,
they would be able to have any kids. But, they said, it would
be stupid to slip again, knowing that the last day of June,
the day set for their wedding, was only a little over a month
away. They told each other that they had found out how
truly wonderful their marriage would be. And he, with pon-
tifical sophistication, told her that perhaps they had been
wise to ascertain their sexual compatibility. This cool statement annoyed her. They agreed that it would be nonsense
to take such a risk again.

But they did slip again, of course, as perhaps both of
them suspected they would. They slipped three times beside
the same stream in the same valley, and when she found he
had come prepared for the possibility, she was angry with
him and accused him of having no character. It took him a
long time to convince her that he did indeed have character,
a respectable amount of character, and he had equipped himself in much the same frame of mind as a farmer might
have while purchasing a lightning rod for his barn. You
didn't expect lightning to strike. But if it did . . . Surely,
working in an insurance office, she could understand that.
And when she was comforted, he indulged in a little self-
analysis, wondering if perhaps there wasn't some Freudian
implication in the analogy he had invented. He stopped
wondering aloud when he realized his flight of fancy was
making her uncomfortable. He had begun to learn that when
he voiced some of the oblique flights of fancy that went on
in his mind, she would become restless and slightly resentful
of him. But this was a most minor flaw, if indeed it could
be considered a flaw, in the fair Joan Browning. She was
staunch and honest and almost invariably gay. She was affectionate and neat and as personally tidy as a cat. And, best

of all, best of everything, her physical hunger for him was as great as his for her.

So the wedding finally came, and they were married in her home in Watertown, and the most obvious cases of snuffles were on the part of his sister, Marian, and Joan's father, and two stone-faced maiden aunts of Joan that she claimed to have seen only twice in her life before. Bill Garrett had unloaded his speculative houses and came in a new suit and an almost new Cadillac, and Carl wondered what badly needed piece of equipment the company had been forced to forgo because Bill Garrett felt he needed a Cadillac.

Dr. Browning's wedding present was five hundred dollars, and the present from Carl's parents was initialed luggage for both of them.

They got away after the wedding lunch and drove up to Cape Vincent and took the ferry to Kingston and stayed the night there, and then drove the next day to Ottawa and there found a big room in a pension, with a great feather bed and a long view through big windows. And decided to stay two nights rather than one. And ended up staying twelve nights in all, while the marked road maps lay in the bureau drawer, forgotten.

During those twelve days and nights he began to learn her the way a soldier might learn a strange terrain. He learned her tempos in love and discovered which things most pleased her. She liked great hot steamy baths, and to have her smooth back scrubbed, and to come to bed all pink and humid from her bath and be made love to. After the first few days, when she was more at ease with him, she reverted to her private custom of padding around nude, and teased him when she found he had a funny streak of modesty which prevented his doing so. Whenever she brushed her hair, she had her underlip caught behind her teeth. Sometimes she was as boisterously playful as a puppy, cuffing and pummeling him, then fleeing in mock fright, wanting to be caught, wanting, after being caught, for the playful violence to turn into something else.

All during the drive back to Syracuse she sat close beside him, her shoulder and hip touching him, her hand resting on his thigh. She was content, and she hummed small songs, and her eyes had a look of sleep and love. And, as an index to the efficacy of honeymoon, it was very fine indeed.

He thought of the honeymoon girl, and he thought of the woman in the hospital tonight, seventeen years older, twenty pounds heavier—but the same person. Incredibly the very same person, a girl who thought of herself and reacted to others in the same way as the honeymoon girl. If she was awake she would be looking into the darkness and being afraid. But it was a fear she would not show. Because of that staunchness.

So many things had changed. He wondered how he would have felt on that wedding day if he could have looked ahead and seen how the future would be for those of the wedding party.

His sister, Marian, who had wept, seemed now quite beyond tears. There was no more softness in her. She was in New York now, a crisp and cynical and too aggressive divorcee, a highly paid television consultant in one of the major advertising agencies.

Bill Garrett had lived up to the rather plaintive promise of his almost new Cadillac. During the war he had done cost-plus work at a huge airbase. As soon as the war ended, he went into small home construction and rode the crest of a rich wave, sinking everything from each development into the next one and making each one bigger. In late 1954 he had suffered a mild heart attack, and had immediately sold out for a figure that would enable him to live in Sarasota in comfort for the rest of his life. The latest photograph that Betty had sent showed the pair of them, in color, on his small dock. They looked brown and smiling and healthy. They were barefoot, and Bill was proudly holding what, according to the legend on the back of the photo, was a fourteen-pound snook.

Dr. Browning had diagnosed his own case of cancer of the lower bowel in 1943 while Carl was overseas, and had died nine months later. Walt Browning, who had survived the war, was a brilliant fifty-year-old Navy captain, now lecturing at the Army War College.

Everyone would want to know about Joan, he realized. As soon as he got the good word from Bernie Madden on Tuesday he would get on the phone and let everybody know. Kip and Nancy and all the rest of them.

He sat up and plumped the pillow and stretched out again, trying to find a position in which he could sleep. It was two-thirty by the luminous dial of the bedroom clock. Too late to take a pill. It would make him too dopey tomorrow.

He realized that by thinking of old times and old places he had been carefully preventing himself from thinking of Cindy Cable. But what harm could there be in thinking about Cindy? The poor kid was in a mess. And they were good friends. He wondered if she was also awake. And, if she was asleep, in what position did she sleep? Joan liked to sleep on her left side, with her left hand under the pillow and her right hand resting near her stomach, clasped into a slack fist.

And what did Cindy wear while sleeping? Joan slept nude. He wore pajama tops. Wasn't there some sort of conversation several months ago? What had Bucky said? Oh, of course. "Cindy is the old-fashioned type. Nightgowns. In the summer they're made out of cobwebs and in the winter they're made out of outing flannel. I tell you, you see her in the winter with her hair in braids and that outing flannel tent on her, she looks like she came over in a covered wagon."

And, remembering it, he seemed to hear a sneer in Bucky's voice that he had not noticed at the time.

So why not think of Cindy?

And, thinking of her, wondering about her, he slid quite readily into a sleep so deep that when the alarm went off at seven-thirty he felt rested and refreshed.

FIVE

Carl Garrett had been transferred from Camden to the Hillton Metal Products Division of Ballinger in June of 1951 when the plant was first opened. A team of specialists from the Industrial Management firm that had designed the plant remained for several months after it was opened. The production areas were long windowless rectangles, and inside them, in the air-conditioned interior with its controlled lighting, systematic and colorful paint scheme, the flow from raw material storage through processing to final assembly, inspection, crating and shipment was severely logical.

The plant was designed to handle a multiplicity and diversity of small metal units and assemblies with economy and flexibility, and a maximum of control, and a minimum of confusion. Inside the production areas the light and the climate was always the same. From the catwalks above the pastel production lines, the production control specialists could look down into the whirring, clacking, chittering, grumbling, buzzing production areas and see, not confusion, but the steady operation of a master plan of elegance and purpose. Hard metals, spinning at ultra-high speeds, bit and peeled and pierced and polished softer metals, while both the heat of cutting and the reek of hot oils were whipped away by the wide-mouthed suck of the air-conditioning system. Women in trim and functional coveralls, in varying shades to denote department and function, tended the semiautomatic equipment, pushed the glittering, roller-bearing racks, fed the conveyors, took the samplings for the statistical control of inspection, fed the hoppers, yelled for stock, screeched for setup, briskly busy with only the automatic half of their minds on the job at hand. Above and around and below the shimmering roar they traded bawdy gossip, formed cliques, bedeviled the weaker ones, all with a continual hip-rolling, oblique-eyed, arrogant awareness of men. All men. The foremen and the visitors and the specialists on the catwalk and the engineers and the stock boys and the factory reps and the repair specialists.

Down on the floor the setup men changed the bite and timing and tolerances of the waiting machines, and other men threaded the automation tapes into the completely automatic equipment.

Behind the catwalk were the glass doors that opened into the rooms where it was all controlled, where girls key-punched the multi-colored cards, where the sorters shuffled and clicked, where the alphabetical and numerical tabulators rattled out the essential lists, where the panel boards clicked and the lights blinked. The tabulation equipment and electronic controls made all of the little decisions. Time to order more of this, and time to stop the run on that, and better make an eight percent overrun on this because the tolerance is close, and time to cut three turret lathes on the A line over to order 66-81-F rather than pile up dead time.

In these rooms the floor noise was slightly muted so that the shrillnesses were taken out, and the sounds seemed deeper, a chuckling and mumbling.

Carl Garrett liked to leave the main offices and walk over to one of the production areas and climb to the catwalk and lean on the rail and look down at the acres of movement and activity, and amuse himself with insane conjecturings. Would it not be nice if, parallel to this building there was another building where the neat shipping cartons were unpacked and the clever fabrications went then through uninspection, disassembly—were torn back down and re-formed into the basic rods and sheets and coils and blocks which were then sent back to be run through again? Of course the personnel in this building would know nothing of what transpired in the neighboring building. It would be a closed circuit, endlessly efficient. Or, on the other hand, let them know what was being done. A few, a very few, might wonder what the hell it was all about, but the rest of them would shrug and go ahead with the job and draw their pay and bitch to the shop steward about coffee breaks and work standards and seniority and how come I got moved over onto the damn grinder and they give that Rayzek bitch my place on the bench and when are they going to do something about that john that's running over so it's like a lake in there anyhow?

He would look down and look at the Chinese red of the moving parts, and the sea-gray of the housings and hearty buttocks in azure blue, and bleached hair tied in a green bandanna, and come to believe that this was the whole world, that nothing existed from sea to sea but these fluorescent interiors held at a rigid seventy-one degrees, standing jowl to jowl while the forgotten sun shines down on all the blank roofs.

Maybe it was all part of a monstrous conspiracy. Maybe the electronic controls were lying, and there was utterly no use for the gleaming and intricate and clever products of the production lines. So that, day after day, barges carried the taped and labeled cartons to sea and dumped them beyond the continental shelf.

And would shake his head and go back to his own office and his own staff and wonder which was more unreal, the production areas or his own function.

His function was easy. Find out what it costs, per unit, and down to the last fraction of a mill. It took fifteen people and over a hundred thousand dollars of accounting and tabulating equipment to perform the function. There are twenty-six thousand units in an order, say. So merely take the cost of materials, including waste and scrap, and the appropriate labor costs for production, inspection, packaging, etc., and a proportional amount of factory overhead (and keep track of that too, as closely as you keep track of every change in the cost of materials) and then divide the whole shooting match by 26,000 and you can step up proudly and say, "Gentlemen, each widget we made in the last reporting period cost us precisely $1.3931. This naturally includes that order's share of the cost of reupholstering the furniture in the women's lounge. And many other things."

So mighty Ballinger computes the new sales price for the next batch of widgets—and with great guile sells the whole production to itself.

And, in the terribly important and significant annual report, the total unit costs of each of several hundred different products, multiplied by the total in each order, must, of course, exactly match the total operating expense of the Hillton Metal Products Division of the Ballinger Corporation.

And there is, of course, one other little function above and beyond merely keeping track. That is, by report and memorandum, call attention, in a severe and acerbic way, to those areas where costs are climbing too rapidly, and those areas where it would appear that a saving might be effected —without alienating entirely the devoted gentlemen in Production, Purchasing, Engineering, Design, Maintenance, Labor Relations, Inspection, Stock Control, Storage and Shipment.

Watchdog all potential leaks because, should in the next reporting period an identical widget cost $1.4338, that is a serious matter. It is a 3% jump in the cost of making widgets in a reporting period when overall production costs advanced a mere .07%.

And what makes a widget stand out like a sore thumb? Too much scrap or too many rejections? Clamp down on Production or Inspection. Someone must explain. Ah ha! Now we have it! Stock Control goofed. Submitted an incorrect report on the present level of Compacted Gezundamite in stock, and so to avoid an interruption of production, Purchasing had some flown in by air express, and the widget order was debited with the expense involved, thus raising the unit cost by 3%. Appended hereto is the buff copy of the report from Stock Control explaining the situation and what steps have been taken to prevent a recurrence in the future. A new reorder level has been set. There is every expectation that on the widget order now in process of production, the unit cost will drop to the approximate level reported on May 8th to your office, covering the April reporting period. Signed, Carl A. Garrett.

A staff of fifteen, twelve of them female. Fifteen hundred square feet of working area for clerical personnel, eleven hundred square feet for files and electric accounting equipment, four hundred square feet for male staff assistants. One hundred and sixty-eight square feet for Carl Garrett, assistant to the plant manager in charge of factory cost accounting. An office twelve by fourteen. Name in dark red on the blond face of the flush door with the spun aluminum doorknob. Two casement windows through which can be seen, beyond the parking lot and the gritty old shoulder of the Pike Wire and Cable Company, the white span of the new bridge three miles away, and a glint of river, and the summer smog over the city beyond.

One standard sepia photomural of an aerial view of the plant. One air-conditioning grid in a high corner, humming almost inaudibly. Plywood paneling in pale birch. Wall-to-wall carpeting in a tufted blue-green. One gray steel executive desk with dark blue linoleum top. One stubby gray desk lamp, shaped like a toadstool. One heavy chair with arms, behind the desk, upholstered in gray plastic. Two other comfortable chairs. One straight chair. One machine for dictation, standing against the wall behind the cattycorner desk, standing waiting on slender legs. On the side of the desk, a gray phone hanging. On the desk a dark gray intercom, a double pen set, a ceramic pot containing a half dozen needle-pointed yellow pencils, Venus No. 3, points upward, an in-basket and an out-basket, a memo pad, a framed snapshot of Joan with the kids, a large glass and leather ash tray with a grid of brass wire across the top.

Seated at the desk, the chief of section, in gray dacron, button-down collar, green tie with small black figure. He has swiveled his chair a quarter turn so that he looks rather blankly at a bank of gray filing cabinets against the far wall. The door to the corridor is closed. A financial report is open on his desk. He has a yellow pencil in his hand and he is gently stroking the rim of his right ear with the eraser end.

Enter through the open door at his left, Mrs. Brisbie, his secretary. Garrett is Captain of the command. Finch, Goldlaw and Sherban are his junior officers. Mrs. Brisbie is his master sergeant, a tall woman in her thirties with black hair, a cold, pale and elegant Italianesque face, a long white neck, thin legs and tiny and delicate ankles. But between the neck and the legs, there is an astonishing and startling abundance of big round warm thrusting breasts, and a protrusion of rounded meaty buttocks. Mrs. Brisbie carries herself as though all these feminine riches are an oppressive burden, an affliction she did not ask for and must endure, a grotesquerie she must continually attempt to ignore, despised burdens forever bobbling about, flaunting themselves in a continual state of bawdy insurrection. No man will make the mistake of being misled by her abundances, because there is about her the arid flavor of the voluntary spinster. She is a cold and utterly humorless and vastly efficient mechanism, which dresses itself with utmost severity and exudes a faint aroma of disinfectant. From the side her figure forms a startling and unlikely letter S, so pronounced that even though she tries to hold herself erectly, when she walks it appears that she is bent slightly forward from the waist. There is much office speculation about the un-likely fact of there ever having been a Mr. Brisbie. Some suspect that he is a myth. It is known that she lives with a maiden aunt, that she collects antique glass and crystal.

When the Hillton plant first opened, she was in the stenographic pool. It is remembered that an unwary stock boy, deluded by the splendor of the hips clenching their way down the corridor directly in front of him, perhaps bemused beyond caution, administered a dreadful tweak. Mrs. Brisbie whirled like a striking snake and irrevocably flattened his nose against his face with a small white fist clenched to marble hardness.

She walks noiselessly to the desk, and makes a small correct sound in her throat. Carl Garrett starts slightly and swivels his chair back and looks up at the white face and feels for the ten thousandth time as though the stupendous breasts are aimed at him like twin howitzers.

"Yes?"

"I just wanted to remind you of the meeting in Mr. Hardy's office at eleven, Mr. Garrett."

He looked at his watch. "Thanks. Better take off right now, eh? It isn't really a conference, Mrs. Brisbie. We just sit around and match quarters." He watched her expression, saw the customary look of bafflement, then a faint flush, then comprehension that this must be one of Mr. Garrett's jokes, saw the artificial smile, and heard the flat and deadly ha-ha. She walked back into her office and he stood for a moment, wishing he could stop himself from ever making any kind of light comment to Mrs. Brisbie, no matter how inane. He knew it was painful for her to have to cope, and it was painful watching her. As he walked down the corridor he wished he could get rid of her. He wished he could, just one time, have the guts to be unfair. She was ferociously competent and utterly loyal. But, by God, she was a deadening and stultifying influence around his shop. He realized dolefully that he would never have the heart to get rid of her. She wouldn't be able to understand why. And she was healthy as a horse. Never missed a day. Just as he reached Jim Hardy's office he realized that he might in all probability have to endure Mrs. Brisbie for another twenty-three years. He found the idea more distressing than he would have thought possible. He and Brisbie would grow old together. They would wither and fade, until nothing was left of either of them but wisps of dryness. Everything would fade but the Brisbie breasts. They would remain unchanged—vast taut globes, flushed with life and youth, quivering rebelliously.

"I like people to walk in here smiling," Jim Hardy said. "What's so funny?"

Jim Hardy, the plant manager, was an amiable and reasonably able man in his middle fifties. He had a guilty secret and did not suspect that most of his staff was quite aware of it. He knew he bore a certain resemblance to President Eisenhower, and because of his deep admiration for the man, he had been, for several years, patterning his smile, speech, dress and habits accordingly. Hitherto a duffer, he had even gone to work on his golf game with such application and diligence that he had gotten it down into the middle eighties. And he had done such extensive reading in the field of military literature that he was able to use battlefield analogies in discussing HMP problems. Behind his back he was known as Little Ike, and even though Carl was terribly afraid that one day someone would slip and use it to his face, he did want to be a witness when that happened.

"A daydream, Jim. Or I guess you'd call it a mental image concerning my Mrs. Brisbie."

Ray Walsh, doodling on one of the yellow pads at the small conference table, chuckled and said, "She's got one advantage as a secretary, Carl. No wife, meeting her, is ever going to be alarmed when her husband has to work late at the office."

"Everybody here?" Jim said. "All right, men. Tim here has been planning the order of battle on this extrusion problem, and now he's come up with a flank attack that looks mighty interesting to me. Tell the boys about it, Tim."

Carl left the office at twenty after five on Monday. He drove into the city planning to eat at Herman's Rathskeller on Grant Avenue. But, when he stopped for a drink at the bar, he ran into Gil Sullivan, a Crescent Ridge neighbor, and they got into a discussion about the school problem, and he had several drinks and then suddenly realized he wouldn't have time to eat and get to the hospital by seven. So he had another drink, and when he drove out to the hospital he realized, to his surprise, that he was slightly tight. He drove with extra caution and so it was a little after seven when he got to room 314. Rosa Myers was in her bed by the windows reading the book Cindy had brought Joan. Joan had her bed cranked down and her eyes were closed.

She opened them and smiled and said, "Hi, dear. Crank me up, please."

"How are you, honey? You look a little pooped."

"I'm exhausted and I'm famished. I could eat a horse, but they won't let me. And you smell like a still."

"I was going to eat at Herman's, but I ran into Gil Sullivan and we went around and around on the school thing. I'll eat after I leave here."

"Was there anything interesting in the mail?"

"I haven't been home yet."

"Oh, I was hoping there might be something from the kids. Aren't the red roses lovely, darling? Molly brought them this afternoon."

"Who else came?"

"Molly and Cindy and Jane Cardamo, and that horrible Martha Garron. I haven't the faintest idea why she'd come see me. Her dress was absolutely filthy and she was high as a kite. We thought she'd fall off the chair, didn't we, Rosa?"

"That one was a beaut," Rosa said.

"Did Cindy stay long?"

"About fifteen minutes, I guess. She didn't look very well to me. And I thought she acted a little bit odd."

"Did she?" he said casually. He wondered why he so instinctively decided not to tell Joan what Cindy had told him. He was not accustomed to keeping secrets from her. Certainly this was not a guilty secret. And nothing could have been more innocent than having a beer with Cindy. He told himself that it was best not to tell Joan because she might fret about it, and this was no time for her to have anything on her mind. During the hour and a half of visiting hours, he had ten minutes alone with her. When he left he said, "Is the time still set for ten?"

"That's what Bernie told me again today."

He bent over the bed and kissed her and squeezed her arm. "I'll be around. I'll get here by nine-thirty anyway. Don't be scared, baby."

She frowned. "I don't think I'll like this spinal thing."

"They'll have you so doped up you won't mind it a bit."

He kissed her again. When he walked down the hall toward the elevators his eyes suddenly filled with tears. She looked so damn helpless. They were going to cut her and she was scared. He knew that the five or so drinks were making him more emotional than usual. And he suspected that he had stopped counting his drinks because he was frightened too.

He ate again at the drive-in and went back to the empty house. The mail was dull, and there was nothing from the kids. That made him feel less guilty about not thinking of the mail before going to the hospital. The effects of the drinks had worn off but for a slight headache. He went across the back yard and was surprised at the sharpness of his disappointment when he found the Cable house completely dark. He hesitated, and then went to where he could see into the car port. It was empty.

After a few minutes he was able to be amused at himself for being so annoyed with Cindy for not being home. What she did, where she went, was no part of his business.

He decided he would read for a time and go to bed early.

SIX

It was twenty-five to eleven when he thought he heard her drive in. He lifted his head and listened, and heard the thud of a car door near by. He put the book down and walked over to a west window. When a light came on in the Cable house he could not see the window, but he could see the reflection of the light on the leaves and on the night.

He stood there for a half minute, and then went back to his book. He had been having difficulty concentrating on what he was reading, but now he found it almost impossible. He slapped the book shut and put it on the table beside his chair. He went into the bedroom, undressed and showered and put on his robe.

Suddenly he thought, Why in hell am I dithering around? I'll be making mountains out of molehills. I'll be giving this a lot of significance it doesn't deserve. The Cables are good friends. Cindy is a good friend. And probably just as damn lonesome and just as upset as I am. That's when you use your friends, isn't it?

So he put on fresh slacks and moccasins and a blue golf shirt and opened a can of beer and walked to the red maple. The kitchen lights were on, but she was not in the kitchen. He hesitated a moment, and then went to her kitchen door and rapped. The door was open. Through the screen he could hear the hushed roar of the shower she was taking. In that instant he visualized her so clearly and so perfectly that he might have been staring into the shower stall rather than into that particular corner of his mind. He saw her long flanks and the secret curvings of her and the soapy freshness, the cones of abrupt breasts, and the belly's gentle convexity and the long complex curve of her back and the wiry pyramid of pubic hair between satin thighs. In the instant of his visualization desire came to him, savage and ready, and he knew that it was not new. He knew that it had been with him for a long time, and that he had never permitted himself to accept it, to even be consciously aware of it. He thought of all the times he had looked at her, very calmly and casually and thought, Cindy is a damn good-looking woman. There was no ordinance against making such an observation, against admiring her objectively, or enjoying being with her and talking to her. And because desire had been so long suppressed, it had a violence that startled him.

He could remember only one time in their relationship when, for a few moments, he had been stirred by something beyond friendship. It had happened last New Year's Eve at the Timberlane Country Club, the small family club to which so many of the Crescent Ridge people belonged. They had not gone to the party with the same group as the Cables. At midnight, slightly fuzzy with drinks, after having exchanged the ritual kisses with the other women in his party, Carl had come upon Cindy in the small hallway where the nickel slot machines were. Her silver eye mask was pushed up onto her forehead, and he stopped her, and took her by the shoulders and grinned at her, weaving slightly and said, "Old Cindy. A fine new year to old Cindy." And laid his mouth on hers, and felt the heat and fragrance of her heavy level lips, and felt a sudden alarming tingle of an intense awareness of her, and released her quickly and rather awkwardly and avoided her eyes and dug out a nickel and put it in the nearest machine and said foolishly, "Pull the handle, Cindy, and find out how good your luck will be in fifty-seven."

She yanked the handle and the wheels spun and stopped at a lemon, an orange and a bar.

"That will give you a clue, Carl," she said and walked away from him, tall in her formal gown, swaying with her slow grace, not looking back.

Now he knew that in some dark way he had managed to thrust the incident completely out of his memory, and had not thought of it again until this moment of revelation.

He knew she could not have heard his knock, and he knew that the most intelligent thing he could do would be go home. Fast. As he stood there, the shower stopped abruptly. Then he thought what good is it to run away? Hell, a man would be abnormal if he didn't feel a yen for Cindy Cable. God knows she's the unwilling target of enough drunks at parties. Just because I have a sudden itch, it doesn't mean I have to do anything about it or would, God help me, ever try to do anything about it. Poor kid has enough on her mind without another clumsy pass by a balding neighbor. Smart thing to do is prove to myself that I can continue to carry on the same old relationship without giving myself away.

He knocked again and called, "Cindy!"

Her voice was remote. "Who is it?"

"Carl."

"Oh, hi! Come in and get yourself a beer. The door isn't hooked. I'll be right out."

He finished his can and threw it in the wastebasket and got a chilled bottle from the refrigerator. He stood by the sink and looked out and tried to see the red maple but he could not. There was a cup and saucer in the sink and it had been run full of water, but the pink-orange mark of the shade of lipstick she used was still on the cup. He looked at that mark and wondered why he should feel curiously touched, why it should appear helpless and pathetic and young, and why he should feel tenderness toward the mark and toward her. A very stupid reaction, considering that the smallest fleck of red on rim of glass or cup in a restaurant would disgust him.

"Hi there," she said, coming into the kitchen.

He turned and looked at her and said, "Lady, you've had some sun!"

"I really got it, didn't I? This afternoon I decided all of a sudden I wanted a swim, so I threw a suit in the car and drove way over to Pond Lake to the public camp grounds. I didn't leave until the sun did. I lived on hot dogs and coke and jumped in the lake every time I got too hot."

"Maybe you got too much."

"Not me. I've got a hide like a rhino. Tonight it's red, tomorrow it's tan."

She opened herself a beer and got a glass and they went to the booth and sat as they had the evening before. She had put on a black denim skirt with large white buttons on the slash pockets and a yellow sleeveless blouse. Her hair was casually piled on top of her head and pinned in place.

"How was Joan this evening?"

"Tired, but she seemed pretty calm."

"You'll be there when they operate?"

"Of course."

"Stupid question. I guess I'm just making talk. I was going to come over and see you, but I decided I got home too late for that. I talked too much last night, Carl. I've felt uneasy about it all day."

"I don't think you did."

"I can only claim one thing. I didn't make the situation sound worse than it is. But I do think that talking to you got me closer to making a decision, and I'm glad of that, and I think that because I nearly talked you to death, I do owe it to you to tell you what I've decided. Not really decided, but what I think I'll decide."

"What's that?"

"I'm going to make one last college try. I'll go along on this second honeymoon idea and I'll wait until the time is just right and when he's in the right mood, and then I'm going to put the cards on the table. I'm going to make a final glorious effort to make him understand how I feel and what I want out of my life and out of my marriage. And what I don't want. And then, if I can't get it across to him, I'm going to start thinking of breaking it up. And that will be a royal mess, I know, but not as bad as the eventual messiness of trying to make a hopeless marriage work. But I'm fool enough to think that maybe I can get through to him. He's not a bad man, you know."

"Sounds sensible to me."

"And then his dear mother can refer to me as that impossible girl our Bucky was married to. A complete neurotic, my dear. And a horrible housekeeper. Bucky is well rid of her, let me tell you. My God, I can even hear her saying it. If anybody is to blame in this mess, Sarah Cable is. She didn't want Bucky to grow up, so he never did. The first time we stayed there after our marriage, I felt like a wanton woman. I could see that she couldn't quite bring herself to believe that that girl had any right to be in her darling Bucky's room and sleep with him. All his airplane models and his little gilt cups and his football pictures were on display. It was her little museum, devoted to Bucky. She kept popping around corners at us. One time Bucky kissed me in the hall, and when I looked over his shoulder, there she was, halfway up the stairs, looking at me with truly shocking malice. But then, very quickly, she put on her social smile and laughed her social laugh and said, 'You young people! My lands! Bucky, dearest, there's a hole in the elbow of that sweater. You take it off this minute and Mother will mend it.' The inference was that I'd do much better if I'd spend less time kissing and carrying on and more time mending. So Bucky is just a little boy. He wants people to look after his clothes and his food and clean up after him and scold him when he's bad. His job is a toy, and that airplane is a toy, and I was supposed to be another toy, but I won't co-operate. I won't stay put in the toy box."

"If it doesn't work out, what will you do?"

"I don't know. I'll think about that later. What is there about you, mister, that gets me off on a talking jag? Don't answer that question. It's because I haven't had anybody to talk to. I don't mean what passes for conversation at the average Crescent Ridge cocktail party."

He grinned at her and said, "I know what you mean."

"Let's grab some emergency beer rations and go out in the yard, Carl. Maybe it's my burn, but it feels so hot in here."

She turned off the kitchen lights as they went out. They stood in the darkness until their eyes adjusted to the night and then walked across to the lawn furniture. They sat on two aluminum chaise longues with plastic webbing placed at an angle to each other so that their feet were close but they were about three feet from each other, each half facing the glow of Hillton on the sky. He could see the pallor of her yellow blouse, see the glow of red against her face when she drew on her cigarette, hear the clink of glass on glass when she poured her beer. The breeze came from her direction, bringing with it a hint of perfume and soap.

They talked idly and comfortably about the school situation, about neighbors and parties and friends. It was effortless conversation, yet throughout it, like a single scarlet thread in a tapestry, he could not cease being aware of her physical presence and his desire for her.

At last she said, "Now I'm going to do my good deed and send you off to bed as requested."

"Please can I stay up, huh? Please? None of the other guys got to go to bed this early."

Her laugh was a low warm sound in her throat. "No back talk from you, young man. March! I think I'll go in. Maybe I can get to sleep while I'm still cooled off. Bucky keeps trying to promote an air-conditioner for the bedroom. But I hate the horrid things, whining all night and huffing air at you that smells like it came out of a subcellar. And, knowing Bucky, I am perfectly aware that he would keep it at maximum volume. I love the summer nights, and the smell of summer coming into the room."

They got up and she gathered up the bottles and the glass and her cigarettes and he walked her toward the back door. Ten feet from the chairs she tripped, fought for balance and fell hard. He grabbed for her, but not in time. She gave a thin wail of pain. He dropped to one knee beside her.

"Are you hurt?"

She pushed herself into a sitting position. "Darn it, darn it!

Graceful, co-ordinated Cindy. I flounder around like a rup-
tured elk."

"What happened?"

"That damn sprinkler head. We can't just use a hose. No,
Bucky has to have little men come and bury pipe in the yard
so we can have little booby traps sticking up all over."

"Where do you hurt?"

"Right on the point of my chin where I cleverly chunked
it against one of these damn beer bottles." He clicked on his
lighter and looked at it.

"It isn't cut. Good thing the bottle didn't break."

She took his hand and he helped her up. "I just can't seem
to help being the glamorous type," she said. She took a half
step and winced and said, "Ow! The complete treatment. I
must have turned my ankle too." And she laughed, a sound
of helpless annoyance.

He got on the other side of her and said, "Put your arm
over my shoulders."

"I'll manage in a minute."

"Go ahead. We'll get you into the kitchen and get a look
at you."

He put his right arm around her, his hand on her supple
and narrow waist. She took six limping steps to the back
door. He knew he should release her. But he had the odd
feeling that all this had happened before, just exactly as it
was happening now. And he turned her into the circle of his
arms and began to kiss her.

She stood rigid and shocked and unco-operative in his
arms, not fighting him, but, whenever her lips were free, she
said, "No. Please, no. Please, Carl. No." But her reluctance,
her passive resistance seemed to him to be something far
away and of small importance. And, after she had stopped
speaking, he felt her give a prolonged shuddering sigh, and
turn to meet his mouth with hers, turn slightly in a fluid and
practiced way so that their prior awkwardnesses of knees that
bumped and elbows that were in the way were gone so they
fitted sweetly and tightly and with a perfection. Her right
arm was around his neck, her left arm around his waist, her
palm and fingers firm against the muscles of his back, her
mouth working against his. He had somehow anticipated, perhaps because of the difference in their ages, a girlishness
about her, possibly a demureness. But this creature arched
so closely against him was a mature woman, mother of two,
with the humid and silky tautness of perfect health, without

sexual restraints or fears or ignorances. She seemed there, in the warm night, to open like a tropic flower so that the scents and fragrances of her were enhanced. For the space of a second he was taken aback, startled, possibly somewhat alarmed—like a petty thief who opens the stealthy drawer and sees the heavy stack of currency. But then her response aroused him further, and the night seemed to wheel around them, tilting and breathless. They lost their balance, as though the grassy earth was trying to pull them down. He staggered and caught himself and she whirled away from him and moved three steps, limping slightly, to lean against the side of the house.

He sat down on the step in front of the kitchen door. He could hear the muted galloping of his heart. She was breathing so deeply he could hear her. He could see her, not clearly, in silhouette, feet braced, head lowered, arms folded across her breasts.

"My God," she said softly, giving it more the cadence of prayer than of curse.

He lighted two cigarettes, held one out toward her. She reached and took it from his fingers without touching him, and moved back to her former position.

"It was my fault," he said. His voice sounded clotted and rusty and strange, as though he had not spoken aloud in weeks.

"Let's not follow that line of conjecture, please. It's so damned barren. Your fault, my fault. So what? I wanted you to. For many dirty sneaky shameful months, I've wanted to be kissed by you. Kissed for real, because I was curious. And so maybe I thought about it just enough so subconsciously you got the message. That isn't the point. The point is how we undo it. How do you go about getting unkissed?"

"I don't know."

"Don't you see? It's so damn cheap. That's the thing about it. It's such a horrid and typical little suburban game."

"So," he said heavily, "maybe we can leave it that way. A little experiment on a summer night in suburbia. And forget it."

"Can we really do that?" she asked in such a subdued way he could barely hear her.

"Now who's helping?"

"I'm sorry. I don't know what I mean, Carl. One of the things I've been cursed with all my life is a passion for complete honesty and frankness. Plus an unhealthy amount of curiosity. Maybe, if we're frank with each other, we can open up this little infection and let it drain. Or maybe, God knows, we can talk it to death."

"It started last New Year's Eve, Cindy."

"I know it did. When you were drunk. I wanted you to be too drunk to remember."

"And ever since then I've been telling myself I feel one way about you, and hiding the other way so that even I couldn't see it."

"You hid it so well I couldn't see it either."

"But it was there. And here's another thing I'd like to believe about myself. That hidden . . . response to you started to come out in the open last night and tonight. But it's as though we'd been tricked some way. I mean that when Joan and I planned the time she'd be in the hospital, I had no way of knowing you would be alone here."

"I can play that game. When Bucky had the sprinkler system put in he had no way of knowing I would trip and fall at such a terribly strategic time. But maybe I'm wrong there. Maybe my subconscious mind was aware of the location of the sprinkler head and steered me into it so that I would get special attention from you."

"I don't think so. It's just the timing. It's a sort of trap that was set for us, Cindy."

"What I want you to know and believe, Carl, is that I am a good person. By that I mean I'm not mischievous, or flirtatious or experimental. And by that I mean that I'm not trying to turn this into a dramatic game because I've seen too many movies. Or because I'm bored, or restless or discontented. I am restless and discontented; but I think I'm honest enough with myself to keep from using you as a temporary remedy."

"You don't have to explain that to me."

She snapped the cigarette out into the dark yard. "We're not getting anywhere with this. I'll be clinical. I happen to be physically very darn vulnerable right now. Not only because the physical side of my marriage has been . . . personally inadequate for quite a long time. So all this is a big fat rationalization. It's just an animal need, so I'm cloaking it with a lot of fancy words."

"Do you believe any part of that?"

"Now who's not helping?"

"All right. I'm sorry."

They were silent for several minutes. He heard the insect sounds in the night. His heart had slowed. He felt tired.

"Carl?"

"Yes, Cindy."

"If we're going to be honest, you must know something. A kiss is not supposed to be a shattering affair. I had never known I could be so thoroughly shook up by a kiss. I couldn't have imagined that any kiss could make me so . . . damnably and almost obscenely . . . ready."

"I sensed that. The readiness. And I keep wondering if maybe in trying to be honest or talk it to death or whatever you want to call it, maybe on another level we're merely trying to maintain . . . all that awareness."

"That's a stinking thing to say!"

"If we're going to be honest, let's be completely honest. I'm sitting here perfectly aware of the fact that this little talk has its inevitable ending. That's the scene where we tell each other it can go no further, that we are both people of character, that we are too fine to get involved in any sticky little infidelity, and we can't hurt Joan this way and we have responsibilities to our families and ourselves and so on. And we shake hands on it, or something. Hell, I'm aware of that and so are you. It's the only way the conversation can conceivably end. But that does not deny the fact that I can sit here and try in desperation to think of some way I can take you to bed and still manage to save my face and yours, that I think there is some glittering rationalization just out of my mental reach, and if I can grasp it and explain it to you, then we might feel that it was our God given right to pile into the sack and have at it."

"Don't. Please don't."

"What good is honesty if it only goes so far? Then it's as bad as the thoroughgoing lie. Maybe worse. Let's not, for God's sake, dwell on the fine textures and subtle flavors of our souls. We're a man and a woman and we were stupid enough, or I was, to lift the lid on the box and let the monsters out. And we aren't going to be able to do a damn thing about it. And that won't be the result of character, it will be the result of emotional logic."

"All right, all right," she said, and her voice was tired. "I should have slapped your face and marched into the house. And now I think I better go in. Maybe if we expose this to some daylight it won't seem so enormous and dramatic. Maybe in the daylight, Carl, it will look small and cheap and beery and . . . manageable. But it certainly doesn't look manageable right now, does it?"

"No."

"But it's got to be."

"Yes, I know that. Good night, Cindy."

He stood up and stepped back, aware that he should not get too close to her. She went in without word or gesture, her shoulders at a weary angle.

He paused at his back door and went to the red maple. The kitchen lights were on and he saw her go from the yard into the kitchen with the bottles and glass she had dropped. He watched her sit in the booth, and then he saw her lower her head to her outstretched arms. He could not tell if she was crying.

His own house had an odd look to him. He could not identify the strange feeling he had about it. And then he remembered a time in his childhood. He had been about eight and Marian had been about four, and the family had gone on a long motor trip one summer, to far away places. They had returned on a Sunday afternoon. And when they had gone into the house it had a dusty locked-up smell, and everything had looked strange to him—slightly out of proportion and of a different hue than he remembered. Even his own room and his toys had been distorted by an alien magic. It was as though, while they were gone, the house had been completely destroyed, and then rebuilt by people who had been able to get it almost right.

As he prepared for bed, he saw the mark of her lipstick on the corner of his mouth. He rubbed it off carefully and looked at the smear on the piece of Kleenex. It seemed a symbol of all deceits, a painful clue to all infidelities, an index of the faithless.

In seventeen years of marriage, he had committed but one infidelity, and that affair had been of an intensity which, he believed, had cured him for all time. He had learned that he could not survive in the emotional climate of infidelity.

And he remembered Sandy . . .

SEVEN

Carl Garrett had been drafted into the army in March of 1942. The Carrier Corporation had attempted to have him deferred as essential to the war production effort, but it had been denied. Carl, himself, had asked for deferment on the basis of Joan's pregnancy, but it had been a half-hearted request, made out of a feeling of obligation to Joan. He had wanted to serve in the armed forces, and had the feeling that if he did not, he would forever feel as though he were not quite a legitimate member of his own generation.

Kip was born in August of 1942 on the first day of Carl's compassionate leave from OCS. After he was commissioned in October of 1942, he was assigned to the Signal Corps and ordered to report to Washington. After a frantic search he found a small and shabby apartment in Alexandria, and Joan closed the Syracuse apartment and joined him. He was in Washington eight months, and, in June of 1943, as a first lieutenant, was given fourteen days' leave before reporting to Camp Anza near Riverside, California, for overseas shipment to the CBI theatre. The leave they granted him gave him time to get Joan settled with his parents in Youngstown.

He went out to Anza by train, and had six days in the harsh dryness of the yellow sun and in the cold purple shade before embarking on the *Brazil* for Bombay. He shared a small cabin with seventeen other first lieutenants, and the forty-one day voyage with stops at Hawaii, Wellington, Melbourne and Perth made all the accustomed things of his life seem very far away indeed. He felt not only an almost uncomfortable freedom and lack of responsibility, but like a most impartial observer who could watch everything about him, and also observe his own behavior with remote interest.

From Bombay he was flown by ATC to New Delhi, billeted in a room for four in the Victoria Hotel, and assigned to the staff of the Theatre Signal Officer.

India gave him the impression of being a vast circus grounds a week after the circus had left. Dust and smells and debris and the sun-parched grasses. He could never get used to the poverty—the bloat and the stick-limbs of the starving, the fly-clotted pus around the eyes of a baby in arms, the fungoid sores of the beggars, the great sour reek of the market places. The Indians had an insinuating and disturbing servility about them.

Here, amid the filth and turmoil of New Delhi, were the great arid buildings of British H.Q. and United States Theatre Headquarters. There seemed to be to him no purpose or reality in the staff work he was asked to do. They were forever making out lengthy requisitions for Signal Corps supplies for mysterious Chinese forces termed Xray, Yoke and Zebra. The estimated manpower of these proposed forces fluctuated wildly from week to week, as did the estimates of what tonnage could be airlifted over the Hump into China.

The Victoria Hotel was a concrete structure with huge barren rooms, plagued by mice, by petty thievery and by drunken officer personnel. Their room bearer was named, inevitably, Ali—and he made a specialty of being unavailable whenever there was any legitimate use for his services. On too many nights Carl would lie in the lumpy bed under the mosquito bar and listen to the slow creak of the ceiling fans and the distant hootings and laughter from other rooms. Sometimes at night the jackals would invade the city and run in gibbering packs.

When he arrived there was a thick packet of letters from Joan. He sorted them chronologically, and the third one he opened informed him, a little too bravely and blithely that she was again pregnant, with a tentative date of January of 1944. Her letters were chatty and warm and loving and amusing.

He tried to fit himself into the routine of New Delhi. He managed to acquire a ponderous khaki-colored bicycle on which he braved the curious traffic problems of the New Delhi streets. He wrote long descriptive letters to Joan, and he tried to make sense of the staff work he was asked to do. He made friends and played bridge and volley ball. He drank gimlets and a strange British concoction called a Suffering Bastard. He made trips to the station hospital for treatment of athlete's foot and prickly heat. He ate butter that tasted of goat. He went to the coffee shops and walked through the market places and procured a guide book and dutifully visited places of historical interest.

But he felt oddly unreal, as though he were a two dimensional man, a purposeless figure in a mythological place.

Her name was Sandara Lahl Hotchkiss and she was called Sandy. She was an Anglo-Indian girl, or, as the American officers termed that racial mixture, a chi-chi. She was from Calcutta, and she was employed in CBI Headquarters in the Special Services Section as a civilian. She was five feet five, twenty-four years old, with coarse and shiny black hair, a sharp-featured, handsome but rather sallow face, very dark eyes, a cute, fragile-looking figure, a confidence and self-possession that amounted almost to arrogance, and a very very British accent that was faintly contaminated by the curious singsong cadence of the Anglo-Indian.

He had noticed her around headquarters, but the first time he had talked to her was at a dance at the hotel when, on impulse, he had cut in when he saw her dancing with another officer he knew rather well. She had looked very pretty in a pale blue gown, her black hair in an intricate styling, her bright eyes shadowed, her smile quick. There was an intense, quivering aliveness about her that intrigued and stimulated him.

The officer she had come with passed out, and Carl, after considerable delicate maneuverings, managed to be the one to take her home. She lived but four blocks from Theatre Headquarters, in an upstairs apartment in a building on the south side of Conneaut Circus. She was very argumentative and opinionated, and on that evening they sat in the front room of the apartment and argued bitterly in hushed voices to keep from disturbing her roommate.

The next day was Sunday. He met her by prearrangement and they took a tonga ride through the more pleasant suburban part of the city and returned to her place in the late afternoon. Her roommate was out. A half hour after they had entered the apartment, he possessed her on the shabby settee in the tiny front room of the apartment, and again, an hour later, in the more spacious bedroom of the apartment.

During the next week the first building to house junior officers was completed, and Carl was moved out of the hotel. At about the same time Sandy's roommate disappeared. "She had to go back to her people in Agra because of sickness," Sandy explained. She wanted to look for another roommate. She did not make enough money to carry the apartment alone. Carl persuaded her to let him pay fifty rupees a month toward the upkeep of the apartment.

After the affair had gone on a month, Carl knew her very well and knew that she was very unsuitable. She was arrogant and selfish and lazy. She was quarrelsome and demanding. She was half-educated, and coarse, and she treated the Indian servants with a vicious contempt that continually embarrassed him. She was such an inveterate, incurable liar that it was impossible for him to piece together any coherent personal history. She demanded dozens of small, intimate attentions, and became furious when he was not as obedient as any servant. Their quarrels were violent and exhausting, and it was a rare week when he did not plunge out of the apartment, vowing never to return. She had a fishwife temper and her tantrums were like those of a small child, rolling and drumming her heels and screaming.

But she was completely and compulsively sexual, inventive, demanding and experimental, shameless and greedy and aggressive, insatiable and bold. When he was away from her he would feel shame when he thought of the sweaty tableaus he had endured, but at the end of the day he would find himself waiting at the end of the corridor in headquarters where they met, and feel the sick thumping of his pulse when she would come teetering and clicking down the corridor on the high heels she loved, hips swaying in an absurd parody of a ladylike walk, her welcoming smile eager and knowing and anticipatory.

It was a sickness in him, and the most evident symptom of his disease was the continuing ability to meet all of her demands on him.

The affair lasted over eight months. During that time, when the news came announcing the birth of Nancy, he felt as though it were something that had happened on a remote planet, a birth to a woman he did not know, but had heard of somewhere, a long time ago.

The affair ended on a Sunday afternoon. There had been gin, too much gin, and a turbulent and meaningless quarrel, and then they had made love, and then he had slept. He had awakened first, with dried mouth and fast pulse and sweat cold on his body. She was beside him, facing him, still asleep. Her mouth was open and she breathed at him the stale spices of the foods she had eaten, and that scent was mingled with the distinctive acid tartness of her perspiration. He looked at the black tangle of hair and the sallowness of her and the large dark brown nipples and felt so suddenly, so strongly repelled that his stomach twisted and he thought he would be ill. He dressed quietly and collected the things in the apartment that were his, and crammed them in the musette bag he had once left there and put it by the front door. Then he shook her awake. While she was still dazed by sleep he told her he was leaving for good. She jumped up and followed him, naked, to the door, screaming at him, calling him foul names, beating at his back with her small hard fists, but he would not give her the pleasure of walking more quickly. When he reached the street entrance he could still hear her voice.

He had not anticipated how difficult it would be not to go back to her. He had not known the spell of evil was so strong, or that he was so vulnerable to it. During the next week he exhausted himself with hard exercise, and tried resolutely to keep her out of his mind, but she kept creeping back in, and in each pose there was more provocation than the last. But he fought it successfully and, ten days later, when he was transferred to General Dorn's headquarters in Kunming, he was grateful that it had been taken out of his control.

In Kunming he was given staff work that was more immediate and practical and made more sense to him. He began, once again, to write to Joan with greater regularity and in greater length. He felt as though he had gone to the edge of the world and teetered over the blackness below and had, with the greatest luck, started to find his way back to the center of things.

And it was in Kunming that he worked for a time on a special assignment under a Colonel Gregory Dean who, in peacetime, was a top executive with the Ballinger Corporation. They took an immediate liking to each other. It was Colonel Dean who made possible Carl's promotion to captain and who, over several long evenings of conversation, convinced Carl that he would do well to come with Ballinger after the war. Dean guaranteed him a position at an increase over what he had been making at Carrier.

He saw Sandara Lahl Hotchkiss once more, and for the last time. He was sent down to New Delhi as a courier officer. He found out she no longer worked at Theatre Headquarters, that she had been discharged for some infraction of the disciplinary rules. That evening he loitered outside her apartment for forty-five minutes. She came out with a Navy lieutenant commander, a bulky young man with a red face. Though Carl moved away quickly, there was no need to. She was clinging to the Navy's arm in a possessive way he well remembered, and she was talking up at him, and he saw from the look of her eyes and the shape of her mouth that she was giving him her special variety of virulent hell. The Navy's mouth was clamped shut and his face was perhaps not as red under other circumstances. He stood behind them and looked at the sway and flaunt of her little hips, and the teetering heels and the sinuous waist, and felt nothing. No desire, no regret, no lingering shame, but only a great swelling relief that he had gotten out of it so little impaired.

It had been his only infidelity, yet it had been a most serious one. He knew that he had drifted into it because of his loneliness and a feeling of unreality and futility. And from it he had learned that, under the right provocation, he was a more sensuous man than he had imagined. By the time he was flown back to the States, flown back for discharge at Camp Dix, he had so completely recovered from the impact of Sandy that her face was blurred in his mind. He had phoned Joan from the West Coast, and she had come down to New York and taken a hotel room for them. They spent a wonderful week in New York, and got over their initial shyness with each other. He checked in with Mr. Gregory Dean at Ballinger and was told to report to the Camden plant on November 15th. Then he went back with Joan to Youngstown to see his family and to meet the daughter, over a year and a half old, whom he had never seen. And who managed to adore him on sight.

Now, in the bathroom, the smudge of Cindy's lipstick on the ball of Kleenex seemed to be a symbol of the eight months during which Joan had been, for the only time in their mutual lives, of almost no importance or interest to him.

After he was in bed he tried to dispose of the Cindy problem with great coldness and logic. After all, it was no problem. A kiss was not a problem. A special awareness was not necessarily a problem. They were both adults, and so nothing beyond what had already happened would be permitted.

But, even as he struggled to be adult and reasonable, his mouth remembered the taste of hers, his hands remembered the sinewy planes and softnesses of her back, his chest remembered vividly the high strong thrusting of her breasts. And the fragrance of her was suddenly in the room. Desire moved through him, a dark oiled shifting in his belly and loins, a sudden shallowness of breathing, sweaty palms and staccato heart and a prickling of the skin on the backs of his hands and the nape of his neck.

At three-thirty he got up and took a pill, and when the alarm went off he did not hear it, and when he awakened abruptly it was twenty-five after nine, and Joan would be operated on in thirty-five minutes.

He arrived at the hospital, at ten minutes of ten. The pill he had taken made his head feel as if it were full of vast metallic echoes that smelled of machine oil. There had been no time for breakfast. Yes, Mrs. Garrett has been taken to the operating room. No, it will not be possible to see her. I cannot tell you when it will be possible for you to see her. From the operating room she will be taken to the recovery rooms for post-operative care. She will probably be brought down to her room some time this afternoon. No, Dr. Madden has other operations scheduled this morning, and he won't be free until noon.

"I wonder if I could see the other patient in 314. Miss Rosa Myers. For just a minute."

He was given reluctant permission. Rosa was in a wheel chair by the windows.

"Well, good morning!" she said. "And I might say you look like you had a rugged night on the town."

"I couldn't sleep and I took a pill and then I didn't hear the damn alarm, so I didn't get here in time to see her. How is she?"

"Much as I'd like to have you keep your guilty conscience, Carl . . . I may call you Carl? . . . they started needling her at eight-thirty. By nine-thirty, she was loaded. High. She was so gay and drunky, it didn't fret her a bit that you didn't show. I don't even think she remembered you were supposed to."

"That makes me feel better, Rosa."

"Now the big trick is to find out what goes on up there. They seem to like to keep it a state secret. There's a small waiting room on the fifth floor, and when the surgeons leave the operating room they pass by it. You can tell them by the green outfits they wear. They look like oversized elves."

"Thanks, Rosa."

"Ask me anything. I feel like I've been in this place for years."

He did not check in again downstairs but went on up to the fifth floor. He found the waiting room. It was quarter after ten. He felt very alone.

Suppose it was not as routine as Bernie had indicated. Suppose when they opened her up they found . . .

"Carl, sit down. I hate to have to tell you this."

"Do you mean . . ."

The fantasy assumed the vividness of reality in his mind. He could see just how it would be, how their friends and neighbors would react, how the people at the shop would react. Suddenly they would be tragic figures, the woman doomed, the man stern and heartbroken and brave, determined to make the little time left to her as happy as possible, but always aware of the great emptiness he would face after she was gone. Telling the kids would be horrible. Kip's only acquaintance with death had been when Joan's father had died in '43 when Carl had been overseas. But he had been so tiny then it had been meaningless. This would strike dreadfully close. Joan would not be told. She would think that she was getting better. But then, one day, she would read it in his face, perhaps see the gleam of tears in his eyes in an unguarded moment . . .

And quite suddenly he was sickened by the selfish bathos of his fantasy, realizing that he was getting a certain amount of curious satisfaction out of thinking of himself as a tragic figure. He wondered what kind of a man he was, what unsuspected streak of coldness could make it possible for him to indulge himself in this shallow game at Joan's expense.

It was a good marriage. It had been and it would continue to be good. The world was a cruel and lonely place, and disasters struck in a disconcertingly casual manner, and if you could find one other human being who was irrevocably committed to you, then you were ahead of the game. They had achieved a rare contentment.

But he was still disturbed that he had been able to project the fantasy so vividly that for several hypnoid minutes he had been reconciled to hopelessness and death. He wondered if it could be merely a protective device, a kind of self-anesthesia which could partially soften the jolt were the news bad. Or was it a basic coldness in him, a remoteness?

Joan had often complained about this remoteness, his spells of keeping himself to himself. Though his parents were both warm, outgoing people, both he and Marian had been moody children, shy and often depressed, with a need for privacy and solitude, without the knack of making and keeping friends.

As he had grown older he had learned the tricks of friendship, acquired a somewhat spurious degree of that extroversion necessary to be at home in a smiling rotarian world. But he had never felt at ease or at home with most of the trappings of goodfellowship. He envied other men their ability to cope with utmost sincerity with the bawling of sentimental songs at service club meetings, their bluff locker-room manners, their ability to chortle at the bawdy and unfunny joke, their casual and meaningless use of the leggy girls who livened their business conventions.

He had conformed insofar as it was possible for him to conform. He had learned to address a meeting or a group with an ease of manner that masked the weak feeling in his knees, the sweaty palms, the feeling of being a damn fool. He had laughed at all the jokes and had told some of his own, and he played golf and joined the clubs and played his expected part in the nonsense of cocktail parties and cook-outs, but too often he would sense that the smile he wore was pasted there in a grotesque way, that he was actually from some alien world, less hearty, less sweaty and more skeptical.

Joan had grown accustomed to his apartness. His reluctance to give her all the normal, casual gestures and words of affection no longer caused her to feel the need of reassurance of his love for her. She was physically, actively affectionate, with frequent little pats and hugs and words of endearment.

He had convinced himself that despite his surface restraints, he loved her deeply. And that he was capable of love. And had convinced her. And he had adjusted himself to accept, as a condition of his life, those frequent moments when he would feel completely unreal, as though in his secret heart he were an impostor condemned to live out his life as Carl Andrew Garrett.

So, there in the waiting room, he eased his conscience by telling himself that his fantasy had been meaningless, that it was just another evidence of the same offbeat imagination that had prevented him from committing himself to his maximum capacities to the destiny of Ballinger.

And to prove it, he devised another game. This was a hospital in a world designed on a different basis. He had this day been constructed out of the raw stuff of life, built, clad and equipped with all the memories of a life he had never known. And now he waited until they completed the construction of the female entity who would be his wife. From this day on they would progress backward through time. Each day would be in normal chronological sequence of hours, but the day after each Christmas would be December 24th. So, together, they would move back through all the memories, powerless to change any word or action, back, inevitably, to the day before he met her, back then through school and childhood, back to the misty grasping mind of the infant, and then into the pre-birth blackness. Each man and woman in the world would be in the same trap. There would be all the conventions about growing old, providing for the future, accepting the inevitability of eventual death, but they would all know, but could not say aloud, the truth that they moved forever backward through artificially imposed memories to the first and final day of their lives.

But he tired of that game, and the time moved with a dreadful slowness. He thought of what they might be doing to her, and his mind would slip and veer away from images too vivid.

At eleven-thirty two men in pale green operating costumes came down the hall, talking to each other. He got up quickly, but sat down again when he realized neither of them was Bernie Madden. Nurses went by, walking briskly.

At twenty minutes after twelve, Dr. Bernie Madden came down the hall. Carl hurried toward him, and when he saw how sick and gray the usually vital face looked, he felt as if he could not catch his breath. Madden looked at Carl as though he were a stranger. Then he nodded and said, "Hello."

"How's Joan?"

"Joan? Oh, Joan is fine. No problems." He leaned against the door frame and took out his cigarettes. "I just lost a kid in there. Eleven years old."

"When will I be able to see Joan, Bernie?"

Bernie did not seem to hear the question. "See her? Wait here a minute." Bernie came back in five minutes. "She's doing fine. They'll take her back to her room at about two o'clock. You can go get some lunch and come back."

"What did you have to do to her?"

"Took out those fibroid tumors and one ovary. Those

tumors were good sized, but I'd say there's nothing to worry about on the lab reports. We'll have the reports day after tomorrow. There's a flock of tiny tumors on the uterus, too small to get all of them. Took a biopsy, but I didn't perform any hysterectomy. I thought about it, as long as I was in there, but I've never been as damn anxious as some of my colleagues to perform a hysterectomy. When they aren't in menopause it's a hell of a shock. If the little ones are as slow growing as the ones we had to take out, and I'm pretty damn sure they are, it'll be fifteen years before anything would have to be done. And maybe never. She's fine, Carl. Go have some lunch and come back at two. They'll let you see her, but she'll be pretty groggy. I'll order special nurses around the clock for a couple of days, and we'll keep her on demerol until she's more comfortable."

"Thanks, Bernie. Thanks a lot."

He nodded absently. Carl knew he was thinking of the child again. When Bernie walked slowly down the corridor, he looked small and stocky and defeated.

He had lunch near the hospital and discovered he was ravenous. He felt in a holiday mood. He felt as though great weights had been taken from him, and he caught himself grinning at nothing at all. He had not realized the full extent of his fear and worry until it had been taken from him.

At two o'clock they let him see her. One of the special nurses, a Miss Calhoun, was on duty. She looked up at Carl and smiled and got up from the chair beside the bed. The curtain between Joan's and Rosa's bed was drawn. "Mr. Garrett?" she said. "I'm Miss Calhoun." Her voice was polite and hushed, and she was a small-boned, pretty woman. "She's doing wonderfully."

Joan lay flat. When she smiled at him, her eyes were oddly wide and staring and her smile didn't seem to fit. "Hello, darling," she said in a faraway voice.

He kissed her forehead and said, "How did the other guy look?"

"Gosh, I could feel them sort of cutting and tugging and talking to each other, but it didn't hurt and it wasn't even scary." She tried to shift in the bed and grimaced with pain.

"Hey!" he said.

"I'm supposed to move. But it feels as if . . . everything would fall out."

"I talked to Bernie. He says you're fine."

"Did they . . . do anything else to me?" She had a worried expression.

"Just the tumors, honey. That's all they did. That's all they had to do."

"Are you sure?"

"I'm positive."

"They try to kid you. I know that. Everybody tries to kid you along."

"I wouldn't kid you, honey. You know that." She shifted again and grimaced, her lips whitening. She looked gray and sweaty.

Miss Calhoun stood beside him and looked at her. "Time for another shot, I think. You hurt, don't you?"

"Not very much."

"Your wife is a very stubborn patient, Mr. Garrett. She's supposed to tell me when she hurts, but she won't."

"You tell the nurse whenever you feel uncomfortable. That's an order."

"Yes, darling," she said.

He kissed her again and said, "I'll be back in a little while."

He went out into the corridor with Miss Calhoun. "Have I stayed long enough this time?"

"She'll go to sleep as soon as I give her the next shot."

"When can I come back?"

She looked at her watch. "She should sleep pretty heavily. Why don't you wait until about seven?"

"Will she be allowed other visitors?"

"Oh, no! Probably not until tomorrow evening."

When Miss Calhoun went to get the shot, he went back into the room. She found his hand and held it tightly. Her hand felt damp and very warm. "Gee, I'm glad it's over. I'm glad I can stop thinking about it."

"After you get your shot, you'll have a good sleep."

"That nurse is nice. I wondered why she was staying with me. I asked her about it and she said she's a special nurse. Aren't they terribly expensive?"

"Not to us, dear. The hospitalization takes care of it."

"Oh, good."

When Nurse Calhoun came in with the hypo, Carl said good-by to her and left. The two-thirty sunshine looked bright and joyous. A man was weeding the flower beds. Two boys in swimming trunks rode by, dinging their bicycle bells, towels tied to the handle bars. All in all, he decided, it was an excellent Tuesday. The best of Tuesdays.

It was too late to go to the plant. He drove home and went into the quiet house and made the promised phone calls, five of them, Kip and Nancy first, then his parents in Sarasota, then Joan's brother's wife, Charlotte, in Falls Church, and finally Marian at the agency in New York.

He was talking to Marian over the living room phone when he heard the rap on the front screen door. He looked over his shoulder and saw Cindy standing, looking through the screen, so he motioned to her to come in.

". . . and take good care of her, Carlos," Marian was saying. "She's your anchor to windward."

"And when do you acquire an anchor, Sis?"

"Remember me? I tried that once. I'm a fading grass widow, and sublimely happy, thank you. Thanks for letting me know."

As he hung up he said, "That was the last call."

Cindy had collected a stack of ash trays. She was wearing blue ranch jeans and a red canvas halter, and her hair was tied back in a pony tail. "I heard enough to be glad about it, Carl."

She carried the ash trays into the kitchen and he followed her out and stood watching her wash them out.

"How's her morale?"

"Good, but she's pretty dopey right now. She hurts, but they keep giving her stuff."

"I was worrying about her and I called the hospital at about one, but they gave me the usual double talk. When I looked out a little while ago and saw your car, I came right over. You've certainly used every ash tray in the house, my good man."

"I'm just not neat."

"You were able to get the kids on the phone?"

"Without any trouble. They'd made some sort of arrangements at the camps. Want a beer?"

"Sure. I'm thirsty. I've been baking myself in the sun in the back yard."

He opened two cans and when he went to the cupboard for a glass, she took one can out of his hand and said, "It's fine like this. I just don't like to drink out of bottles." She smiled at him and looked away, just a little too quickly to achieve the casual manner she was evidently trying to assume. He sensed that she had come over with the intention of being casual and impersonal, of burying the incident of last night under a new layer of polite and courteous and neighborly conversation.

He knew it was a good idea, and knew he would co-operate with her.

EIGHT

They went into the living room. Cindy redistributed the ash trays. He sat on the couch that was set at right angles to the fireplace wall, with the low coffee table he had made in front of the couch. Cindy hesitated visibly, and came and sat on the other end of the couch and put her beer can on the coffee table. He sensed the strategic reasons for her hesitation. To have sat far from him would have merely underlined the possibility in her mind of a recurrence of the physical attraction of the previous evening. To sit too close might give the impression of inviting a recurrence. She wanted to avoid giving either impression.

"It must be a terrible weight off your mind, Carl," Cindy said.

"I didn't know just how much until it was over. Then I felt like jumping in the air and clicking my heels."

She leaned back and crossed her long blue denim legs and said, "I guess the best way to get into this is to say . . . about last night."

"I know. It's daylight now. And we can be all sane and plausible."

"A summer night and a few beers and loneliness and proximity and that damn foolish accident of mine. That's what did it."

"How's your ankle?"

"It was a little puffy last night. I soaked it, and it's gone down. There's a little twinge when I put my weight on it, but not enough to give me an intriguing limp. Anyway, neighbor, we acquired a guilty little secret, and we'll keep it as our guilty little secret. And maybe we can even be a little proud of ourselves."

"For our enormous restraint?"

She frowned. "No, I don't mean that. I mean for being able to be shook up by a kiss. In this day and age. My God, you've been to enough drunken dances at Timberlane to know what I mean. The well-adjusted little housewife lines up a sitter for the kids, and they have a quick knock before they

85

go to their friends' house, and have a couple there, and then have some at the bar, and then there is a great likelihood that in a parked car, or out beyond the swimming pool, or off in the shrubbery by the eighteenth fairway, she'll get herself soundly mauled by the husband of one of her friends and, not too infrequently, screwed by same. Forgive the terminology, but this little routine disgusts me. I refuse to go home all fingerprints. So they get their stolen, shoddy little morsel of hasty sex, and delude themselves into thinking it's a big torrid affair, like in the books and movies. But actually it's just a grubby little incident that occurs because their lives are empty and their marriages are empty, and they've got such a terrible fear of growing old too fast that they take the quickest and cheapest way to prove they're still desirable. Four to one love on the rocks with a twist of lemon."

"So you want to avoid that classification?"

"I damn well do, Carl. And if I ever cheat, it isn't going to be that way. It's going to be all the way. Out in the open. With divorce and remarriage and all the rest of it."

"Which, of course, lets me out."

"I know that."

"You get pretty vehement about it, Cindy."

She drank deeply from the beer can and put it down. "Oh, I have all my little acts. I come on right after the trained seals. I wish that I could believe in all my little acts, Carl, but whenever I hear myself sounding off, I have the horrible suspicion that I'm impersonating somebody. That, maybe, there is no real Cindy—just a collection of attitudes I strike."

"I thought that was my private curse."

She looked at him sharply. "You feel that way sometimes?"

"Too damn often for comfort."

"Birds of a feather, eh?" she said.

"The undeniable attraction of nonentities."

She made a face. "Don't call us that. Anything but that, darl . . . darling." And she looked defiant.

He laughed aloud.

"What's so damn hilarious?" she asked heatedly.

"All these forlorn little mechanisms, Cindy. I was laughing at myself as well as at you. You don't go around calling people darling. But you started to call me darling. You got halfway into the word, not knowing why you started to say it, and then wished you hadn't stopped, which made it overly obvious, and then decided that rather than cover up you'd better go through with it, and so you did, and then, to cap it, you sort of glared at me as if daring me to make anything out of it, daring me to find any significance in it."

She flushed and said, "We're so hopelessly complicated, Carl. We get lost in such intricate interpretations. You read me loud and clear, I admit. And I don't know where the darling came from." She paused and looked at him wonderingly. "That's stupid. Of course you know and I know where it came from. To me you are a darling. And in a curious and hopeless way, I'm somewhat in love with you. And I know I'm looking defiant again."

"You don't have to look defiant. I guess I'm touched. And I know damn well I'm flattered, Cindy. You are a strikingly handsome gal. And I'm a sedentary office worker, biologically if not socially old enough to be your father. I'm getting thin on top and I've got a partial bridge and . . ."

"Stop it, Carl. Stop that this minute."

"Okay. So we chalk it off to the summer night, beer, proximity and so on. And we don't let it happen again."

"That's right. We stay sensible about it. We've got ethical responsibilities."

"And right now, Cindy, we're demonstrating one of the big fat flaws in the logic of the western world. All of us try to attack emotional problems with logic. And logic with emotions. Emotion is more of a physical problem. It's as though . . . you see a man drowning and you stand on the bank and explain to him the mechanics of the flutter kick."

"All right. I might buy that. But what has it got to do with us?"

"I mean that we can stay out of trouble with each other through an exercise of will, but please to God, leave us not try to say we've saving ourselves through logic."

"All right, Carl," she said in a subdued way. "But don't you think that . . ." As she spoke she reached toward her can of beer, but she was looking at him as she did so. She reached beyond it and her wrist hit it, knocking it off the coffee table so that it fell on the floor between them. They reached for it simultaneously, both bending over to rescue it quickly before the beer ran out on the rug. As she grasped it, her hair brushed his cheek, and as she placed it on the coffee table he reached across and cupped his hand on her bare, warm, tan shoulder, her left shoulder, to turn her toward him, to turn her so she would face him.

She sat very still, head lowered, fingertips still touching the beer can. She sat rigidly, resisting the increasing pressure of his grasp. She made not a sound, but he was aware of the lift of her breasts as she took a deep breath. Then slowly, and reluctantly, she let herself be turned toward him, head still lowered. When she was facing him on the couch she slowly raised her head and looked into his eyes, their faces inches apart. Her gray-blue eyes were wide and they seemed to look beyond him, unfocused. He held her there and watched her face change, watched her lips swell and part, watched her eyelids droop in sexual languor, watched her head waver as though it had become too heavy to be supported by her frail throat.

He kissed her, and her kiss was immediately fierce and heavy against his mouth, her arms twining around him, her fingertips working at the nape of his neck, sliding up into his hair. Still holding their mouths together he pushed her back and swung his legs up onto the couch and gathered her legs up clumsily with his left hand, so that they ended up lying face to face with Cindy on the outside, with his back against the back of the couch. And they each made small adjustments to fit their bodies together more perfectly, the endless kiss enduring, breathing quickly and harshly from their nostrils, breath mingling. With fingers working blindly, he undid the snaps at the back of the halter. She made a moaning sound in her throat as he pulled it free and then pressed herself against him with great strength. The catch and zipper were on the right side of the ranch jeans. He undid the catch and pulled the zipper down and then began to peel the tight jeans back and down, rolling and working them off from the round, taut, satiny, globular buttocks as she pressed her mouth more savagely against his and made whimpering sounds in her throat, and her body leaped and jerked and quivered with each touch of his hand as though his touch burned her. Then quite suddenly her mouth was gone, and she was fighting him silently and desperately. When, in surprise, he loosened his hold, she thrust herself back so violently she fell from the couch, knocking the coffee table over. She thudded heavily against the rug, and a beer can rolled to click against the stone of the fireplace.

He sat up and looked at her. She sat bare to the waist, the jeans down around the tops of her thighs. She looked up at him, her face twisting, tears spilling out of her eyes, and whispered, "Not here. My God, darling, not here. Not like this."

And he looked around the room as though awakening

from a sound sleep to unfamiliar surroundings. Of course she was right. Not here. Not in this house, in this room, on this familiar couch. He had made love to Joan on this couch. To have done this to her here would have been a special and unforgivable wickedness. He shook his head to clear it. His breathing was deep and rapid.

"Don't look at me," she whispered.

He looked at her, at the abrupt ivory of her breasts, at a blue vein under rounded snowy texture, at coral nipples fiercely erect.

"Please," she whispered, and held her arm across her breasts. He looked away from her, and he heard her stand up and heard the small insectile clicks of the fasteners, the faint gritty sound of the zipper. She sat heavily on the couch beside him and leaned against him, her forehead against the angle of his jaw. She took a deep and shuddering breath and whispered, "That was so horribly close, my darling. So terribly, terribly close."

"And the next time?"

"I don't know. I don't know. Oh, God, I don't know what to think. It's like I'd . . . turned into some kind of animal. You touch me and I haven't any will or conscience or anything. There's just the wanting. What are we going to do? What are we going to do, Carl?"

He turned and grasped her by the upper arms, holding her strongly, and shook her a little and said, "But you're right. Not here."

"I know."

"Then where? Where and when?"

"Carl. Please."

"Where and when? Say it."

"You're hurting my arms. Please."

He let go of her. She was crying again. She looked at him with grave eyes, looked at him for a long time and said, "Nobody would ever have to know. Please tell me that nobody would ever have to know."

"Unless we have the worst possible kind of luck. Or unless we get foolish and careless. Anybody could have come to that door, you know."

She turned sharply and looked at the front door. She got up quickly, righted the coffee table, picked up the beer cans and the ash tray. She put them on the table and sat down beside him again.

"If nobody knew," she said, "it wouldn't really hurt anything."

"I guess it wouldn't."

She laced her fingers in his, looked down at their joined hands. "I feel so ashamed of us."

"I know."

"We're being animals."

"I know that too."

She looked up at him. "But maybe it's the quickest and best and most final way to get over it. Wear it out. Have a perfect glut of each other. Sicken each other."

"And how many times have people used that as a rationalization."

She shook her head violently. "I don't know. I don't care. All I know is I can't go on this way." She picked his hand up and held the back of it against her cheek, and then turned his hand over and touched his palm with her lips. "Arrange something, darling. But quickly, quickly, please."

"A motel?" he said flatly.

She released his hand and seemed to shiver. "I'd hate that. It's so ordinary."

"Well, it's like this. In real life, I'm actually a millionaire and it so happens my yacht is anchored off Palm Beach and we can fly down and . . ."

"Don't try to hurt me, darling, because you want to hurt yourself. All right. This is clinical. This is pure, unadulterated, inexcusable sexual infatuation. But let's not be cruder than we have to be."

"I'm sorry."

"There's one place that might be all right."

"Where?"

"Scott and Lucy Jessup offered me the use of their place at the lake. I've never been up there, but . . ."

"I have. It's no good. Those cottages are ten feet apart and, at this time of year, loaded with Scott's and Lucy's friends and their kids."

She looked doleful. "This is so ridiculous. Here we are with two empty houses, but . . ."

"I know. We can't use either of them. Too many memories looking over our shoulders."

"Maybe . . . the motel thing would be all right. But a nice motel, darling."

"There's a batch of nice new ones thirty miles east of here, just off the turnpike."

"I know the ones you mean. Those new ones. How will we arrange it? We'll have to be so terribly careful. It can so easily be terribly right or terribly wrong. And maybe it will be terribly wrong in any case."

He lighted a cigarette and stood up and paced slowly back and forth across the living room and stopped in front of her, looking down at her across the coffee table. She looked flushed and thoughtful and lovely.

"How about this. Tomorrow, after work, I'll drive directly out there and get a room. I'll explain the local license plates by telling them carpenters and painters are working on the house, and my wife and I have to have a place to sleep."

"For a few nights."

"Yes, for a few nights. I can get the key then and pay in advance, and after I leave the hospital I can come back here and pick you up and we can arrive out there after dark. And leave early enough in the morning so I can get to work."

"I don't want us to be seen leaving here together, and I certainly don't want anybody to see you bringing me back early. I should take our car, I think."

"All right. When I go out tomorrow, I'll look for a place where we can leave it, between here and there. I'll tell you, and we can use that as a meeting place."

"That should work," she said. "It's as though . . . we're plotting some kind of a murder, darling."

His smile felt crooked. "Maybe, in a sense, we are."

Her face showed quick concern and she got up and came around the coffee table and took his hands and looked into his eyes. "My darling, I don't want you to have any regrets. Nobody will ever have to know . . . about us. We'll take this one little piece of time out of all the days of our lives and use it selfishly for ourselves, and when it is over, it must be completely over forever. But if you think it isn't worth it . . . if you think . . ."

He pulled her close and kissed the side of her nose. "Hey, that's my line, not yours."

"I know, but . . . I feel as if I were the one the most willing to . . ."

"Nobody takes the responsibility. We share it equally, Cindy. This is our affair. Equal partners."

"Our affair. That certainly is the right word."

"Yes."

"Our tawdry, sneaky little affair. We'll keep remembering that there's nothing glamorous about it, Carl. Please keep remembering how messy it is. And, before we start it, I want you to say one thing to me. You can call it a rationalization if you want. It probably is. But I want to hear it said. You only have to say it once, if it's going to be too hard a lie to say."

"I love you, Cindy."

"And I love you, Carl. Was it hard to say?"

"Very easy to say. I'll keep on saying it."

"I think I have to hear that. I think I have to be told I'm loved and wanted, or I don't think I'll be any good at . . . this kind of thing. So even if it's a lie, keep telling me, so for a little while, for a few nights, I can believe it."

"I promise. I'll phone you tomorrow evening when I get out of the hospital."

She kissed him lightly on the lips and turned toward the door. He went to the door with her. Once she was outside she came back close to the screen and said, "I'm going to suffer the conscience qualms of the eternally damned between now and then, darling, but do you know one thing I'm glad of?"

"What?"

"That it's tomorrow night, not tonight. I want all this time to think about it."

"Sensualist."

She winked broadly and gaily and said, "Of course." And was gone across the lawn, long legs swinging, head high, pony tail bouncing, the pelvic basket balanced surely and gracefully on the changing focus of the long round legs.

After she was gone, he could not believe that it would happen. Maybe it was some kind of game she was playing. He could not believe that a fruit of such perfection and ripeness could fall from the high branch into his waiting hands.

The nurses had changed at four o'clock and would change again at midnight. The new nurse was Mrs. Pierce. She had grizzled blond hair, a stocky body and a pugnacious face. She seemed to be giving him grudging permission to talk to his wife.

Joan was still flat, but her color was better. Her eyes still had the staring look. She smiled and held his hand tightly and said, "Darling, were you here before? Really?"

"Yes, I was here before. Right after they brought you down. And I told you what Bernie said."

"I couldn't tell if I'd dreamed you were here. And I can't remember much of the dream. What did they do to me?"

He sat beside her and she kept hold of his hand while he went over it all again. He was with her over a half hour. When he was with Cindy, Joan seemed equally remote. He had the insane impulse to smile brightly at her and say, "Guess what Cindy and I are going to do tomorrow, dear." And then he would wonder if she could read it in his face. He had never been able to lie to her successfully.

He told her what the kids had said and what his mother had said, and about Marian and her sister-in-law. And he read her the letter from Nancy and the post card from Kip and left them in the drawer of her night stand to read over. He told her to sleep well, and kissed her and winked at the stolid nurse and left, feeling guilty and relieved, and filled with a tremorous anticipation that made his belly feel hollow and his head light.

As he had eaten before going to the hospital, he was in bed by nine-thirty, and asleep minutes later.

nine

Everybody he met in the office during the course of work on Wednesday morning wanted to know how Joan was. He found it very difficult to work. He would check a draft of a report and suddenly the words and figures would blur and fade and, where they had been, Cindy would appear, smiling at him, or giving him that broad and wicked and promissory wink. But he managed to get the urgent things out of the way.

At quarter of twelve he phoned Jim Hardy and said, "Jim, I'm pretty well caught up here, so if it's okay with you, I'll work through until about two-thirty and then go on out to the hospital."

"Sure thing, Carl. You didn't have to ask. Give that little girl of yours my love."

"Thanks, Jim," he said and hung up. It was one of the meaningless courtesies of the office. He had to ask Jim, and Jim had to say go ahead, and he never failed to say you didn't have to ask. But if you didn't ask and Jim decided he wanted you for something, then you would have built yourself a very sturdy doghouse, suitable for long wear.

As he drove toward the hospital he realized what a thorough hypocrite he was being. He had not planned to visit Joan during the afternoon visiting hours, yet if he used her as an excuse to leave, he stood a better chance of getting out on the turnpike in time to find a vacancy in a good motel before they were all taken by the summer vacationers. The realization of his duplicity gave him a sour look at himself that clouded, momentarily, his anticipations of Cindy. He wished he could turn off that portion of his mind which continued to make these bitter little reappraisals of the ethics and motives of Carl A. Garrett. Think no longer of loyalty and fidelity and trust, and this violation of them. Is this so crucial? The male is polygamous, they say. And this fine taut unhappy girl is marvelously ready. And she will make no trouble. So feast on what the gods see fit to place before you, and do not question your luck.

Or, in that comforting lexicon of thieves of all varieties, what Joan doesn't know will not hurt her.

And Mencken adequately defined conscience as that still small voice that says somebody might be looking. Nobody will be looking.

It is neither crucial nor unique, is it? When the man of the house was out stalking the saber toothed tiger, somebody went tippytoe into his cave. And on this particular hour the entire planet in its orbit has an imperceptible tremor generated by that same ancient act. We've just erected too many barriers of myth and convention around it. Haven't we?

Or, traditionally, blame it on being in the dangerous forties. And remember how sorry you are for the things you don't do.

Or, for the love of God, just try to stop all this thinking. Think only of Cindy, she of the long golden legs and the blue-gray eyes and the expressive mouth and the dark blond hair.

Nurse Calhoun was on duty again. Joan was cranked up, her hair fixed, lipstick on, her eyes better but still not quite right.

"I told you you shouldn't come out in the afternoon, darling," she said. "But I'm glad you did come, anyway. Just a little while ago they had me sit right up with my legs over the side of the bed. Dangling, they call it. They make you dangle on the day after. Honestly, dear, it's incredible. The day before yesterday I was trudging up and down the halls, and now I'm weaker than a kitten. I couldn't stand up and take a step if my life depended on it."

"Tomorrow you'll be taking some steps," the nurse said. "We'll have you running around the block before you know it."

"How do you really feel?" he asked her.

"Well . . . I still feel as if everything could fall out. And the incision feels so strange. It feels as if a piece of that sort of hard rope, you know, about this big around, was sewed right across here, under my skin."

"Are you in much pain?"

"When I hurt they keep giving me things, but I don't think they're as strong as before. They're pills now, not shots. I had some shots in the night. The night nurse is nice, but I can't remember her name."

"Gallowell," Nurse Calhoun said. "I'll be right back, Mrs. Garrett."

After she had gone Joan lowered her voice and said, "All the money for nurses is making me nervous, Carl."

"I told you before, the insurance takes care of it."

"Does it really? Or are you just saying that?"

"It really does," he lied.

"I was so foggy yesterday. I can hardly remember a thing that happened. And now I'm utterly exhausted, just from hanging my legs over the side of the bed. Are you going back to work now?"

"No. I'm goofing off. I'm using you as an excuse."

"It looks like such a nice day out there. Why don't you play golf, dear? It would do you good."

"The grass is getting shaggy. If I feel the need of exercise, I better break out the mower. Who sent the yellow roses?"

"Oh, they came from the garden club. Aren't they lovely? They must have come from Molly's garden."

Nurse Calhoun came back and studied Joan with a professional eye. "This is a lady who needs a nap, I think."

So, at ten minutes of three he was on the turnpike heading east at sixty-five miles an hour.

As the new turnpike was a limited access highway, the group of new motels were on a parallel strip at one of the exits. As he turned off he was distressed to see how many cars were parked at the motels at this hour of the afternoon. But he was heartened by the vacancy signs. He cruised the strip slowly, turned around in the parking lot of a Howard Johnson's, and, on the way back, turned in at a motel called The Traveler, and parked near the office. It had an imposing façade that faced the highway, a high glass wall, a startling angle of roof. The units, of redwood and gray stone, stretched back in two parallel lines at right angles to the highway. The highway sign told of air-conditioning, television, swimming pool. The pool was a garish blue against a green lawn. There were chairs on the lawn and children in the pool.

When Carl walked in, a man came out of a rear office to wait upon him. He was an imposing man, large and stately, with ruddy face, white hair, a gray military mustache.

"May I help you?" he asked in a rich and measured baritone with a slight trace of British accent.

"I would like a double room, please."

The man placed the registration card in front of him and pushed the pen stand an inch closer. "We can accommodate you, sir."

Carl picked up the pen and said, "We don't want to take occupancy right now. We'll be in later on in the evening."

One white eyebrow went up in question.

"It's like this. My wife and I are remodeling our house. We live . . . just outside of Hillton. The carpenters and the painters started on the bedroom this morning. And we thought we'd rather . . . stay out here than down in the city. With the pool and all. And it is only a forty minute trip." He heard himself talking too much and too rapidly, but he could not seem to stop.

"Of course, sir."

"So if we could take it for three nights. That's the estimate of how long before we can use our own bedroom. I'll pay you in advance of course."

The man gave him a weary and very knowing look, and Carl felt his face get hot, and he knew that this was something that had happened before and would happen again, and that the man had made his decision to accept him not on any moral basis, but merely because he looked quiet and decent and reasonably prosperous.

"The room will be fifteen dollars a night, sir. Would you care to see it before you register?"

Carl saw how neatly he had been trapped. This man would not be the owner, merely a resident manager. If Carl's story was legitimate, he would yelp at the high rate and then be shown a room he could have at their regular rates. If he was setting up a clandestine arrangement, he would swallow the financial penalty without a murmur, and the imposing man could pocket the difference.

"No. No thanks. I'm sure the room will be fine. Very attractive place here."

"Thank you, sir."

In his confusion he forgot his intention of signing the false name he had made up until he had written *Mr. and Mrs. Carl A. Garr* . . . After a frozen moment, he finished the name as Garroway and gave a false and empty laugh and said, "Absolutely no relation to Dave."

The manager gave him a wooden smile. Carl wrote a false address, wrote in the make of his car and the proper license number. He put two twenties and a ten on the counter top, and received a five dollar bill. It left him with eight dollars in his wallet.

The man placed the key in front of him. "Number twenty, sir. In the right wing, halfway down. You'll see the ice machine near the public telephone. I hope you'll be very comfortable, sir."

When Carl walked out to the car he felt shaken and sweaty.
He tried to believe that it made no difference what that man
might believe. Maybe the aura of disbelief had been all in
his own mind. Maybe their rates were that high.

He drove back through the arch beside the office and
parked in the marked slot numbered twenty, unlocked the
room door and went in. The room was about fifteen by
twenty, and contained two double beds. There was a central
air-conditioning system, and a soft sound came from a wall
grid, a sound like an unending sigh. The venetian blinds were
a dark wine red, the wall-to-wall carpeting a deep soft blue-
green. The furniture was squatty and pale and modern. On
the table between the beds was a double gooseneck lamp
with spun aluminum shades. The television set was angled
into a corner, looking out at the room through its single blind
oppressive eye. On the bureau, on a glass tray, was a red
plastic pitcher and two squat tumblers sealed in cellophane.
The room was clean and hushed and impersonal.

He walked to the bathroom, found the soundless mercury
switch. A circular fluorescent fixture went on over the sink,
filling the small room with glaring white. There was a tub
with semi-opaque plastic screens that slid in a channel along
the edge of the tub to turn it into a shower stall. Two bath
towels, two hand towels, two paper bath mats, and a wide
strip of paper that sealed the closed toilet lid and announced
how sanitary it was.

He turned off the light, went back into the bedroom, sat
on one of the beds and tapped ashes into the glass tray on
the dividing table. He could not believe that it could happen.
He could not visualize her in this impersonal efficiency. And
then all the anticipation started again. It started with a
hollow throbbing feeling in his belly that moved up and
fluttered violently under his heart so that he could not take
a deep breath.

He drove out of The Traveler, and remembered the problem of her car. Two hundred yards from The Traveler, at the
corner of the commercial strip and the exit road, was a large
gas station. He pulled up to the pumps and a crewcut boy in
gray coveralls filled his tank and checked under the hood.
As he was cleaning the windshield, Carl said, "Can I park a
car here overnight for two or three nights?"

"Park here?"

"Yes. Leave a car here."

"Sure, I guess so, but we couldn't take no responsibility.

You should lock it up good. There's nobody here after eleven, and we open up at seven."

"Where'll I put it where it won't be in your way?"

"Put it back over there on the grass, mister, right next to my old Chev. Will you bring it in tonight?"

"Yes, tonight."

"Okay, I'm on to eleven every night. I'll tell the boss. Let's say a buck a night. That sound okay?"

"That's fine," Carl said. After he paid for the gas and gave the boy three dollars, he had less than two dollars left.

It was just five o'clock when he pulled into his driveway and parked beside Joan's Hillman. He went out into the back yard and looked down into the back yard of the Cable house. Cindy, in a white sun suit with small red polka dots, lay prone on a rubberized beach mattress on the lawn, her body greased with sun lotion, her book and sun glasses beside her.

He went down the abrupt terrace into her yard. She heard him and sat up quickly, and one hand went to her throat.

"What is it?" she said. "Why are you home? Is something wrong?"

He sat on his heels beside her. "I left the office early and went to the hospital and then went out the turnpike."

She met his glance and looked away. "We shouldn't do this. I can't think of anything else. I can't read or eat or anything. We shouldn't, Carl."

"I know that, damn it!"

"I feel so strange and horrible."

He took the key out of his pocket and showed it to her, a shining brass key fastened to a dark red plastic plaque.

"Number twenty," she said.

"And I've got a place for your car. I'll leave the hospital at eight-thirty. You park at the corner of Crescent Road and Route 80. I'll meet you there, and then you follow me out the pike."

"It's all so . . . cold and conspiratorial."

"Instead of clumsy and careless. What should we do? Go down and check in at the Brower Hotel?"

"I know, darling, I know. But it's so contrived. So sort of cold-blooded. I wish . . ."

"What do you wish?"

"Nothing. I'm just in sort of a flap, I guess. It isn't the sort of thing I'm all practiced up on."

"Shall we skip it?"

"Don't be cross and cruel, please. It's making us both

nervous, but let's not snap at each other, darling. If you want me to take the responsibility, I will. No. We won't skip it."

"I didn't mean it that way. I'm sorry. This horrible grimace is supposed to be a warm and loving smile."

She smiled back at him. "Do you know what I was thinking about when you arrived? The stupidest thing. What to wear. It makes a very special problem of what to wear. How does a girl dress for an assignation? There isn't a word in the etiquette books, honestly."

"I won't be any help. I just hope I remember to notice what you wear. But you should bring something along you can wear in the morning too, when you come back." He stood up. "I've got things to do now. I should be along at about twenty to nine."

"At the corner of Route 80 and Crescent Road."

He went back to his house and got a check and drove to the new shopping center a mile away and got the okay of the supermarket manager to cash it for fifty dollars. From there he went to the liquor store he patronized and bought two bottles of good champagne. As soon as he got home he put the champagne in the refrigerator. He took a long and thorough shower, dressed carefully, packed a small suitcase and stowed the champagne and the contents of two ice trays in the scotch cooler, and put them in the car.

He walked, smiling, into Room 314 at exactly seven o'clock, to spend the entire hour and a half with Joan. Miss Pierce left when he arrived.

Joan looked more tired than when he had seen her earlier in the day. She said she had "dangled" again, that Bernie had stopped by an hour ago to check her over again and he said the incision was coming along fine.

She smiled at him and said, "My goodness, you're certainly all decked out tonight. If I didn't know you better, I'd say you were going out for an evening on the town."

"I got all dressed up to see you," he said, vividly aware of the motel key in his pocket. He looked beyond Joan and, for a moment, caught the bright, wise and skeptical look of Rosa Myers before she turned back to her book.

"Well," Joan said, "if you did go out on the town, I don't think you'd have many problems. You look very handsome."

"As a matter of fact, after I leave here I may go on into town. Jim Hardy is entertaining some of the New York people at Steuben's. I may decide to join them for a drink."

"Then you don't want to hang around here, dear! Why don't you run along?"

"No. I'll stay here. I'd rather."

"Did you decide to play golf or mow the lawn?"

"Neither. I spent the afternoon being a slob."

"Speaking of being a slob, how is Cindy coming with her project?"

"Project?"

"You know, dear. What she said about doing absolutely nothing."

"I guess she's working at it. She was in her back yard this afternoon, sunning herself. I . . . I went over and talked to her for a couple of minutes, told her how you're coming along. She says to give you her best."

"Tell her that I go back on the visiting list tomorrow, will you? I always enjoy Cindy. She says such crazy wonderful things. Bernie says I can let the night nurse go after tonight, and after tomorrow, I can let Miss Pierce go, but I should keep Ruth Calhoun for another few days, to help me with my bath and learning to walk all over again. You know, this is Wednesday, and it doesn't seem possible I can come home next Monday. It doesn't really seem possible."

"You'll mend fast. You are mending fast."

"Did Molly get hold of you yet? They want you to have dinner over there."

"Not yet. Maybe she's tried. I've been on the run."

"I've been wondering about the refrigerator. It was making a funny noise every once in a while and I forgot to tell you about it. Have you heard the funny noise it makes?"

"What kind of a noise?"

"Sort of a thumping, just before it turns off."

"I haven't noticed anything."

"You listen for it. Maybe we ought to have somebody look at it. It's five years old and I don't think a repair man has ever even looked at it. In fact, I know no one has looked at it. Dear, have you been getting enough sleep? You're not staying up reading until all hours, are you?"

"No."

"Oh, before I forget, I wrote the kids. Would you put stamps on these and mail them, please?"

He put the letters in the inside pocket of his suit coat.

"Now don't carry them around for weeks. And really, darling, don't try to come and see me tomorrow afternoon. I don't think you should spend so much time away from the office. And I'm really not sick any more. Look, dear, at the card I got from Jill. I haven't heard from her in ages."

"Jill?"

"Jill Watson, silly. At least she used to be. Now she's Jill Pritchard."

"Oh, the little dark one who got the messy divorce."

"I've heard she's very happy now."

The minutes seemed to crawl by. The visiting hour would never end. At last it did. He kissed her and, from the hallway, smiled back at her and waved, and walked to the elevators, and went down and turned in his visiting card and went out into the twilight.

TEN

The Cable family sedan, a blue two-year-old Buick, was parked at the corner. He touched the horn ring once as he drove slowly by. He caught a quick glimpse of her behind the wheel. When he looked back he saw the car pull out to follow him. He went back onto the turnpike. The evening traffic was heavy, and soon it was so dark he could not tell if the headlights behind him were hers.

He could not establish his usual driving rhythm. He seemed to be going either too slow or too fast. And it seemed a very long time before he came to the sign that announced the next exit one mile ahead, and he saw the bright clutter of the neon along the commercial strip. When he moved right into the exit lane, the headlights behind him followed him. He drove down the long curve and pulled into the gas station. It was brightly floodlighted and, at that moment, very busy. Cindy pulled up on his right and he leaned across the seat and said, "Back it onto the grass beside that Chevy."

He got out as she backed it into place. He opened the door for her. She took a small suitcase from the seat and handed it to him.

"Should I lock it?"

"Give me your keys. I'll do it. You get in my car."

He locked her car, carried her small suitcase to his car and got behind the wheel. She sat far over by the door. She was wearing something dark. Her long hair was fashioned into a flat bun at the back of her head, and there was a drifting scent of musky perfume in the car.

"Hello, Cindy," he said softly as he started up.

"Hello." Her voice was small and tense.

"That's it, just up the road. The Traveler."

"Carl . . . could we just drive for a little while? And come back?"

"If you'd like."

"It's just sort of too quick."

"I know what you mean." He went back to the turnpike

103

and headed east through the night in the fast even flow of traffic. She stayed over on her side of the seat. He glanced at her when oncoming headlights shone into the car. Her face was grave and still.

"It's very odd," she said.

"What is odd?"

"The name of the place. The Traveler. This is a journey, I guess. A trip to a far place. And when you come back, you aren't the same again, ever."

"I suppose."

"We went to Mexico City on our honeymoon, you know. We had a suite at the del Prado. And we found a place to eat that we loved. El Parador. We ate there many times. Do you know what that name means?"

"No."

"The Traveler. They made their martinis with Amontillado sherry. They had hors d'oeuvres that were little hot biscuits with a surprise in the middle. A shrimp or a little cube of steak. It was a wonderful honeymoon, Carl. We were going to be happy forever. I'm telling you this because I don't want you to get the wrong idea from what I said the other night, about the bedroom part being all wrong lately. In the beginning it was so very right. We would be in some public place and then we would look at each other, and all of a sudden the plans we'd made for the day were unimportant and the only important thing was to get back to the hotel, quickly. I know that the . . . physical part of marriage is more important to me than it is to most women. And in the beginning Bucky was thinking of me, too, instead of just thinking of himself, the way he does now. He tumbles into sleep and I lie there with my fists clenched, all tight as violin strings, despising him. But it was good, Carl, very good. And you should know that. And if it was still good, in spite of all the other things, I wouldn't be here."

"I know that's true."

She suddenly slid over and sat close beside him, so that he felt the warmth of her hip. "Now," she said, "there isn't going to be any Bucky and any Joan. You're not Carl and I'm not Cindy. No labels. We're just a couple. And we're in a car. and we're going to be together soon."

"Shall we go back now?"

"We can turn at the next exit. From the sign back there it ought to be another four miles." He dropped his right

hand to her lap. She held his hand tightly in both of hers.
Her fingers were chill.

After he had turned around, using the clover leaf and
the underpass, she said, "Is it terribly silly of me to feel
like a bride? Is it stupid or coarse or anything?"

"No."

"I've got the most horrible case of stage fright. I suppose, rationally, it's because I'm doing something I never
thought I would do. I knew I'd never cheapen myself by
getting into one of these grim little clandestine adulteries.
Cheap and sneaky."

"Then how do you react irrationally?"

"I guess I don't feel cheap. Or maybe that will come
later. I just feel all trembly and scared and hollow and ex
cited. Darling, do I talk too terribly much? Wouldn't vou
rather have a woman of restraint and mystery and so on?
I'm too much the den-mother type to be suitable for intrigue."

"I love to hear you talk."

"I have a great talent for talking things to death. I was a
horrid-looking child, you know. All strings and knobs, and
when the other little girls mv age were having dates, I was
still trying to scrounge turns on the post rifle range and
taking my horse over the highest walls I could find. As a
defense, I chattered. Endlesslv. I remember, when ` began
to look a little more human, a boy wanted to kiss me. He
was a colonel's son and his name was Benny something,
and that was when Daddy was stationed at Fort Ord, California. I knew he'd maneuvered me into a walk in the woods
for the purpose of kissing me. And `` verv much wanted to
be kissed, so that   could sort of ìoin the group, so to speak.
We were both horribly nervous. I started talking before we
got to the woods and I talked all the wav through the woods
and out the other side and all the wav back to the frort
porch of our house on officer's row, and then went plunging
in and fell across mv bed and cried my eyes out."

"Poor Benny."

"Well, he did try again, poor thing, and took advantage
of the first ten seconds of silence I gave him. After we got
over the nose-bumping problem, we acouired quite a taste
for it. I was fourteen at the time, and Bennv was fifteen.
We managed to get in a great deal of kissing and fumbling,
and though I was heartbroken when thev were transferred,
it was probably a verv lucky thing, because in another few
weeks we could have gotten into some real trouble. I think

we wrote each other every day for as long as three weeks."

"I would have liked to have been the first to kiss you, Cindy."

"Would you now? How old were you when I was fourteen, twelve years ago."

"Thirty, damn it."

"They would have been after you with a net. Can you remember your first kiss?"

"Distinctly. Back in Youngstown when I must have been twelve or thirteen. I went to a birthday party and they got around to this game of playing spin the bottle. I had the vague scared feeling that I would like to kiss a little dish named Florence. But the luck of the bottle sent me out into the hall closet among the coats with a monstrous girl named Irene Brechtoller. She was half a head taller and weighed twenty pounds more than I did, and she had the beginnings of what is probably, by now, a handlebar mustache. And no dainty peck for Irene. She took her cue from the movies. I felt like I was being simultaneously smothered and crushed. I was terrified, but dead game. I got into the game again on the off chance of getting to kiss Florence. But I got Irene again. After my second tour of duty in the closet, I said I had to go home. For months afterward, it seems, everytime I looked behind me on the way home from school, there was Irene waddling along wearing a wide hopeful smile."

"Poor little man!"

"I think we've done enough driving for the day. There are some good-looking motels up ahead, Mrs. Garroway, so let us go get us a room."

"Garroway?"

"That's what we're registered as."

"A good thing to know."

He drove through the arch. The pool was lighted. A man and woman were swimming side by side, their slow strokes in perfect rhythm. He parked in front of twenty. It was nearly ten, and most of the units were dark. He unlocked the door and found the light switch just inside the door, and a very bright ceiling fixture went on. He put the two suitcases down and went out and carried the cooler in and shut the door and fastened the night chain.

Cindy stood with her back to him. She turned as he walked up to her. The garish light made the room look harsh and ugly. But it could not make her look less desirable. She wore a tailored black suit, a white blouse with a severe collar, white pumps with high heels, small gold hoop earrings. Her dark blond hair was pulled smoothly back at the temples. Her makeup was careful, her face flawless.

With wry and crooked smile, she said, a strained note in her voice, "Well, here we are! Isn't that what one says?"

He took her in his arms and kissed her. She was awkward in his arms, and the kiss she returned him was quick and tepid. She moved out of his arms and said, "I had quite a problem. Would I try to look girlish and innocent? Or slinky and seductive? Or maybe all frilly? So I settled for sophistication. Like me?"

"You inspire a certain amount of awe. But yes, I like you."

"Let's do something about the horrible lighting effects, at least." She turned on the gooseneck lamps between the beds and he turned off the ceiling light. It was immediately a much more attractive and intimate room.

She sat rather stiffly on the side of a bed and said, "This isn't what I expected. I didn't think about it too much, but I sort of had the idea of a sort of grim cabin effect, with one naked light bulb and a lot of trucks growling by just outside the door. This is . . . almost too formal. I don't even feel like taking off my jacket. But I have to because you have to see this sneaky blouse."

She got up and took off her black jacket. The blouse consisted of the severe collar and a front and a small area around her waist. It left her smooth and honey-tan shoulders and back bare. She pirouetted slowly and said, "Sneaky, hmm?"

"Delightfully." She went to the closet and hung up her jacket, then noticed the cooler.

"What do we have here?"

"Maybe it's a little on the corny side, Cindy. It's champagne."

She came to him and kissed him lightly, and moved away before he could take her in his arms. "You're a darling," she said. "I think champagne is going to be practically essential, the way I feel right now."

He took out a bottle, stripped the cellophane from the two glasses, twisted the wire loose and thumped the cork out. It popped off the ceiling and struck her on the shoulder as it fell.

"I think that's supposed to be lucky," she said.

She took her glass and they clinked glasses. They sipped, and then she began to stroll restlessly. He sat on the bed and watched her. The skirt of the suit was high waisted and superbly fitted to the narrow waist, the roundness of hips.

"I just wish I could stop feeling so damnably awkward and strange," she said.

"Come here and be thoroughly kissed."

"Not just yet, please, darling. I have the ghastly feeling that I want to run like a big rabbit. I feel so dang . . . immature."

"You're lovely, Cindy."

"Thank you kindly." She went and refilled her glass, drank it down thirstily, refilled it again.

"Hey!" he said.

"I'm seeking a little moral anesthesia, pal. I've got a painful abscess of the conscience. Joan and Bucky are riding my back."

"We weren't going to mention them."

She sat on the other bed, facing him, and crossed long legs in the narrow skirt and looked at him somberly, and said, "You're being very patient with me, and I do appreciate it, my darling."

"I don't think it was supposed to be exactly like this."

"We're both awkward, aren't we? Poor stuffy fools. Lost lambs, or something. I think it's because it's all so planned. It wasn't at all planned the other two times. I'm completely unaware of the protocol, Carl. I'm facing the awkward problems of just how we go about getting undressed. If I hadn't worn such silly complicated clothes with girdle and all, you could undress me and maybe that would be all right. Look, would you care to start giving some orders around here?"

"All right. We have one more drink, and then I shall go out and look at the starry night. And then I will come back in say fifteen minutes."

"All right," she whispered. She blushed then and looked down at her glass and said, "Might as well get all the embarrassing little matters out of the way. You won't have to worry about . . ."

"I understand." He poured another drink for them and took her glass to her. They touched glasses again. They drank in silence, and when the glasses were empty, he left.

He walked slowly out to the pool. It was empty. He sat on a lawn chair damp with dew and smoked a cigarette and looked at the high and sterile stars. They were there ten thousand years ago and they'll be there ten thousand years after the last memory and trace of me is gone. Under their pale light, anything I do is meaningless, of too little significance to be considered good or evil, right or wrong.

When he went in and locked the door behind him, she was in bed. She had twisted the neck of one half of the double lamp so that it threw its cone of radiance down toward the floor, and in the reflected glow he could see her shadowy face, her hair spread and tousled on the pillow. He undressed in the shadowy corner near the closet, and went to the bed and slipped in beside her.

"Leave the light, dearest," she whispered.

He reached for her between the crispness of sheets and laid his hand on the tender concavity of her waist, felt the warmth and softness and electric aliveness of her, felt the deep lift of her breathing. And all at once she came into his arms, all the trembling, gasping, silken length of her, throbbingly warm, vivid, so stirring in her eagerness that any lingering restraints were swept away, and he was involved and lost in her textures and customs and pliancy, involved in all the secret places of her, wracked and pulsed by her thirsts and her needs.

Once when he awakened he reached for her and she was gone. He awakened entirely and sat up. The light was still on and he saw her, tall and pale and vague in the shadowy place near the windows, standing and looking out between the slats of the blinds, her back to him, white across the buttocks where the sun had not touched her, with a lesser band of white across her back.

"Cindy," he said.

She whirled and looked toward him. And came swiftly to him, chanting, "Darling, darling, darling, darling . . ." keeping it up until he stopped her lips with his own.

Another time he awakened and she was curled beside him, an arm across his chest, a leg linked in his—sleeping deeply, her chin touching his shoulder, her slow exhalations warm and sweet against his throat, stirring the strand of her hair that lay there. He tilted her head gently so he could reach her lips, and in that gentle way he awakened her from sleep and awakened her again.

When he awakened the last time, morning was in the room, and she was sitting on the floor by the bed, her face close to his saying, "Ding, ding, ding, ding, ding. Good morning, my honey. I am being an alarm clock. Ding, ding, ding, ding."

"I shall turn you off."

She wore red denim shorts, sandals, a crisp white blouse with round red buttons down the front. Her hair was tied in a pony tail with a red ribbon.

"What happened to the sophisticate I came here with?"

"That crow in black? She took off. She sent me in to sub. She explained that you're very dull, but sort of sweet."

"What time is it, anyway?"

"There have been thirty little men out in front chunking car doors for hours. It is now ten minutes beyond seven. Time to get up, dear. Time to go be an executive type."

He pulled her close and kissed her. At seven-thirty he got up, picked the red shorts and the red-button blouse off the floor and hung them on a chair back. He showered and shaved hastily. When he was dressed he went over to the bed. She looked up at him and said, "Nobody would ever know, dear."

"Are you going to get up?"

"I was thinking there isn't much point in it. When I'm ready, I can walk down to the gas station." She reached out and caught his hand and tugged him off balance so that he sat on the edge of the bed.

"I want to be serious," she said. "I know that this is wrong. I know it's sin. But I feel absolutely wonderful. I feel like a happy bride. I love you terribly. I love you with all my heart. That's all I want to think of now. I want to save all the remorse until after it's all over."

He leaned over and kissed her. "It's a deal. I love you."

She wrinkled her nose at him. "I know, I know, but am I any good in bed?"

"Breathtaking. Incredible. A great unsung talent."

"Spread the word." She pushed at him with her knee. "Now get on your horse. And I will expect you home here no later than ten after nine tonight. No dilly-dallying. No stopping off in low dives for a quickie."

"Nag, nag, nag," he said, and kissed her again and left.

It was a little after eight-thirty when he stopped at the house. Marie Pounders, the cleaning woman, was sitting on the low terrace wall, a sullen and stubborn bulk in the sunshine. She stood up with a weighty abused sigh and said, "I was figuring I better maybe walk down and catch the next bus back, maybe."

"I'm sorry, Marie. I had to go out early today. I should have left the house open."

"You don't want to never leave the house open. There's thiefs everywhere. How's the missus?"

"She's coming along just fine."

She followed him into the kitchen. "I don't expect it's much messed up around here, you being here alone and the kids gone and all. But I got to do the windows and that'll take up the best part of a day anyhow. But if my back gets to aching me like it has lately I'll have to lay down a while."

"That'll be all right, of course."

"I'll be gone before you get back and I'll go out the front door so it locks itself and the missus said you'd pay me before you go. That's nine dollars plus forty cents on the bus."

He paid her and went into the bedroom with the intention of rumpling the bed, but was glad to see he had forgotten to make it from the night before. When he left, Marie was banging around in the closet where the cleaning materials were kept, mumbling to herself. He wished Joan could find someone more pleasant. But Joan insisted that Marie was dependable and thorough, and after all, she came to clean not to be entertaining.

All during the fifteen-minute drive to the office, he dwelt on the sensual memories of the long night. Their immediate physical rapport had been startling. It dizzied him to remember how well she suited him. She was midway between the somewhat reptilian fascinations of Sandara Lahl Hotchkiss and her somewhat repellent devices, and the cozy and placid competence of Joan. Just one of the three nights was gone. It seemed as though an infinity of Cindy lay ahead, an endless time with her.

His day of work was a vague and misty time for him. Cindy stood at his elbow all day long. At four in the afternoon Molly Raedek phoned him and said, "If you aren't the hardest man to locate, Carl Garrett! I called you a dozen times last night and I guess I just missed you by a whisker this morning. Ted and I want you to come to dinner tonight. I've just come from seeing Joan, and so that's an order, not an invitation. I'll feed the kids early, so there'll just be the three of us."

"Molly, that's darned sweet of you and I appreciate it, but I made another date not a half hour ago."

"Oh, darn! Well, tomorrow night then?"

"If it wouldn't foul you up too much, Saturday night would be better."

"So Saturday it is. About six?"

"Fine. And thanks."

After he hung up he suddenly wondered why he and Cindy had restricted themselves to three nights. He remembered her saying, in the hospital room, that after Bucky finished his Big Swing he was going to a convention in Memphis over the weekend. If Joan wouldn't be released until Monday, they could have five days instead of three. He decided to talk to Cindy and, if she agreed, then he could think of some way of getting out of the dinner with Molly and Ted.

And even after the five nights, it wouldn't be sensible to say that was the end of it forever. There might be other times when it would be safe. Just as safe as this arrangement. But he guessed that it wouldn't be wise to mention anything like that to Cindy until these three nights—or five nights— had ended.

It was an endlessly dull day. His attention wandered so badly in a conference that the others became aware of it and kidded him about it. But Jim Hardy's kidding had an edge to it. And he longed to tell Little Ike to go straight to hell.

Mrs. Brisbie got on his nerves more than usual and he snapped at her and felt ashamed when she looked at him like a kicked dog. Goldlaw had made a stupid error in a report. Carl had not caught it, but it had been caught in New York and sent back with a very sarcastic note of query. Once, during the day, he went out to the production areas and leaned on a high railing, hoping that the churning floor would soothe him with its flavor of frantic nonsense, but the familiar magic did not work.

He left just as soon as he dared. The sky was gray and a slow viscid rain was falling. When he crossed the Governor Carson Bridge he caught a glimpse of the Silver River, dark and metallic, poisoned by a hundred kinds of industrial filth, and wondered what it had looked like when it had first earned its name.

But by the time he was halfway home his feeling of depression had lifted, and he thought of Cindy, and he remembered vividly her curious cry of completion, a surprisingly low-pitched sound, not loud, that seemed to tear her throat and burst from her lips against her will. Her car was not in the car port.

He showered and put on slacks and a short-sleeved sports shirt. The rain had nearly stopped and it threatened to be a sticky night. He decided it would be better to leave her earlier and come back to the house to shower and change for the office. He drove down to the new shopping center and looked for a gift for Joan. He found a game box of a dozen mechanical puzzles imported from England, and bought it. Joan took a childish delight in solving puzzles. While paying for it, he decided it wasn't enough, and bought her a tiny and expensive bottle of perfume in the same drugstore.

He arrived at the hospital at seven o'clock, bearing gifts, and digesting a huge steak.

ELEVEN

Joan had been cranked almost straight up. She was bright-eyed and full of news. Rosa was going home tomorrow. Molly and Jane and Cindy had visited her in the afternoon. She had walked around the bed, leaning heavily on Nurse Calhoun.

She opened her presents and raved over the puzzles and put them aside with a certain reluctance, and opened the perfume and smelled it and decided it was just right, and gave him the two letters that had come from the kids directly to the hospital for her. Nancy had enclosed a snapshot of herself looking rather small but confident atop a large white horse.

"Did Molly get hold of you?"

"Yes. She phoned me at the office."

"Then you're going over there tonight?"

"The date is for Saturday night."

"But she told me she wanted you for tonight."

"I know that, but I'd already made a date with Gil Sullivan. Madge is visiting her folks, so he's alone too." He knew that Madge was out of town, and he made a mental note to get Gil to cover for him, just in case. It would be an awkward request to make, but if anybody would catch on immediately, it would be Gil.

"But you don't even like him!" Joan said.

"Gil is okay."

"He loves to go out and whoop it up. Don't you try to drink along with him, and for goodness sake don't you let him do the driving. It's a miracle he walked away from that accident two years ago. Gee, I wish you were going to the Raedeks instead, dear."

"I'm a big boy now. I don't think you have to worry about me."

"When do you have to meet Gil?"

"Any time. Down at the grill room of the Brower."

"Will there be anybody else along?"

"I don't know, honey. I just said I'd meet Gil. That's all."

114

"You certainly aren't dressed for the Brower Hotel."

"I've got a jacket in the car."

"You should wear a necktie."

"It's July, honey. And I'm off duty."

"Well, you don't have to snap at me, do you?"

"I'm sorry."

"I wish there was some way you could call me when you get home."

"For God's sake, Joan!"

"Oh, all right. I guess I'm just fussing. I guess it's just because I don't like that Gil Sullivan. I don't trust him."

"You look pretty good tonight, Joanie."

"I feel much, much better. I'm beginning to believe I might get out of here Monday, after all."

"What time of day will you be getting out?"

"I don't know. I'll ask Bernie. Did Marie come?"

"Yes, she arrived, full of sour looks and dark mumblings."

"Does the house look nice?"

"It looks okay. She was going to do the windows."

"It always rains when she's going to do the windows. The rest that Cindy is having is doing her worlds of good, Carl. She looked absolutely radiant today. I don't think I've ever seen her look so pretty. She's getting a marvelous tan, and her face looks so rested. A person would swear she wasn't over twenty-one. We had a nice visit. She told me that as far as she knows, you're getting to bed early. But I'll bet you won't get to bed early tonight. Not if you're out with that Gil Sullivan."

"Joan, I . . ."

"All right, dear. I won't bring it up again. Are you going to cut the lawn over the weekend?"

"That's when I plan to do it. And clip the raggedy hedge."

"If it's terribly hot, don't try to do too much."

He left at eight-thirty. He was ashamed that he had been irritable with her. But all that Gil Sullivan talk had gotten on his nerves. He felt both relief and intense anticipation as he straightened out on the turnpike, heading east. He found a news program on the car radio but turned it off as soon as he realized he could not follow what the man was saying. He was too engrossed in his thoughts of Cindy.

She swung the door open the moment he knocked, and, as soon as he was inside, she threw her arms around his neck, straining tall against him, kissing him with a fierce and joyous abandon. She wore a black sheath blouse that left her shoulders bare, a colorful pleated skirt. She was barefoot.

She led him by the hand to the bureau and said, "Look. The very best people drink their champagne from champagne glasses." The slim-stemmed glasses were fragile and handsome. "And the champagne is iced, sir, and our stock is back up to two bottles again." She hugged him. "Oh, I'm so glad to see you. This day has been a horror."

"Just like mine."

"Do you want to hear about mine first?"

"Tired man gets home from office and his woman immediately starts complaining."

"Hush. Just sit right there and listen. I'm not burdening you with this. It's my problem and I'll handle it myself. When I got home I wasn't in the house ten minutes before the phone started ringing. It was Bucky, calling from St. Louis. The first thing he did was shout, 'Where the hell were you last night?' 'Right here, dear,' I said. 'Oh, no, you weren't. I started calling at nine and I called until two in the morning. And I called again at six this morning.' So I said, just as coldly as I could, 'I was right here all the time. The phone must have been out of order.' 'Phone, hell,' he said. 'At two o'clock I had the operator try the Garretts and there wasn't any answer there, so I had her try the Stocklands. Bill Stockland got up and went over there while I waited on the line. No car, no lights, and no answer when he pounded on the door.' By then, darling, my knees were shaking, really, but I managed to say, 'So that's what that was.' He asked me what I meant. I told him I'd heard somebody thumping on the door in the middle of the night, but I certainly wasn't going to get up and answer it. I told him the car wasn't there because it was in the repair garage, overnight. I think I quieted him down, but he was furious at first. He gets very jealous sometimes."

"That's just dandy," Carl said. "That's fine."

"Don't worry about it. If he's calling tonight, I'll lie again. I find I have an entirely new knack of lying. I think I could become an expert."

"I don't like it."

"We just won't think about it."

"What will the Stocklands think about it?"

"I don't really care."

"Eunice will have you pegged as a loose woman."

"Has it not occurred to you, darling, that perhaps I am?"

She had fixed the lights. He opened the champagne and poured it. They sat on the two beds, facing each other, the bottle on the floor at his feet.

"You saw Joan today," he said.

"I thought it would look horribly strange if I stayed away. But it was twenty minutes of hell. I've never felt like such a complete louse. I mean to sit there and chatter, just as though the world hadn't suddenly been turned upside down. She's a dear, you know. She's the one who must never, never find out about this."

"She said the rest was doing you good. She said you looked radiant."

"I didn't know it showed. She asked me to be sure you were getting enough sleep. I've been very naughty about that, Carl. All you got last night were little bits and pieces of sleep. But I shouldn't make a joke out of that. I suspect it is not in the best of taste. So I sat there and when she smiled at me, I felt perfectly willing to run out and cut my throat. It's such a foul thing to do to her. And she's such a warm sunny unsuspicious little guy."

They drank and talked and soon the talk began to die, and the last of the bottle was divided between them. Her glass was empty first. When his was empty she took his glass out of his hand and took the glasses and bottle over to the bureau. Then she came back and stood between his knees and put her hands on his shoulders. The angle of the light shadowed her eyes.

She said, in a very low voice, "Last night, I was all tricked out in that terribly complicated clothing. Tonight I'm very very easy. No shoes, no bra, no panties. This pulls over my head and this I step out of. But at the moment, dearest, I'm terribly, terribly lazy."

He stood up and pulled the sheath blouse up over her head, and free of her upstretched arms. He unbuttoned the side of the skirt and unzipped it. When it dropped she stepped out of it and then stood there looking at him quite gravely, her head slightly tilted to one side, her mouth soft and level.

"You're glorious!" he said in a husky whisper.

And when he put his arms around her, his palms flat and firm on the planes of her back, her fingers worked quickly and efficiently at the buttons down the front of his sports shirt.

"I'm getting horribly bold and brazen," she whispered.

"I like you this way."

He pushed Bucky into a forgotten corner of his mind until morning when he was ready to leave her.

"What if Bucky calls again?"

"Then I shall lie again. And there's nothing he can prove, is there?"

"You don't want him to suspect, do you?"

"Don't look so grim. The way I feel this morning, I'd like to throw it all in his face. I'd like to brag about it. And don't look so alarmed, beloved. I won't. But I'd like to."

"What are you going to do?"

"Take a lovely little nap on this lovely Friday morning, and if I have any luck I'll dream of you, and then I'm going to slosh in the pool. I brought a suit yesterday and came early and swam in the rain. It was lovely. And then I shall go eat a mountainous breakfast, and then go home and wander around the house feeling like half a person because I'm not with you, and then I'll go buy something to wear just for you, and then I'll come back out here as early as I dare, and have my swim and then go eat at Howard Johnson's, and then come back and make myself as pretty and fragrant as possible, and then lie right here and think of you and how soon you'll arrive and get myself all humid and bothered just thinking about you. Satisfied?"

"It will be the last time."

"I won't let myself think about that. And if I think about it at all, it's only to tell myself that next time will be as much better than this time as this time was better than the first time."

"We could stay two more nights. Saturday and Sunday. Joan comes home Monday. Bucky will be at the convention in Memphis."

She sat up in bed, holding the sheet against her breasts. "I wouldn't dare! I think he'll get away Sunday and come back. But, darling, one more night! Oh, yes, we could have one more night. Oh, darling!"

"I'll arrange it when I arrive tonight."

She looked at him and said, "I would like to have enough nights here so that I could find out when it levels off, when it stops getting forever better for us. Already it's the best there ever was, by far. Hurry back, my lover."

The day was crisp, clear and bright, washed clean by Thursday's rain. As he drove west along the straights and the sweeping engineered curves of the turnpike with the morning sun behind him, he could not for a time identify his feeling of unease. And quite suddenly he realized that he regretted having brought up the idea of another night, and was disturbed that she had accepted it. Bucky's suspicions troubled him. Her lies, which had seemed agile when she recounted them, now seemed clumsy.

But it was more than worry about Bucky, more than the feeling that their conspiracy had started to leak at the seams. It was, he sensed, the first awareness of the possibility of a surfeit of Cindy. Too much of her. She was sixteen years younger. And her ardors were becoming too . . . arduous. He smiled wanly at his own pun. He was wearied by two nights of sketchy and intermittent sleep, and he remembered, on this past night, being brought reluctantly and somewhat querulously up out of the sooty velvet of deep sleep by the mischievous insistencies of her fingers, the incandescent bloom of her lips, the furry whispering of a strand of her hair drawn across his face. She was at a pneumatic peak of supple health, and on this past night pride had been forced to take the place of wanting. Her energies were so shockingly impressive that what had been exciting had now started to become a little alarming. He felt like the man in the legend who had undertaken to empty the Seine with a sieve.

And he felt a sudden hot resentment that right now she should be back there snug in that sheeted battleground, restoring herself with the deep blurred sleep of satiety. He knew that he could survive one more night of their intricate gamboling, knew that by evening he would be eager again, but the thought of an additional night brought more despair than pleasurable anticipation.

He knew that today she would again visit Joan, and in the callous light of morning it seemed to him a shocking thing, wife and mistress exchanging pleasantries amid the sterile bustle of the County Memorial Hospital. She looked radiant.

Though he drove as fast as he dared, by the time he had changed, there was no time to stop for breakfast before he had to be at the office. At ten-thirty he had a chance to send Mrs. Brisbie out for a cheeseburger, coffee and a large vanilla milkshake. He was eating and working at his desk when Ray Walsh came in with the draft of an idea he was bird-dogging. It involved a substitution of materials on one of the basic items. He had gotten an okay from Production, Design, Purchasing and Engineering, and needed Carl's approval of the cost picture. Ray pulled a chair over beside Carl's and they went over the breakdown. The change-over would cause an increased unit cost in the beginning, but when it leveled out it would mean an eventual saving. After Carl initialed his approval, Ray Walsh leaned back and grinned at him. Ray was a man in his middle thirties with prematurely gray hair, an open friendly manner, small shrewd blunt eyes. It was the general opinion that Ray would do very well for himself indeed, and it would be healthy to keep your guard up, but not to keep it too obviously high because if Ray climbed over your head one day, he would have a long memory. So he was treated with caution because of the extent of his ambition, and respect because of his abilities.

"Well, well," he said. "Black circles under the eyes. Big energy-building milkshake in the middle of the morning. You must be taking this golden opportunity to really bounce the fillies around, Carl."

Carl felt a dull anger which he was careful not to show. He smiled and said, "I'm the steady type, Ray. Just haven't been sleeping too well."

Ray winked and knuckled Carl's shoulder and said, "Hell, man, who can sleep next to one of those lovely little tidbits? If you want to get lined up with a real jewel, and incidentally help get her off my hands, I can give you a . . ."

Carl heard himself say in a direct and gritty voice, "What I do or what I want to do doesn't seem to me to be any of your God damn business, Walsh."

The friendly Walsh smile turned to stone and faded quickly away. He picked up the draft of his proposal and stood up. "I appreciate your approving this, Garrett." He headed for the corridor door.

"Ray! Wait a minute."

Walsh turned and waited, expressionless.

"I apologize, Ray. My nerves are on edge."

Ray took two steps toward the desk. "So your nerves are on edge. Maybe you better wake up and look around you, boy. You're tabbed as an odd-ball. You've built a home away from home. You've got everything so flattened out you don't have any pain or strain. You've got a nice easy routine."

"What are you trying to say?"

"This isn't the most aggressive outfit in the world, but once in a while they like a few changes here and there, for the better. A lot of people think it's pretty damn funny that you're supposed to be the big costs boy, but you never come up with anything constructive. You make big contributions, you do. You've got a specialty. You sit around and make hilarious comments. Don't you believe in what the hell you're doing, Garrett?"

"Do you?"

"That's just the kind of odd-ball reaction I'd expect. You're perfectly right. What you do and what you want to do is none of my God damn business. I've seen your type before. You're another hunk of dead weight the rest of us have to haul around. Wake up, boy. Check the next conference. Nobody expects anything constructive from you. And your jokes don't get much of a laugh. You just sit in."

"You better knock it off, Walsh."

"Gladly," he said, and banged the door when he left. Carl knew that he had not made an enemy by his irritable response. He had just brought resentment and enmity out into the open. But the trouble with that was that now Ray would feel entitled to carry the knife openly. And Ray Walsh could be dangerous.

The most uncomfortable part of it was the sneaking knowledge that Ray was right, up to a point. He had contented himself with the function of merely measuring and reporting. And though it had never been explicitly stated, he was also expected to come up with cost-cutting ideas and follow them through.

He pressed the switch on the intercom and said, "Mrs. Brisbie, come in here a moment."

She came in with the usual look of competent inquiry on her pale thin face, her implausible breasts cantilevered in front of her.

"Round up Misters Finch, Goldlaw and Sherban and send them in here, please."

"Yes, sir."

He realized that it had been a very long time since he had had a departmental conference with his three assistants. When things were running smoothly he thought nothing was as inane as a meaningless conference. Nothing seemed as ridiculous as a think-fest.

Finch and Goldlaw came in and sat down on invitation and they talked idly until Will Sherban arrived. The meeting lasted forty minutes. After they left he was faced with another sour self-appraisal. They felt that he had a private policy against any constructive suggestions affecting operations outside the department. There were too many of their memos to him that had died in the files. Lou Goldlaw, of the phenomenal memory, had cited chapter and verse. He had sensed in them the resentment toward him which is the inevitable reward of the bureaucrat.

He had said the only thing he could—that all such memos would be given specific and immediate attention, but not to go running off in all directions to the extent that normal procedures would deteriorate. He felt as if he had begun to erect a defense against the machinations of Ray Walsh, but a rather frail one. And for the first time in several years he felt the nervous flutter of insecurity, saw himself waiting in a hundred anterooms for the hopeless interview, collar too large on the scrawny neck, broken shoes highly polished, clothes neatly mended and pressed. We're sorry, Mr. Garrett, but our policy prevents our employing anyone over forty.

He brushed the plaintive and ridiculous image out of his mind. His New York contacts were good. Ballinger seldom released an executive except at his own request.

But it would be very very wise to take a more aggressive attitude. And to try, for God's sake, to convince himself that the destiny of the Hillton Metal Products Division of the Ballinger Corporation was the most important thing in creation.

During most of the day he was able to compartmentalize Cindy, to keep her stowed in a locked cupboard in the back of his mind. But in the late afternoon she broke out and from then on she moved, slow and naked, through all his thoughts, her head tilted slightly, gray-blue eyes wide and touched with lust, lips apart in provocative question, tousled hair falling to her fragrant shoulders. And she made a stirring in his loins, made him feel breathless and sweaty. And guilty.

When he got home at five-thirty, he went to bed, setting the alarm for seven-fifteen. When it awakened him he felt drugged and sullen and sticky, with a furry taste in his mouth. A quick shower did little to throw off his feeling of depression.

He did not get to the hospital until eight o'clock.

TWELVE

When he saw Cindy sitting beside Joan's bed, he felt as if his heart had stopped, and then, reluctantly, assumed an accelerated beat. Joan saw him first and smiled at him as he came in the doorway. Her smile was warm and genuine. Cindy turned and smiled also. It was an apologetic, tremulous and slightly frightened smile. She wore a sleeveless red blouse, a crisp white skirt, sandals with white thongs tied around her slim brown ankles.

He went around the bed and bent over Joan and kissed her, conscious of Cindy's eyes on him. It seemed incredible to Carl that there was not some current between him and Cindy so tangible that Joan could not help but detect it and be aware of their relationship.

"Where have *you* been?" Joan said chidingly.

He sat on the foot of her bed. "It seems I took a nap."

"I could have guessed," Joan said. "It always makes you look so puffy and grim."

"I see Rosa regained her freedom."

"This afternoon, and after the stories she told me, I'm terrified to think of what sort of case they might put in that empty bed. No more private nursing, dear, except Miss Calhoun for a few more days, maybe until I leave."

"I think you should keep her."

"It does mean you get a lot better service."

Cindy stood up and said, "Well, people, I will be running along. It's good to see you looking chipper again, Joan."

"Thanks for stopping by, Cindy."

She smiled at both of them and left. Carl walked back around the bed and sat on the gray steel chair she had vacated. The warmth of her was still in the metal, and even this served to awaken the little clawings of desire.

"Did Cindy come both times today?"

"Yes. She's been very sweet. I had scads of company this evening, but they all came early and didn't stay long. So that Gil Sullivan kept you up until all hours so you had to have a nap."

He realized he had forgotten to get in touch with Gil. "It wasn't such a late evening. One o'clock maybe. Or two."

"Or three. Or maybe you didn't get home at all."

"Oh, I got home all right."

"You look tired, darling. Did anything go wrong today?"

"A showdown of sorts with Ray Walsh. We're out in the open now."

"Oh, I'm sorry. But he can't really do anything to hurt you, can he?"

"No, not really."

"When I get home, I'm going to feel as if I've been away for a year."

"It feels that way to me too, honey."

"It's such a different world, being in here. I guess it's like being on a boat or something. You can't do anything about it. The world goes right on, but you're out of it for a little while.

"Did you have a chance to eat yet? I guess not, if you took a nap. You're not losing weight, are you? You look sort of gaunt, darling."

"I always do. Remember?"

"Please try to eat properly. Go get a nice meal somewhere. I'd think the neighbors would be feeding you more often."

"A lot of them are on vacation."

"I know."

He looked at his watch. "I sort of goofed off tonight. I'm sorry."

"Your sleep is more important than spending the whole hour and a half here. You can sleep late tomorrow, dear."

"And I'll see you in the afternoon, Joan."

"Get a good dinner, now, and get lots of sleep."

He kissed her and left. The evening visitors were leaving, moving out through the main doors to the parking lot in the July dusk. Sunset was vivid over the hills beyond the city and the river. He looked toward his car and saw Cindy standing beside it, tall and quiet, waiting for him.

He did not speak until he was close to her, until they were twenty inches apart. "Why did you do that?"

"A lot of reasons. One was that I thought it might seem odd if I never visited her in the evening."

"It was a jolt."

"I know. It was bad before you arrived. Then it was worse."

"But it went off all right."

"And that was one of the things I wanted to know."

"I don't know what you mean."

"I'll tell you when we're alone."

"You're acting pretty subdued and kind of strange, Cindy."

"I feel subdued and I feel strange and I want to talk to you."

"What about Bucky?"

"He hasn't phoned again, not that I know of. But I haven't spent much time home."

"Well . . . I'll see you there."

"Have you eaten?"

"No."

"I'll stop on the way and pick up some food. Don't forget to tell them at the motel office. About tomorrow."

"Do you think . . . we should?"

"Why not? Three days, four days, a month. We were guilty after the first hour."

"Well . . ."

"Here's the key, darling. I'll take longer than you will."

When he went into the motel office after parking the car in front of twenty, the same man came out of the back room and said, "Good evening, Mr. Garroway."

"We'd like to stay another night. Tomorrow night. The . . . paint isn't dry yet." And he wondered why he found it necessary to make any explanation at all, particularly one which sounded so awkward and feeble.

The man picked up his fifteen dollars and said, "I hope you've been comfortable."

"Yes, we have. You have a very nice place here. Very nice."

"Your wife has been enjoying our pool."

"Yes, I know."

"She's a beautiful swimmer, Mr. Garroway."

"Uh . . . thank you."

"Good night, Mr. Garroway."

"Good night."

Back in the room he turned on the bedside lights. Her black and yellow swim suit hung on a towel rack. He touched it. It was slightly damp. Her blue-handled hair brush was on the glass shelf over the lavatory, her yellow toothbrush next to his green one in the rack. He went out and sat on the bed and lit a cigarette. The closet door was ajar and he could see some of her clothing hanging there. There was a book on the night table. He opened it and read in it at random, flipped it shut.

He opened the door when she knocked. She carried a brown paper sack, and she kissed him on the corner of the mouth as she went by him toward the bureau. "Goodies," she said. "Monstrous thick hamburgs, and some goopy pecan rolls with a little thing of sweet butter, and some big things of black coffee."

"You're gay all of a sudden."

"I'm a creature of mercurial moods. Haven't you noticed? Where'll we eat? Say, pull that luggage rack over here. This is lovely. No dishes to wash. I detest and despise all dishes except the kind you throw away."

She refused to be serious. As they ate she chattered about the people she had met by the pool that afternoon. His spirits lifted to match her air of gaiety.

After they had eaten he looked across at her as he sipped his coffee, looked into the gray-blue eyes that had become suddenly grave and felt unaccountably uncomfortable.

"Carl, I said I had a lot of reasons for visiting Joan again this evening."

"Yes?"

"I didn't tell you the most important one. I had to find out how selfish I am."

"I'm not sure I follow you."

She indicated the room and all that had happened in it with an expressive wave of her hand. "Hasn't this been perfect?"

"You know it has."

"Too perfect to let go of, Carl."

"Now wait a minute, Cindy."

"Now please let me say all of this, and it isn't easy to say. I've been going over it in my mind all day. My marriage is a farce. I know that so much more clearly than I did before we came here. I love you and I want to be married to you."

He looked at her and could not deny her terrible sincerity. "But . . ."

"And I decided another thing too. I decided I would spring this on you, and then I wouldn't let it turn into a discussion. This isn't the time for it, darling. Or the place. I know that it isn't just an attempt on my part to rationalize a situation that might look awfully messy to any outsider. Man creeping off with his neighbor's wife and all that. It is a messy thing, but it doesn't seem messy to me—at least not so messy that I've got to build up a big marriage thing. My conscience isn't hurting me that badly. My conscience is pretty tender, but nothing like I thought it would be. It's just that I can't bear to think that all of this will be over after tomorrow night. And it isn't just the sex thing. That's been entirely colossal, I'll admit, but it's just as importantly the times in between, the talking and the jokes and the fun. We fit together in all ways. And that is something so damn rare, something so few people ever find in life, that only the damnedest of damned fools would let it slip out of their fingers once they find it. Oh, I know how messy it would be—all the scenes and recriminations and how could you do this to me? But your kids are old enough to adjust, and mine are so little it won't much matter. Don't say a word. We aren't going to talk about it now. You do as much thinking about it as I've done, and then we'll talk. But not here. This is the clandestine place. We'll talk on Sunday in my house or yours, very sanely and objectively. And if you say no . . ." Her smile was twisted and sad. ". . . I might survive it, but at the moment I don't see how. And now finish your coffee, darling, because I'm getting positively feverish just sitting here and looking at you."

He left the motel at eleven o'clock on Saturday morning and arrived home at quarter of noon, feeling torpid and drained of all vitalities. After he had showered he put on a robe and phoned Gil Sullivan on the bedroom phone.

"Gil? Carl Garrett."

"Well, how you doing, boy? Haven't seen you since we settled the whole school problem in one hour at Herman's. What's on your mind?"

"Is Madge still out of town?"

"I've got one more week of debauchery, if I can last that long, boy."

"If it should come up, and I don't expect it will, I . . . I was with you Thursday night, Gil."

After a short silence Gil said, "Oh, no, pal! Not you!" And started to laugh.

Carl waited him out. "Is it all right?"

"Anything for a friend. Where were we?"

"We met at the Brower and started from there."

"What I want to know is, did we have a good time?"

"Just dandy. Thanks, Gil."

"Don't thank me. I thank you for brightening up my little sordid day. Is she anybody I know?"

"It probably won't come up."

"But if it does, my friend, I will do the most beautiful cover job you ever saw—the kind I expect from my friends and they never come through with."

After Gil he phoned Molly Raedek, planning to make some excuse. But when she answered, he quietly hung up the phone. It would be just too damn awkward to get out of it at this late hour. It would be better to go and leave as soon as he decently could. Cindy would certainly understand.

He dressed in work pants and a T shirt, made a stale bread sandwich and drank a can of beer with it, then trundled the yellow power mower out of the storage compartment of the garage. It started on the third pull. As he followed it back and forth, settling into the dull rhythm of the work, his mind was freed to think of Cindy.

At one time in the night it had seemed almost possible, a new marriage, a new young bride, an escape from all the established routines, from Mrs. Brisbie and Ray Walsh and the school problem and the mortgage payments. At one time in the long night, when his head was pillowed on her sweet resilient flesh and he could hear, commingled, the steady trudge of her sleeping heart, the depth of her breathing, the whispery hush of the air-conditioning, the barely audible night-drone of transport trucks on the turnpike beyond the locked windows, it had seemed to him that this could be the beginning of a second life for him, a rare chance to live two separate existences, too valuable to miss merely because of emotional scruples. Cindy was a link to all the long-ago dreams that had been given up, making vivid once again all the islands he had never seen, the far places and the magic.

But now, as he walked behind the rackety chug of power mower, that half-asleep man so tenderly cradling the sleeping flesh in tired arms seemed a ludicrous stranger.

He cannot be me. Not as I mow this lawn I planted on this land I own. Not here at this small green place where my children have played, where I have worked while Joan, kneeling in the sun, has grubbed with green trowel at the roots of the planted things so that I, crisscrossing the lawn behind this whirling blade, have glanced at fabric tight across her and felt the familiar and accustomed pulse and tingle of contented connubial desires. All this, with Cindy, could not have happened to such a man as I believe I am.

If there was magic with Cindy, it would soon be gone. Nothing could long endure so precariously founded on heartbreak, on remorse and regret. He remembered a couple he had met when they had last visited his parents in Florida. Nelson Helvey had been a life-long friend of Bill and Betty Garrett. At forty-three, after a turbulent and reckless affair, Nelson Helvey had divorced his wife after twenty years of marriage and married a twenty-one-year-old girl employed in his building supply business, a dark and vivid and restless girl named Veronica.

Perhaps, for Nelson Helvey, there had been a time of magic, a resurgence of youthful juices. But when Carl had seen them again in Florida, Nelson was sixty-six, Veronica forty-four. He had retired after his second mild coronary, and he was a feeble and pasty old man, grotesque in shorts and sandals and Italian sports shirt, wearing an empty smile. The provocative Veronica had been dried and withered by the years to a brown little simian woman with a face deeply grooved by discontent and petulance, with the purpled tinge of dye in her black hair, her manner fraudulently vivacious, her speech filled with habitual venom. It was apparent that their time of sexual infatuation twenty-three years before had condemned them to a loveless pact, a dry endurance wherein she despised him for the wastage of her younger years, and he resented her as the symbol of the loss of contact with his children and grandchildren. Bill and Betty Garrett, in their warm and wholesome affection, their time-mellowed little jokes and gestures, had provided a striking contrast. Carl's mother had told him that though the Helveys lived less than a mile down the key, they had only seen them three times in two years. She said the Helveys traveled with a younger group.

Carl felt alarmed when he thought about Cindy's compulsion to talk of marriage. He thought that he knew why it was necessary to her. There was a basic decency about her. They had been trapped into the situation by strong physical desire. But once the keenest edge had been taken from that desire, she could not accept this picture of herself as suburban adulteress. She could not reconcile her vision of herself with the kind of motel affair endemic to a Martha Garron or a Gil Sullivan. Since she could not endure being so classified and could not accept such a harsh reappraisal of herself, then it became a most necessary rationalization to begin to play for keeps. That would justify the affair, and rub out the stain of cheapness. And, of course, it made it much more dramatic. And, in her restlessness, in the disappointments of her marriage, she had a quickening need for the dramatic.

But understanding her motivations perhaps better than she understood them herself did not produce any solution to the problem.

He finished mowing the lawn at two o'clock, took a quick shower and went to the hospital. The curtains were drawn around the other bed. Joan, in a hushed voice, told him that it was a Mrs. Mincher, a seventy-four-year-old woman who had tumbled down her own cellar stairs, breaking her thigh and wrist, cracking her pelvis and fracturing her skull. Miss Calhoun had gotten the information on her, and her condition was listed as serious. It was not yet known whether she would live. She was under heavy sedation, and the most severe fracture had not yet been set because she had been in deep shock when brought in.

Joan said, "The poor old thing moans so."

"Will she disturb you?"

"Oh, no. It isn't very loud. You've been in the sun."

"Just for a little while. I just finished mowing the lawn."

"Did you sleep late this morning, darling? You look more rested than you did last night."

"I got up about ten-thirty, I think it was." (And she was taking a shower when I woke up, and later she came out with a towel wrapped around her wet hair, turban-fashion, and came smiling toward me, and when she is naked and knows I am watching her, it changes her walk so that she appears to place her feet more delicately and precisely, stepping a little higher, like a sleek and spirited horse in a show ring.)

"Why don't you play golf this afternoon? It looks like a lovely day."

"It's getting pretty hot."

"What time do you have to be at Molly and Ted's?"

"Around six. We'll probably all troop over here and see you and then go back and eat." (And I haven't told her yet.)

"This morning, dear, I walked down to the elevators and back. I felt as if I'd walked around the world. I was utterly pooped."

He smiled at her. He could think of nothing to say to

her. He felt like an impostor, a man carefully trained to make Joan Garrett believe that he was her husband, but who now had run out of all the lines and comments they had taught him, and dared not say more for fear of saying the wrong thing. This Joan Garrett seemed to be a very nice woman. Carl Garrett must have been a lucky man. Too bad that it had been felt necessary to eliminate him and send, in his place, this articulated robot with its taped voice reel and its chromium heart and its frozen plastiform grin. And it seemed quite sad that this warm and merry Joan Garrett should have to be the most recent member of that vast group of wives on whom this plausible deception has been worked, condemned to spend the rest of her years with a clever mechanical device equipped with electronic relays which permits it to make all the expected responses, but which because of the limitations of manufacturing technique could not be equipped with a heart or a soul.

"Do you feel all right, dear? You look kind of . . . somber."

"I guess I'm lonesome."

"When they send me home Monday you'll wish the house was empty again. It's going to make me very irritable to have to stay in bed most of the day."

"I won't mind that."

When he drove back to the house, he checked next door and found the car was not back yet. He knew he would have to tell Cindy about going to the Raedeks for dinner. She had said nothing about when she would drive back home, or even whether she would come back at all. He realized that she had seemed curiously evasive about her plans—almost coy, in fact. And he suddenly realized that she expected him to drive back out to the motel in the afternoon. He wondered at his own dulled perceptions.

The motel pool was empty. He knocked at the door of the room. He had the feeling that the room was empty, and was slightly shocked at the extent of his own feeling of relief. He knocked more loudly and waited. The lock clicked and the door opened and she looked out at him through the six-inch gap, her face thickened and dulled by sleep.

She gave him a blurred smile and looked cautiously beyond him, then swung the door open for him and turned and padded back to the bed, the tan of her long flat back in vivid contrast to the white flexing of her buttocks. She sprawled on her back and pulled a corner of the sheet across her middle, yawned vastly and said, "I hope you didn't stand out there knocking too long. I was so dead I couldn't figure out where I was, even."

He had closed the door and he sat on the other bed, lighted two cigarettes and gave her one. She yawned again, and indulged herself in a long lithe and tawny stretch that ended in a shudder.

"I'm glad you woke me up. I was having a foul dream. What time is it, darling?"

"Twenty to five. What was the dream?"

"It's all sort of mixed up, but it was awful. I got a present in a long white box, the sort of box cut flowers come in. It arrived while I was having a party, a rather big party, and whenever anybody arrived, I kept hoping it was you. Then somebody gave me that box and said it had been delivered to the door and they gathered around to watch me open it. I didn't know if it was from you or from Bucky, and it was terribly important that I know, because if it was from Bucky I could open it in front of them, and if it was from you, it was going to be some kind of a message, a sort of symbol, that I wouldn't want them to see. It was as light as a feather, as though nothing was in the box, and I knew that if nothing was in the box, then it was from Bucky. My God, I'm beginning to realize just how Freudian this is. I better not tell the rest."

"Go ahead."

"Well, I had to open it. There was tissue paper and when I folded that back, I saw a horrible thing. I stood so the others couldn't see into the box, and I knew I had to pretend that it wasn't horrible. It was your arm, darling, severed at the elbow but not bleeding, and your fist was clenched. I knew that if I could pick it up and wave it around as if it was light as a feather, then they would all believe it was from Bucky and everything would be all right. But when I tried to pick it out of the box it was hard and cold and very heavy—made of bronze or something. I had on a long white dress like a wedding dress, sort of, but very tightly fitted, and I had made it myself, and I hadn't had time to do more than baste the seams. I wasn't wearing anything under it. Each time I strained in desperation to pick the arm up, I felt seams in the dress split, and they had all begun to laugh at me, and I knew the dress was falling off me. I was half crying and trying to pick it up, but each time it

would slip out of my hands and thump back into the box,
and then the noise it was making turned out to be your
knocking on the door, thank God."

"That's a damned strange dream."

She looked at him, and then pulled more of the sheet
across her so as to cover her breasts. "Is it?"

"Don't you think so?"

Though the daylight in the shuttered room was dim, he
saw her face darken. "The symbolism is so damn obvious.
And so physical. You know what the arm represents. And
the virginal wedding dress. My God, I must have a mind like
a sewer."

"Not necessarily."

"The interesting thing, Carl dearest, is my frantic efforts to
keep the others from knowing about you. And how I couldn't
keep them from knowing about you. It will be wonderful not
to have to hide what's happened to us, darling."

"The dream says you want to hide it. Maybe the dream
says you should hide it."

"The dream says we can't hide it."

"Cindy . . . we have to talk about this."

"I said we could talk later, darling. Not in this place."

"Maybe this is the place where we should talk. We have
to talk sometime. I've been thinking about how to say things.
But when I frame the sentences in my mind, they sound tired
and trite—like lines from all the bad plays in the world."

"What do you want to say?"

"That . . . I don't want to change anything. I want to keep
the marriage I've got. I couldn't explain just how we happened to get into this situation, but it was going to be just a
case of . . . of grabbing all we could and then . . . forgetting
it."

She threw the sheet aside and went to the closet and
slipped into her robe and belted it. She adjusted the slats
of the blinds so that the room became brighter. She sat on
the bed, facing him, and pushed hair back from her forehead
with the back of her hand and smiled in a slightly self-con-
scious way and said, "I couldn't lie there and talk. Give me
another cigarette, darling."

"It all makes me feel as if somehow I had been put in a
bad light, Cindy, by not wanting to go along with . . . this
marriage thing. But that wasn't the arrangement in the beginning. I mean I didn't count on it starting to turn into
something else."

She leaned forward for the light and then leaned back again, huffed a gray column of smoke toward his chest. "Be more explicit, dear," she said in a cool voice. "We both wanted to get laid. And we had a perfect opportunity. No regrets, no recriminations, no sticky emotional mess. So we did, and now we forget it."

"That's pretty blunt . . . but . . . yes. All right."

"And then all it is, all it ever will be, is a tired, tawdry, sneaky little spot of adultery—à la motel?"

"Isn't it more than that, somehow?"

"Is it?"

"You keep asking questions."

"Give me time and I'll make a statement," she said. She got up quickly and paced back and forth by the foot of the bed, elbow cupped in her palm, upright hand with cigarette angled back, frowning at the floor six feet ahead of her slow pacing. At last she whirled toward him so quickly that the wide skirt of the robe swung out from her bare ankles.

"All right, Carl Garrett. Statement from Cindy. I try, so help me, to be reasonably honest with myself. I said, Cindy, I said, you want to make a big deal out of this so that you can think of it as a many-splendored thing instead of a little extracurricular coupling with a handsome neighbor. And, my girl, all this futz about not being able to endure the thought of living without him is just the window dressing your sick emotional mind is using to obscure the basic fact that you are at this point a pushover. Maybe any man would have done, Cindy. I told myself that. It didn't work, Carl."

"I had that same idea," he confessed.

"I expected you would. So, because it didn't work, I had to take a longer, colder look at the emotional facts. We're both miscast, Carl, in life and in marriage. Your Joan is a warm, sweet, lovable, loyal little woman. Neither of us want to hurt her. She lives in a constricted little world of children, cooking, housework and garden club. You get as much intellectual stimulation from her as you would from an amiable airedale."

"Now wait . . ."

"Hear me out, and then you can make your objections. Take a look at what your marriage has done to you. You have damn near become a vegetable. You don't commit yourself to your work. You've slid into a t.v. and do-it-yourself existence. You avoid having any ideas, because they are uncomfortable things to have around. You've managed to almost turn yourself into the typical suburban Dagwood, the lovable guy with an itch for complete security. All your opinions have become secondhand stuff you've gotten out of the cheap analyses of our environment that you can read in any newspaper. You're afloat in your little warm puddle of security, Carl, with your eyes closed and a big contented smile on your mouth. You aren't dead, but all you are doing is marking time until you are. And if I want to give up, that's the same thing my marriage will do to me. Darling, they only give us one quick turn around the track, and it's a stinking shame to have to spend the good part of it asleep on your feet. When you love, you want to give something. I want to give you back . . . your awareness and risks and dangers and . . . the feeling of being intensely alive."

She stabbed her cigarette out, knuckled wet eyes in a child's gesture, and then sat opposite him and half-smiled and said, "Big speech. Now you talk."

Even as he gauged the depth of his own anger, he knew that it was partially caused by an element of uncomfortable truth in what she said.

"That's a fine speech, Cindy. And it's a very young speech. We're supposed to clutch each other's hot hands and canter off toward adventure, leaving behind us two adults and four kids who would never know exactly what hit them. We're supposed to strike brave sparks off each other, and live gallantly and furiously."

He stood up to pace as she had done, speaking as he walked, glancing at her from time to time where she sat with still face and averted eyes. "It's young, all right. It's the kind of thing that fills the quaint little bistros of all the art centers of the world with girls who wear black sweaters and bangs and talk about Colin Wilson. God damn it, Joan is no mental giant, but she is sound in what she believes. I'm no mental wizard either. What the hell do people like you think marriage is? A discussion hour? An ideological argumentation period? Marriage is mostly having somebody on your side, somebody who, throughout your life, gives you the incredible gift of being acutely and specifically concerned with what happens to you—your health and your work and your happiness. Marriage is having somebody near you.

"Maybe you are right about my having slipped into a nice comfortable rut, Cindy. Sure, I feel a sense of being wasted. Who doesn't? I titillate myself with that precious little sorrow every now and again. It's one of the great pleasures of man—to say to himself, boy, what I *could* have done. A bitter-sweet pleasure. But in my more rational moments I think of the cost of a continual complete expenditure of myself. I might have gained a certain fame in small circles. I might be, by now, a rich man. And I might have ulcerous holes in my gut and a stumbling heart muscle too. People like to talk about compromise. That word has a sickly stink to it. It has a dishonorable sound. I've arrived at an equation, not a compromise. I have carefully judged my point of diminishing returns. At this point in my life I receive the maximum gratifications and the maximum leisure for the minimum output. I take a deep and, I assure you, very strong pride in my wife, my home and my kids. This is my turn around the track as you call it. One hundred years from now it won't matter a damn whether I was Chairman of the Board of the Ballinger Corporation, or a stock clerk. So I'm going around the track at a pace I find suitable for me."

He stopped and looked at her. "What would you have me do and be? Who the hell ever heard of an avant garde accountant? We run off and make beautiful music together, but I think that it would be music as sterile and contrived as Bartók. Thank you, but I'll stick to my safe, corny, comfortable Strauss waltzes. I can whistle all the melodies."

Then he saw the glint of the tear tracks down her cheeks and he felt a keen guilt for having spoken so savagely, for having made of it an attack on her immaturity.

"I'm sorry, Cindy," he said softly.

She said, brokenly, "If . . . that's what you think . . . then why . . . all this?"

He sat opposite her and took her right hand in both of his. Her hand was cool and without response. "I can't give you a happy answer. I can try to make it an honest answer. If you'll accept the possibility of a man loving two women, I love you. I wanted you. I wanted what you represent. A young woman, eager and available. Putting Joan in the hospital made this a sort of time of reappraisal for me. I felt a sort of restless itch. Maybe a feeling that time is going by too damn fast. A sort of disenchantment with the predictability of my life from here on in. But I would never have deliberately tried to create this situation. It just sort of happened. It was, as we said before, a mutual vulnerability, a sort of devilishly exact timing."

Her lax hand clenched itself into a hard fist and she sobbed audibly.

"We are both, Cindy, in our separate ways, going to regret that this happened to us. And in other ways, I hope we'll be glad it happened. I'm glad for one thing that has just happened. I had to answer the little speech you made. In answering it, I somehow crystallized my own feelings, Now I think I know where I stand. This is the second time I've ever been unfaithful to Joan. And, I'm sure, the last. I don't want her to know about it. I don't want her to be hurt that badly. And, in a selfish way, I don't want our marriage to be less than it has been. And if she finds out, I think it will be less."

"I'll never tell anyone," Cindy whispered.

"In some crazy way, what we've done has made me happier. I'm grateful to you for that. And I wish it could work out that way for you too. Maybe it will."

"Not with Bucky. Not with anyone but you."

"I wish you hadn't said that. It isn't true, you know."

"It is true."

"But you accept the way I feel? You do understand why it all has to stop here?"

She nodded with a jerky abruptness, not looking at him. He felt intense relief. She had removed the horrible mental picture he had of her going to Joan to ask her to release him.

"Now there's something else that came up. I have to go to the Raedeks for drinks and dinner. I have to leave pretty soon. Now that we've had this out, Cindy, maybe it would be better for both of us if I took off right now and didn't come back here from the Raedeks."

She pulled her hand free then caught both his wrists and squeezed them with surprising force. She shook her bent head so violently that it whipped the dark blond hair against her cheeks.

"No?" he said.

"Stay with me now," she half whispered, not looking at him, her voice raw with tears, "and we'll both know it's the last time, and then just leave me, without saying anything. Just leave me then, when it's over. I'm sorry I . . . was such a fool."

"You weren't, Cindy."

She lifted her head and looked directly into his eyes. And made him a twisted smile. And said, "Just don't let

me think this was cheap. Just don't let me think it was like
. . . any other two people with a lech."

"It hasn't been," he said as fervently as he could, but in
his mind was the awkward question: If not, precisely what
is the difference?

THIRTEEN

Carl arrived at Molly and Ted's on Governor's Lane at six-thirty. Molly had seen his car turn into the drive and met him at the door. She was a big-boned, big-bosomed blond woman with a strident and infectious laugh, a generous heart and a touch of genius with all growing things.

"The party has grown, but not much," she said. "And you are one drink behind everybody and probably two drinks behind my guzzling husband. Jane and Paul Cardamo are here."

They were drinking on the small screened cage off the west wing of the house. Heavy plantings shielded it from the road and from the neighbors. Ted Raedek had wheeled his small bar out there and was standing behind it, mixing a drink.

Carl said hello to Jane and Paul Cardamo and went over to the bar. "The surgical-type bachelor!" Ted roared. He was a vast, earthy, swarthy man, Production Chief at the Link-Latch Plant. "Boy, you're hard to get hold of."

"Just look in all the low dives, Ted. Scotch on the rocks, if available. Hey! Take it easy!"

"You've got some catching up to do, fella."

Carl carried his big strong drink over and sat on a sun cot beside dark pretty little Jane Cardamo. Paul, her cadaverous bespectacled husband, was draped in a near-by chair. The Raedeks sat on another sun cot at right angles to the one Carl and Jane were on. For a time they talked about Joan and when she would be coming home and how she would probably feel when she got home. It was decided that they would all run over to the hospital in Carl's wagon after seven-thirty and then come back and eat vast quantities of Molly's barbecued spare ribs.

Ted said, "Say, I understand from Al Washburn that you're coming over to the Center on Monday night and give us Board members the word on the school setup, Carl."

"I'd forgotten all about it. Damn! And Al said he wanted

139

something in writing I could leave with the secretary. I'll have to whip something up tomorrow."

"It isn't just the Board. It's an open meeting of the association, with a question and answer **peri**od."

"Al didn't tell me that."

"It was only changed the day before yesterday. So there'll be a couple of hundred people frothing at the mouth over high taxes if we incorporate."

"Oh, fine!"

And just as he said that he heard Jane Cardamo say, in the middle of a sentence, "Cindy Cable." Jane had been talking with Molly and he had been paying no attention.

"If you make your report explicit, Carl, there shouldn't be too many questions. And Al does a good job of running the open meetings."

"I know."

Jane said, "You know Eunice Stockland, the way she is. She was practically foaming she was so anxious to tell us about Cindy."

"Do I hear you using our neighbor's name in vain?" Carl asked in what he hoped was an indolently casual tone.

Jane turned and made a face at him. "What big ears you have. This is girl talk. In other words, gossip."

"What happened?"

"I can't tell you what happened. But I can tell you what Eunice Stockland reported at lunch yesterday. And you know how Eunice gets carried away. Seems that fair Cindy has packed her kids away to stay with Bucky's people until the end of August. And Bucky is away on a longer trip than usual. So last Thursday night he tried to phone Cindy. No answer. He kept phoning and finally at two in the morning he phoned the Stocklands. Bill put a robe on and went to the house. You can imagine how he was grumbling. No car and no Cindy. Eunice told us it upset her so that she couldn't sleep, so she went and sat near a window where she could watch Cindy's house. Just when Eunice was working herself up to report it to the police, at ten-something the next morning, Cindy came driving in. When Eunice tried to phone her her line was busy. Finally, when she did get her, Eunice said that Cindy said thank you, she had already talked to Bucky. Eunice said she tried to find out where Cindy had been, but she practically hung up on her."

Big Ted Raedek smacked his lips and said, "Any red-blooded American boy would like to cut himself a slice of that Cable baby."

"Shut up, you," Molly said. "All you men are alike."

"Not this man," Paul Cardamo said in his lazy voice. "That little lady would be trouble."

"And just how?" Jane asked coldly.

"She's a neurotic. I don't envy old Bucky. She'd want to play for keeps."

"And how would you know that?" Jane asked even more coldly.

"Don't sweat, honey baby. I acquire my vast knowledge through observation, not experimentation. To coin an old cliché, I have more than I can handle at home."

"Then let's go to your house," Ted said, and bellowed at the old joke.

"Eunice added one more little morsel," Jane said. She eyed Carl in a feline way and said, "About you."

Carl felt chilled and managed to say, "I plead innocent."

"While watching for Cindy, she saw you drive in after daylight, my good man."

"Don't tell Joan, but I got tied up with Gil Sullivan. I'm supposed to have gotten in about two."

"Wouldn't it have been just juicy if you and Cindy had driven in at the same time?" Molly said. "Wow! Eunice would have added two and two and gotten eighty-nine."

Carl did not realize he had emptied his glass until Ted got up and took it out of his hand.

"There must be some explanation other than the obvious one," Jane said, frowning. "I know that our Cindy is a sort of an odd type, but I can't see her playing around somehow. She seems to have her own kind of integrity. As witness the episode of Barry Sanson."

"What about Barry?" Carl asked.

"Didn't you hear about that? I thought everybody knew that one. It happened last summer. I guess you must have been on your vacation. Anyway, there was a dance at the Timberlane and Barry managed to maneuver Cindy Cable outside to look at the moon or something. You know how he thinks he's the smoothest operator in the state, and God's perfect gift to discontented wives. Cindy came striding back in, pale as water, and Barry didn't come back at all. Turned out she didn't slap him or kick him; she busted him smack in the eye with her fist. He wore dark glasses for more than a week. But to get back to Eunice, it was Wednesday night Bucky called. She got back late on Thursday morning and later still yesterday morning. And Eunice will have a complete report on this morning too. That woman has eyes like an eagle. Carl, why don't you brief us on Cindy? You and Joan know Cindy and Bucky better than anybody. And I don't *think* Eunice Stockland is crouched out there in the brush taking notes. Do you think anything is going on?"

"I . . . I really couldn't make any guess."

"They haven't seemed as happy as they used to," Molly said. "Is the marriage all right?"

"They may be having a little trouble. I wouldn't know what about. Cindy isn't the sort of person who would find housekeeping and taking care of two little kids very . . . rewarding."

Jane laughed and said, "I went to see her one morning quite a while back. That little girl, Bitsy, was about eleven months old, I think. The house was a shambles and Cindy didn't seem the least bit apologetic about it. She was in the kitchen, drinking coffee and reading. Bitsy was in her play pen. Cindy had strewn a double handful of puffed wheat or something in the play pen, and Bitsy was crawling around doggedly eating it grain by grain. Cindy said it would keep her quiet for over an hour."

"I still say," Ted said lasciviously, "that if a cleancut American boy could get close to that, he'd have himself something."

"Cut that out!" Molly said. "You sound like such a lecher. My God, if anybody ever met one of those clumsy passes of yours more than halfway, you'd run like an overweight rabbit."

"Something like a rabbit, anyway," he said comfortably.

"Why would a woman send her kids away for so long?" Jane asked. She looked inquiringly at Carl.

"I don't know. Maybe she wanted some time to herself. You know. To sort of rest up."

"I know one thing," Paul Cardamo said. "If I was away and phoned Jane and there was no answer by two in the morning, and if I owned a little green airplane as Bucky does, I would be in my little green plane heading for home."

"And," Jane said, "you'd pull out your little ole thirty-two and go rooty toot toot and me and my lover would fall dead, dead, dead."

"Damn well told," Paul said contentedly.

"Let's start to think of putting this here now show on the road," Molly said.

"One more for the road," Ted said. "Let me sweeten that up, Carlos."

As they drove into the western sun toward the hospital, Carl realized that the drinks were hitting him. The last of the daylight had an unreal look of clarity. His lips felt slightly numbed. He wondered how it would be if he wedged his way into the next gap in the conversation and said, "About Cindy Cable, I left her in room twenty of the Traveler Motel about thirty miles up the pike, just a little over two hours ago. While I dressed she cried without making a sound, and her long hair was all tangly on the pillow, and she had covered herself with the sheet, and her robe was on the floor beside the bed where I had dropped it. I picked it up and laid it across the footboard of the bed and then I kissed her eyes and her lips and left. When I was driving out I could taste the salt on my lips, and then I had tears in my eyes and I really couldn't say why. But it blurred the road, and I turned on the car radio and found that the Cincinnati Reds and the Dodgers were all tied up at five and five in the bottom half of the eleventh. But then somebody got on on an error and Hodges doubled him home for the ball game, and by then the tears were gone and the girl back in the room was like something that had happened to me a long time ago, like something nestling way back in your memories, fragile and scented and very touching when it happened, but something to take out rarely and look at and wonder about."

And he felt as if he had come close to blurting that out to them, dangerously close, but knowing all the time that he had never been in the slightest danger of saying it, or anything that would provide the slightest hint to it.

The Gray Lady on duty let him go up with Molly and Ted, while Jane and Paul waited in the lounge off the lobby. Eunice Stockland was with Joan, her chair pulled close to the bed, muttering intently. She seemed put out at being interrupted. She was a small woman with a curiously large head, mousy hair, and pinched gray features. She had a knack of licking her lips in punctuation of nearly every sentence.

Carl said, "Sorry, Eunice, but we've got to oust you. Regulations."

"Well, it's perfectly all right to be sure," Eunice said. "I'll tell you all the rest of it tomorrow, dearie."

"Please don't bother to come in, Eunice. I'll be home by Monday."

"Well, I think you should know."

After she left Joan smiled at them and kissed Carl and squeezed Molly's hand. "Honestly," she said, "that Stockland woman gives me the creeps. Do you know, she's really . . . evil. I didn't realize that before. She's got some crazy story about Cindy staying out all night every night with a man while Bucky's away. And I know that's perfectly absurd, and so do you, Molly."

"She gave Jane the word yesterday at lunch."

"Cindy hasn't come in yet today, but when she does, I'm going to ask her about it."

"I wouldn't do that," Carl said quickly.

Joan stared at him in an awkward silence. "Why not, dear? Certainly if Eunice Stockland is slandering her, Cindy should know."

He floundered in quiet desperation and said, weakly, "I mean I think Cindy knows about it. She . . . told me about not being home Wednesday night when Bucky phoned her."

"Did she say where she'd been?"

He suddenly remembered that Cindy had told Bucky that she had been home and that she had heard the knocking and that her car had been in the repair garage. And he knew that was the story Cindy would tell Joan if questioned.

His smile felt clumsily stitched in place. "I may have it wrong, you know. I haven't been listening too well to what people tell me. Maybe she was home."

"But she told you she wasn't home, didn't she?"

"That might have been some other night."

"I'm going to tell her about Eunice anyway. I don't see why you think I shouldn't."

"I guess you should, honey. I guess it would be a good idea."

He glanced sidelong at Molly and thought Molly was looking at him with a rather curious expression.

"Did you play golf, dear?" Joan asked.

"No. Too hot for it."

"Hell it was," Ted said. "It was fine out there this afternoon. Rudy and I took a full fifteen-buck Nassau off Quinn and Hallister. I birdied seventeen and Rudy birdied eighteen and afterward we clipped 'em with the bar dice. It was a great day out there."

Molly took hold of Ted's arm. "Come on, you big louse,

let's give the Cardamo kids their chance. We'll send them right up, Joanie."

"I didn't even know they were down there!"

"This has turned into a dinner party for five. Barbecued ribs, a bushel of them."

"Gee, I wish I could come too," Joan said, wistfully.

"There will come a day," Molly said, "and soon."

As soon as they were gone, Joan said, "Have you had a lot to drink?"

"You know Ted's drinks."

"Count them, darling. I worry about you driving around full of drinks."

"I won't be driving around. Just from their house to ours. What is it? A half mile?"

"A little longer than that. You're acting funny. You acted funny about my talking to Cindy about Eunice. Why?"

"I didn't mean to act funny. I just mean that I think Cindy is . . . upset about something. Something to do with Bucky. Everybody knows how Eunice is. Nobody pays much attention to her. I just thought it would worry Cindy."

"I think she should know."

"Then you ask her about it."

"Hi, Jane! Paul! How nice of you to come see me, you darlings."

Jane kissed Joan and Paul grinned at her. They sat and talked about nothing for about ten minutes. Joan insisted that she'd had enough visiting, and they should go on back to the party. Molly and Ted were probably getting terribly bored downstairs.

Carl kissed her good night and they left. He told the Raedeks and the Cardamos to go on out to the car, that he had remembered a call he had to make. He used the pay booth in the corridor. It took longer than he expected for information to find out which exchange the Traveler was on. A woman answered the phone and connected him with room twenty. After it had rung five times he became convinced that Cindy was on her way in, and might stop to see Joan. Just when he was wondering how he could get to Cindy first, she answered.

"Yes?"

"This is Carl."

"I thought it would be."

"The phone rang so many times . . ."

"I was in the shower."

"You sound pretty abrupt."

"What do you want?"

"I goofed, slightly. Eunice Stockland has been running a time check on you, the times you've come in."

"That's typical."

"She was with Joan tonight. I'm phoning from the hospital. The Raedeks and the Cardamos are waiting for me out in the car to go back to the Raedeks'. I said to Joan, without thinking, something about you telling me where you were when Billy Stockland came over to check. I forgot you told Bucky you were home all the time."

"So?"

"Joan is going to tell you about Eunice. And probably ask you where you were. I . . . I wanted you to know what I'd said. Cindy, Cindy, are you there?"

"I'm here," she said in a tired voice. "What do I tell her? What do you suggest? The truth?"

"You know better than that."

"I know, I know. I'll tell her I've been taking long drives and walks and so on and so on."

"Deposit thirty cents for another three minutes, please."

"Good by, Cindy."

"Good by. And please don't come back here later."

The line went dead. He hurried out to the car. She knew damn well he had no intention of coming back later. It was all over. Maybe she got a big boot out of using the tone of voice of a funeral director. Maybe she thought it was dramatic.

He was glad to be back in the screened cage with one of Ted's strenuous drinks in his hand. Ted had turned on the outside spots and floods, dramatically lighting the plantings that thrived under Molly's care. A little while before they ate she asked him to come to the end of the yard to look at a new plant.

He admired it and praised it properly.

"Carl."

Her tone of voice alerted him. "What?"

She turned toward him, one half of her face in shadow. "I was raised on a farm. I guess you know that. We had a spaniel pup that fell into the habit of sucking eggs. My sister and I caught him at it. He knew darn well he was doing wrong. You wore the same expression tonight that Waffle did when we caught him."

"I don't know what you mean."

"I hope you don't. I hope it's an overactive imagination. I hope I'm not talking out of turn. I'm no gossip, Carl. You know that. And I don't meddle. And I'm even a pretty tolerant type. If you and Gil Sullivan went and got yourselves fixed up with a pair of semi-pro cuties down in the city, I wouldn't applaud, but I think I could understand why you would get into that kind of a deal. But I couldn't understand you being so stupid and so callous as to get involved with Cindy Cable. I hope to God I'm wrong. I hope you're not. Because that would be more than dynamite, Carl. That could be an unholy, ungodly mess. The four of you have been pretty close. I . . . I just hate to think that anything like that could happen to you and Joanie and the Cables. Because you're all rather nice folks."

"But I . . ."

"Now don't say anything. If my guess is right, I don't want to put you to the trouble of lying about it. And if I'm dead wrong, then you'll feel more flattered than abused." She laid her hand on his arm. "But if I am right, Carl, try to get out of it just as quickly and cleanly as you can. Now let's go back and get that one last drink before the ribs."

She wouldn't let him say anything. And afterward, he was grateful to her. He could not honestly say whether, had he been given a chance to talk, he would have lied with fake indignation, or tried to shift some of the guilt by telling her the whole thing.

He was grateful, but at the same time she had distressed him. For a time he could not understand why her words had left such a sour aftertaste. And finally he realized that, for the first time, he had been privileged to hear the opinion of an outsider. And it gave him a sharper, deeper view of what had happened. It was as though his own vision had been a single beam which, in a surrounding darkness, illumines the figures it shines on, but also flattens them out into a design as stylized as a frieze. And now, off to one side, the second beam of Molly's perception had been focused on the deed. And the episode had come to life with a dreadful dimensionality. He had been partially drugged by the hypnoid limitations of his own vision, and now for the first time, because of Molly's comments, he could stand off and look at Carl and Cindy as though he were an outsider, rather than merely looking at her from within himself.

No longer could the incident by the back door of her house, the episode in his living room, the interludes at the motel be viewed in retrospect with any flavoring of grace or magic. They had become awkward fumblings and sweaty couplings which, through the gilding of delusion and rationalization, they had managed for a time to believe were unique, sensitive and necessary.

Now, like a visitor at a fair or exhibition, he looked down into the little lighted display and pressed the button to activate the exhibit and saw then, with the clarity of sickness, the timeless and comic surgings of the beast with two backs. It gave him a special sharpness of guilt and shame and remorse, because he saw clearly that it was merely but another shoddy gratification of one of the ageless hungers of man. In any historical sense it was meaningless—as empty as the act of animals or savages. But in the immediate and personal context, it was an act of destruction, a violation of faith.

The final drink before dinner blurred his reflexes, tangled his speech and shredded his memory. He had a memory of eating, then of blundering into a coffee table and tipping it over, of a disjointed argument with Ted about whether he should drive, of standing in his own bathroom and making faces at himself in the mirror and talking to himself. And then a feeling of alarm as he saw the speedometer needle shimmying above eighty. He dropped it back to thirty miles an hour and sat erect behind the wheel, one eye clenched shut so that there was but one yellow line dividing the lanes of the turnpike.

Then he was pounding on the door. And she opened it, vivid in anger, hushing him, pulling him inside.

He planted his feet and stood swaying and grinning at her, and the room had a swimmy, swarmy look, all a-swing and a-tilt, and then a taste as of sour apricots bulged into his throat and he plunged toward the bathroom, rebounded from the door frame, clattered his knees painfully against the tile floor and was then torn and convulsed by the endless choking spasms.

FOURTEEN

The first time he awakened on Sunday morning his heart was knocking against the inside of his chest in a hard, fast, alarming rhythm. There was a first breath of daylight coming through the slatted blinds, and his watch said five after six. His body felt grainy with dried sweat. There was a horrid taste in his mouth, and a hard focus of shimmering green pain over his right eye. He turned his head slowly and saw Cindy in the other bed, her back to him, the hip-mound high in the classic pose of the sleeping woman. As he somberly contemplated the vast efforts which would be required to get up and dress and leave, he drifted slowly down into sleep again.

She shook him awake, gently, at quarter after nine. His heart had slowed and the pain over his eye was less acute, but the taste was the same, and the feeling of stickiness was the same, and he felt vastly thirsty. He braced himself up on his elbows and made a grimace of pain.

"Bad?" Cindy asked.

"I might live." She handed him a glass of cold water. He gulped it down and handed her the glass and said, "Could you do that again?"

She brought him another glass and put a pitcher of cold water on the night stand beside him. She sat on the opposite bed and lighted a cigarette. She was dressed in a full black and white striped skirt, a black blouse with white buttons, collar and cuffs. Her hair was pulled severely back into a plaited rosette, her face carefully made up, her manner cool and efficient.

As he poured a third glass, clinking the pitcher against the rim of the glass, he said, "You seem to know first aid."

"Bucky's always thirsty after he ties one on."

"This isn't my standard operating procedure."

"I know. I don't know how you got here without killing yourself. After you passed out, I went out and moved your car. I'm glad I looked out."

"Where did I leave it?"

"Up over the curbing with the front bumper against the building."

"I was pretty bad, I guess."

"You were stinking drunk. Helplessly, disgustingly drunk. I told you not to come back here. Why did you?"

"I don't really know. I think I got it in my head that I had something to tell you. Something very important and necessary. But I don't know what it was. Did I say anything?"

"I couldn't understand you. You were sick in the bathroom and then you passed out in there. I pulled you out here and finally got you onto the bed and undressed you. Then I cleaned the bathroom."

"I'm sorry, Cindy."

"Why did you get so drunk?"

"That's right. I have to have a reason, don't I? Maybe I felt so ashamed of myself I sought oblivion. You know. Big escape act."

"You don't have to be nasty. You've done enough without being nasty."

"*I've* done enough!"

"Oh, skip it, for heaven's sake, Carl. We just seem to be doing such a wonderful job of ending it on the sourest possible note. Remember, I'm much too young to have mature attitudes. You told me that. Why don't you take your shower and get dressed? I'm all packed. You can drive me down to my car when you're ready. Your clothes are dry. I scrubbed the stains off your shirt and slacks an hour ago."

"Thank you."

"They're hanging in the bathroom." She got up and went to the front windows and stood with her back to the room. He got out of bed, took his shorts and socks from the chair and went into the bathroom. He felt as if he stood too tall on his legs, tall, fragile and insecure.

He was in the shower and had rinsed away the soap and was standing braced against a cold stinging spray, hoping it would renew him, when she said, "Carl! Carl!" and rapped against the plastic sliding partitions sharply.

He toed the lever that diverted the shower into the tub faucet and pushed a partition part way back and looked out at her.

"What's the matter?"

Her eyes were wide, her mouth trembling, and she looked greenish under her tan. "Oh, my God!" she said.

"What's the matter?"

"Bucky. Bucky's sitting out by the pool."

"You're crazy! How could he be?"

"He is. I don't know how he could be there, but he is. I was looking out the window and I saw him and I couldn't believe it. It was like a bad dream. He seemed to be looking right at me. He's still there. Oh, God, what are we going to do? What will we do?"

He turned the water off, knotted a bath towel around his waist and walked, dripping, to the front windows. He looked out through the crack between slats of the venetian blinds and saw Bucky Cable sitting in a chrome and green plastic chair near the pool, with the chair turned so that he faced the door of number twenty, faced Carl's Ford station wagon parked directly outside the door. He was sixty feet away, motionless, expressionless. He wore a pale tan summer suit, a pale blue bow tie. His legs were crossed and his cocoa straw hat with pale blue band was on his knee. His face was a sweaty bronze red, darker than his thinning hair. He gave the impression of having been sitting there for a very long time.

"What will we do?" she whispered, close beside him, as Carl stepped back from the window.

"I've got to get dressed," he said. He shut the bathroom door when he went in. He dried himself, brushed his teeth for a long time, shaved carefully, combed his hair, drank more water, put on his clothes.

When he came out Cindy got up quickly from the chair and said, "What are you going to do?" He ignored the question. He packed quickly and put the small suitcase next to hers by the door, wishing that on the previous afternoon he hadn't been so intent on making his departure according to her terms that he had forgotten to bring along his possessions. And he wished his mind was not clouded by the after-effects of the liquor, and wished his body did not feel so frail and shaky.

He sat in the chair and lighted a cigarette, controlling the tremble of his fingers with an effort. She sat on the foot of the bed, turned toward him.

"We don't know how he found this place, but we can assume he knows we're both in here," he said. "He knows my car, certainly. We can assume he's waiting for us to come out."

"He sits there like he wanted us to see him."

"Don't, for God's sake, get hysterical. There are some choices. They stink, but they're choices."

"Like what?"

"I go out the rear window and circle around and take your car back to town and leave it somewhere, and we make sure there's no trace of me left here, and then you go brazen it out. Invite inspection. Tell him you borrowed my car."

"But the . . . the registration in the office."

"I know. I know. It would be better if you went out the back, then I could give him some song and dance about it being somebody else I'd been with. Martha Garron, maybe. I think her reputation is beyond any additional damage."

"Then," she said eagerly, "I could get to my car and go to the lake or something."

"It'll still be sour, but maybe that's best."

"Do you think . . . you can handle it?"

"I can try."

They went to the rear windows. They were steel casement windows. The panes were small. They had been designed to be opened, but since every unit had individual heat and air-conditioning control, they had been welded shut. The bath-room window was high. It opened on a sliding rod, and at its widest, it presented no more than a five-inch gap. He decided it could be broken to open farther, but before doing so, he stood on the edge of the tub and looked out. The ground fell away behind the units. She would have a fifteen-foot drop onto a ragged shale slope.

"Can't you *do* something?" she whimpered.

"We both walk out the front and announce our engagement, maybe? Shut up and let me think." After a few moments he said, "Maybe you don't have to be actually, physically gone. If we can hide you some place in here, and I carry it off all right, then you can leave later on, after we're both gone."

She laughed nervously. "It's like one of those . . . continental comedies."

"Yes, this is a very hilarious situation."

"Please, Carl."

"Let's see now. I've got to assume he'll bull his way in and make a quick inspection. If so, he'll look in the bath-room and the closet, and in the tub behind those sliding things. But I have a hunch he won't look under the beds. That would be too damn trite. It would be an undignified thing for him to do. Look, if I pull this sheet crooked so it hangs almost to the floor . . ."

"But . . . I couldn't."

"Then think of something. Think of some other place."

She chewed the edge of her thumb. After a while she looked at him with a certain shyness and said, "I . . . guess it's the only thing, isn't it?"

"It's either take a chance on that, Cindy, or walk out together. Funny, but I would have thought that would be what you'd prefer to do."

"I couldn't possibly do that."

They checked the room to see that there was no evidence of her occupancy. He plucked a long blond hair from her pillow and, along with her lipsticked cigarette butts, flushed it down the toilet. She sat on the floor between the beds, then slid under the bed and pulled her small suitcase in after her. He adjusted the dangling sheet, then walked around the room, trying to see her. He could not see her.

He stood near the bed and said, "All set?"

"I . . . I guess so."

"He'll come in here, I think. Do you think there's any chance he saw you?"

"I . . . don't think so, Carl."

"Hold tight. I'll get him away just as soon as I can."

"I'll be all right."

He picked up his suitcase, gave a last look around the room, fixed the inside knob button so the door would lock, and went out, room key in hand. He did not look toward Bucky. He noticed out of the corner of his eye that there were only three or four cars left at the motel.

He unlocked the left-hand door of the wagon, tossed the suitcase into the rear seat, got behind the wheel and rolled the window down. Just as he was putting the key in the ignition Bucky appeared beside the open window.

"Hey, Bucky!" he said in simulated surprise. "What're you doing here?"

Bucky was bent from the waist to look in the window. "That's the question I was going to ask you, neighbor." Bucky's voice sounded hoarse. He was smiling. For a moment Carl took assurance from the feeling that this was the same old amiable Bucky Cable, the diligent, likable and uncomplicated young sales executive. But Bucky's smile was not quite the same. And Carl had never realized how curiously flat Bucky's pale gray eyes were. They seemed to reflect no light.

His shoulders were heavy under the tan suit jacket. His face was florid, with a square jaw, and the beginnings of slackness under the chin. His crisp blond hair had receded in a widow's peak. One thick hand rested on the car door, sturdy fingers yellowed with nicotine, the morning sun bright on the pale hair on the back of his hand and fingers.

"Anything I say at this point might tend to incriminate me," Carl said. "I'm just checking out. I was just about to leave the key at the office. Do a neighbor a favor and forget you saw me."

"Nice layout they got here."

"It's comfortable."

"And just about the right distance from town. I'd like to see what one of the units looks like. Might have a use for this place sometime. Mind letting me see?"

"Not at all."

"It won't disturb your playmate?"

Carl, as he got out of the car, said, "She left a long time ago."

"Anybody I know?"

"No. One of the girls from the office."

Bucky wore the same odd smile. "You're quite an operator, neighbor. All this time I've been sucked in by your big act. A real home body. No tomcatting around for reliable old Carl. You're real cagey, aren't you?"

Carl unlocked the door and swung it open. "I wouldn't say that. After you, Bucky."

Bucky went in slowly and Carl followed him in. He felt as if he could not breathe deeply enough.

"Well, now. A nice big closet. Air-conditioning." He went into the bathroom. "Tub and shower. Nice place, Carl. Nice picking." He walked back into the bedroom and sat in the chair and crossed his legs, pushed his hat farther back, took out his cigarettes. "How did you line up the office dish?"

Carl sat on the bed that concealed Cindy. He shrugged. "One of those things. The opportunity just hadn't come along until now. But you still haven't answered my question. What are you doing out here?"

The smile did not change as Bucky said, "Looking for Cindy. Looking for the silly bitch I married."

"Out here?"

"Can you think of a better place?"

"I haven't seen much of her, but I think she's been going

up to Scott and Lucy Jessup's place at the lake. They loaned it to you two, didn't they?"

"Sure. Maybe she likes to swim in the moonlight. So she comes home in the day and goes up there at night. She gave up sleeping at home, I find out. I think maybe she likes motels better."

"I don't know what you're driving at, Bucky."

Bucky reached into his pocket, took out a brown packet of paper matches and scaled them over onto the bed. Carl picked them up. There was an exaggerated drawing of the motel and the inscription, *The Traveler. Luxury at a Fair Price. Forty-one miles east of Hillton just off the Governor Carson Turnpike (Route 87).*

"I flew home last night," Bucky said. "Got in at one in the morning. No Cindy. No car. And nobody home next door. So I woke up the Stocklands. Eunice filled me in. Cindy doesn't sleep home any more. Neither do you. Then I started to take the house apart. I don't know what the hell I was looking for. But about five this morning I found those matches right in plain sight on the breakfast table. So I took a cab out. I had him wait. The office was closed. I spotted your car in front of twenty, so I went out and sent the cab back and made myself comfortable. I tried to look in your windows, but I couldn't see a damn thing. So where is the round-heeled bitch, neighbor?"

"I'm sure I don't know, Bucky. Honestly. As far as those matches are concerned, I've been registered in this place for four nights. And I was over talking to Cindy the other afternoon, and I very probably left them there myself. Why don't you try the Jessups' camp? Or just go home and wait. She'll show up, because I think I remember her saying she expected you today sometime."

"How is Joan?"

It took Carl a moment to adjust to the quick change of topic. "Joan? She's doing fine. She'll be home Monday. Tomorrow."

"I sent her a present. I don't know if she got it yet. It's a word game called Jotto. It's supposed to be pretty good. Two can play, or four can play, the clerk said. But if it turns out to be too tricky then maybe that will rule Joan and me out and you two eggheads can have a merry time with it."

"Bucky, I . . ."

"I get so God damn sick of being patronized by you two, you and Cindy. Like you were so damn superior. You wouldn't last a week on my job, and Cindy is no damn good at her job. Come on, old buddy. Brief me on this shack job of yours."

"I don't care to talk about her."

"I always figured you for too damn chicken to step over the line. Too scared of maybe upsetting your nice little red wagon."

Carl looked at his watch. "I've got to get back to town." He stood up. Bucky made no move to stand up. He sat there, smiling up at Carl. "I'll drive you back to town."

"Don't be in such a rush. How come this office-type shack job of yours wears the same perfume Cindy wears? My nose isn't as good as it was a million cigarettes ago, but I smelled it when I walked in."

"I guess it's a coincidence."

"You know, I never figured out what it was about Cindy. Not until now. You know, the way the wolves flock around her at a party. The way men watch her on the street. You know what it is, neighbor? She's got all the instincts of a complete tramp. But up to now she's never let herself go, at least since she married me, because I guess she thinks it's unladylike or something. But now I can see how she'd let herself go with a nice safe solemn type like you. She'd take the chance you wouldn't shoot off your mouth in every bar in town. She can't walk across a room without waggling her tail around. She was ripe for a chance like this."

"You're talking nonsense, Bucky."

"Sure. I'm a crazy man. I even flew at night. Cindy has standing orders never to fly at night. Something dreadful might happen to her pwecious Bucky-Wucky. Wouldn't that be a damned shame?"

"I've got to get back to town."

"I almost have to laugh when I think of how disappointed you must have been, neighbor, when you finally set it up. We could have a long talk about how a woman who looks like she looks can be so damn useless in bed."

"You must be out of your mind."

"I keep forgetting. It isn't you and Cindy, it's you and that office job. You know, from six to nine is a long wait. I wanted to stretch my legs. But I didn't want you taking off, so I opened your hood and took the cable off one battery terminal. That's when a big old limey-talking manager took an interest in me right after I'd finished. I told him I was waiting for the folks in number twenty to get up. The Garroways?

he said. That's right, I said. Tall dark-haired guy in his forties with a young blond wife, also tall. We'd moved out near the pool where we could talk without disturbing anybody. He's a smart old duck and he had you two pegged right from the start, I think, and it was making him nervous to think I might be the injured husband in the case. We admired the sunrise a while and I was so relaxed he stopped being nervous. Said this was your fourth night here. Said Mrs. Garroway had enjoyed the pool and she certainly is a marvelous swimmer, isn't she. The best, I told him. You know. I disarm people. People always talk to me. I listen in a real eager way that makes them feel wanted and important. So I nudged the conversation over onto women's swim suits, and he briefed me on Mrs. Garroway's, and I got a good description of the one she bought last summer that, if I remember rightly, cost me nineteen ninety-five. Sit down again, neighbor. You look unwell."

"The girl from the office . . ."

"I know. She's a tall blonde with the same swim suit and the same taste in perfume. Anyway, I walked on down the road and had some coffee in that diner down there, and then I walked a little farther and I spot my own car parked next to a gas station, back in the grass off the apron. I couldn't figure that for a while until I realized there's only parking space here for one car per unit. Just luck that I happened to see it. They'd just opened up, so I showed the kid my registration and said I was picking it up for the lady, and he was suspicious until he saw that my key worked all right in it, so I drove it out and parked it around behind the bean wagon well out of sight and walked back up here. What did you do with her, neighbor? Boost her out the back window? Maybe she's hitchhiking home, eh?"

"I . . . I . . ."

"God damn it, Carl, why did you do it? Why did you *do* it?" Bucky got up and went and inspected the rear windows. Carl heard him in the bathroom, opening and closing the bathroom window. He came back and sat in the chair again. Carl had not stirred.

"So," Bucky said in a dull tone, no longer smiling, "she couldn't leave. So she's here. And there's only one damn place left that she could possibly be."

Both men sat in the long and unbearable silence that was finally broken by the forlorn and muted sound of her sobbing. Bucky closed his eyes. "So damn clumsy," he said softly. "So stupid. Book matches in the house. Cars in plain sight. Stupid lies. Jesus God, and all you had to do was use your house or mine."

"We couldn't," Carl said.

Cindy rolled out from under the bed, got up onto her hands and knees and then got to her feet. She sat on the other bed, her face in her hands, shoulders shaking.

"Bitch," Bucky said with artificial calm. "Sneaking, filthy, cheap bitch." And the calm broke and his face contorted and he began to weep.

"Bucky . . ." Carl said.

"Shut up! Why did you have to do it?"

"It isn't the way you think it was. We . . . we were in love."

Bucky stared at him, eyes wild and glaring. "Love? Love!" He stood up. "You're going to call it love? Why you simple-minded son of a bitch. Love! You mean your wonderful brains were in tune or something? This hasn't got anything to do with love, buddy. This is a motel, remember? And I'm married to her. And she was hiding under a bed. Jesus! Love you call it. How come a quick piece of motel tail gets to be called love? How can you kid yourself?"

He took one more step toward Carl. Carl saw a flash of motion, but before he had time to duck, Bucky's thick right fist smashed against the left side of his face. He fell across the bed with such force that he was overbalanced. His legs swung up and he toppled onto the floor on the other side and lay with his cheek against the nap of the rug, a sick-sweet flooding in his mouth, feeling all at once stricken, shocked, faint and outraged. He had not been struck in anger in over twenty years. He lay in such a way that he could look under the bed he had fallen across, and see Cindy's sandaled feet and slim ankles, neatly side by side.

He pushed himself up from the floor until he was on one knee, his forearm on the bed, head sagging. He had not known that a blow could sicken him so, could shock him so utterly.

He stood up and turned. Bucky stood there, grinning widely. "Love," Bucky said. "Undying love."

And again there was the flare of motion, and this time a great force caved in his right side and, almost immediately, he was hit on the left side of his face and mouth again. He fell back against the wall and rebounded forward onto his hands and knees and balanced there precariously, looking dully down at the heavy carmine drops that fell from his

face to the rug. He sat back on his heels and felt behind him
for the wall and worked his way up to stand again on mile-
high legs in a buzzing place.

"Tell me of love," Bucky said, and his voice seemed to be
in a cave, far away.

Carl tugged the flimsy strings of the puppet that was his
body, and pulled his arms up and took a wooden step and
swung a drifting paper fist at Bucky's smile. And was hammered back against the wall and tried to come out again,
tried to sail the slow white paper fists like a child's crude
toys at a red face that looked wide as a wash tub, at the
piano smile. And was trundled back against the wall and
somehow held there while in a faraway, drifting and unimportant world, painless blows broke his body and rang his head,
and a woman screamed and screamed, and there was hammering at a door he had never known, and then he dived
down through the fabric of a thousand circus hoops, the
fabric gray at first when he was falling slowly, but deepening
as his speed increased until all the fabric was black and he
was falling so rapidly it was a roaring in his ears. . . .

FIFTEEN

In a shifting queasy darkness something bit evilly up into his nose and into his brain. He tried to push it away and muttered in irritation at the persistence, but at last had to open his eyes. It took him long stuporous moments to realize that he was on a bed, that one eye would not open, that the two hard-faced bored-looking men in uniform beyond the foot of the bed were state policemen.

"What's the date, please," a crisp voice on his left said. The eye on that side was the one that wouldn't open. He rolled his head slowly. The speaker was a young man with a narrow olive face, eyes closely set, a great shaggy mustache, and a sports shirt patterned with palm trees. Beyond him stood the motel manager, an obelisk of massive indignation.

"Sunday. The . . . twenty-first of July." His mouth felt as if it had been torn out and replaced upside down. His voice was gritty and bulbous.

"Name and address, please."

"Carl Garrett. Ten Barrow Lane. In Crescent Ridge." He saw one of the officers write in a pocket notebook, and it was that ominous action that brought back the memory of where he was, the memory of Bucky and Cindy. He tried to sit up and the mustachioed young man pushed him back gently.

The young man reached down on the floor somewhere and put a loop around his head, folded a mirror down in front of his eye, and shone a bright light into Carl's eye. "Look directly at my eye," he said. He took the apparatus off after a few moments.

"What's the word, Doc?" one of the officers asked.

"I better take him on home and get some cranial plates and set that nose and stitch his mouth there."

"He okay now for questions?"

"Try to make it fast, Al."

"Sure thing. Who beat up on you, Garrett?" The notebook was poised and ready.

"I . . . I fell."

"Sure. You fell and you couldn't stop bouncing. Come off it, Garrett. Who was it?"

"I fell."

"What do you do for a living, Garrett?"

"Assistant to the plant manager at Hillton Metal Products."

"How come if your name is Garrett you registered as Garroway? Don't you know that's a misdemeanor?"

"I . . . I think it's done all the time."

"Who was the blond cookie the manager here give us a description of?"

"I . . . I never got her right name."

"You just happened to meet her in a bar some place and you said how's about it and she said okay so you came here. Is that it?"

"Something like that."

"Only it turned out she had a husband and he beat up on you good. He did a dandy job."

"I fell."

The one the doctor had called Al shrugged and put his notebook away. "There's nothing here," he said to his partner. He turned back to Carl. "Look, Mr. Garrett. We know from your wallet you got a wife and a couple of nice-looking kids. And you got a good job. What's the percentage in you messing yourself up like this, I ask you? Why mess around with a married woman? You got enough dough to buy something safe and pretty right down in Hillton. There won't be any stink this time on account of I know why you don't want to press charges, and you are maybe lucky enough not to get hurt bad. But a man like you just ought to have more sense, somehow."

"Wait a moment, gentlemen," the manager said. "We have some extensive damages here."

Carl sat up and this time the doctor did not restrain him. He closed his eyes against sudden dizziness, and when it had gone he said, "Make out an itemized bill and I'll mail you a check."

"There are blank checks in the office, Mr. Garrett. I believe I'll hold your motor vehicle until your check clears."

"Can he do that?" Carl asked the officers.

"I'm not going to stop him," Al said. Both officers looked extremely unfriendly.

"You won't need your car right now anyway, Mr. Garrett," the doctor said. "I'll take you to my place in my car. I wouldn't want you trying to drive just yet anyway."

Al said, "Thanks, Doc. See you around." They left without another glance at Carl.

"Do you think you can make it out to my car?" the doctor asked. "Don't try to rush it. A physical beating is no joke at your age. It's no joke at any age. It can be a hell of a shock to your system. Do you want me to . . . uh . . . phone your wife, or would you like to?"

"She's in . . . County Memorial Hospital," Carl said. It seemed, under the circumstances, a particularly shameful confession.

He stood up and when he wavered and felt faint, the doctor caught his arm quickly and strongly, supporting him. The swarming black dots faded away and Carl said, "I'm okay now."

The door was held open for him. The doctor's car was parked beside the Ford wagon. It was a three-year-old Cadillac, a baby blue convertible. Carl moved like a fragile old man to the car and got in when the doctor held the door for him.

They drove three miles farther east on the turnpike, and then turned north and drove another two miles to the village of Aldermon. Carl had been through it before and remembered it as a pleasant town. They turned into the drive of a white colonial house set well back from the road, with big elms shading the front law. A small white sign in the front yard said *Dr. Omar Kacharian. Office hours 10-12 2-5.*

"Nice place," Carl said.

"I've been here three years. The village elders still think I'm some kind of foreign devil, but they haven't much choice in the matter. I'm the only one they've got handy."

"I hope this isn't inconveniencing you."

Dr. Kacharian stopped the car and turned off the motor and turned toward Carl. "The state cops use me a lot, because I manage to come every time I'm called. It is a slight inconvenience to be called out on a Sunday morning. Allow me to say that even though I am making absolutely no moral judgments on your . . . predicament, it does give me a nice justification for giving you a tidy bill. In exchange you can be assured that I'll hemstitch your mouth expertly." And a white smile gleamed under the shaggy mustache.

When he walked with the doctor to the office wing of the house he felt slightly stronger, but sharp pains in his right side prevented him from straightening up. The small treatment room was well lighted and well equipped. After he had taken off his bloody clothing, Dr. Kacharian had him climb onto the table and lie flat, with a folded sheet across his loins. A chunky and pretty redhead came in and was introduced as Mrs. Kacharian. She assisted the doctor with a quiet efficiency that spoke of nursing training.

"First off," the doctor said, "we'll get some pretty pictures with the handy dandy here. Then we'll do the mouth and then the nose."

He wheeled the X-ray into various positions, going behind a lead screen each time to activate it. His wife went off with the plates. Carl felt nauseated by the blood he had swallowed. The doctor injected him with a local anesthetic and when the lower half of Carl's face was numbed, he wheeled a light into a better position, worked quickly and deftly with a curved needle, then packed the left cheek with gauze. There was a painful grating as the broken nose was shifted back into position. With quick and gentle fingers, Kacharian taped it in place, humming to himself as he worked.

"Now try to keep your tongue away from the stitches, and try to keep from stretching your lips until the numbness wears off. After it wears off you won't stretch them because it will hurt when you do. Now hold on tight because I want to get a look at that eye you can't open." He gently pried the puffed and blackened flesh aside and shone a light down into the eye, then gave a grunt of satisfaction.

"You're not as bad as you looked, Mr. Garrett. Now just lie there and take it easy for a while until I get a chance to look at the wet plates."

Carl could not estimate how long Kacharian was gone, how long he lay there listening to the dull throbbing of various aches and pains. His sense of time had been disturbed by violence. He could not bring himself to think of the implications and the eventual complications of what had happened to him. He was content to lie like an injured animal, conscious only of immediate misery, staring up with one eye at the featureless pale green ceiling.

Kacharian came back and said, "You seem to be all in one piece except for a pair of cracked ribs on the right side. This may hurt a little." He probed at Carl's ribs with questing fingers and Carl could not restrain a gasp of pain. The woman unrolled strips of wide tape and tore them from the reel and Kacharian took them and taped his side firmly.

"Now tell me how you feel."

It was difficult to articulate with any distinctness with the numb mouth and the gauze. "Tired, I guess. And sick to my stomach."

"Try to control that if you can. You'll rip the stitches. Bonny, bring me a robe, please."

He was helped into a robe and helped off the table. He was given a pill which he swallowed with difficulty. He was led to a smaller room which contained a hospital bed. The woman closed the blinds of the single window and closed the door quietly when she left. Within minutes he began to feel the black furry tugging of the pill, trying to pull him down into blackness. He knew he shouldn't sleep. When he didn't show up at the hospital or send a message, Joan would become frantic with worry. He decided to get up and go find the doctor. But even as he was contemplating it, all pain faded and he seemed to float for a time in blissful ease, and then slid over an oiled edge down into the darkness of the pill.

He came awake fractionally, a little at a time, reluctantly taking a long time to identify the doctor and the small room. He felt utterly relaxed. There was no nausea. The pain had become manageable. His mouth felt as if it were filled with crinkled bits of wire.

"Feel better?" Kacharian asked.

"Much," he said thickly. "Whad you give me?"

"Oral demerol. Open wide and let me get that gauze."

After the gauze was gone his mouth felt as if it were still there. "What time is it?"

"Nearly five."

He sat up slowly. "My wife will . . ."

"I took the liberty of phoning the floor nurse and telling her to tell Mrs. Garrett that you wouldn't be in, that you were unavoidably detained and there was nothing to worry about."

He felt his eyes fill with tears of weakness and gratitude. His emotions seemed dangerously close to the surface. "Thanks. Thanks a lot."

"Any headache?"

"No. My face throbs and my lips feel as if they don't belong to me."

"Take a deep breath and tell me how those ribs feel."

He winced. "I get a sharp twinge."

"No feeling of anything rubbing?"

"No."

"You'll want to clean yourself up. Bonny did as well as she could with your slacks, but the shirt was ruined and she threw it away. Come along and I'll show you where you can clean up."

He took him to a bathroom in the main house. Kacharian said, "That old shirt of mine ought to do long enough to get you home. Don't think of returning it. It's ready to be scrapped."

When the door was closed Carl hung onto the sink and looked at his face in the mirror. The socket of the closed left eye was swollen fat with purple-black flesh. The tape across his nose was a gleaming white. His lips were puffed and irregular. He had a dark shadow of beard and tousled hair. He would not have recognized himself. After he had washed in a gingerly way and combed his hair and put on the clothing that had been placed in the bathroom for him, he looked very little better. The swollen lips and puffed face gave him an unexpected look of brutality and stupidity. His expression seemed to be a dull and somewhat sinister sneer, and he could not alter it.

He walked back down the stairs and out through the dining room to the kitchen. The doctor was at the kitchen table, drinking coffee. His wife was feeding a very fat and very redheaded baby in a high-chair, spooning pablum into him between gurgles and crowing noises.

"Coffee?" Kacharian asked.

"Is it permitted?"

"Sure. But stick to soft foods for a few days. Soup, milk toast. Sit down right there."

Kacharian found a cup and saucer, filled it from the pot on the stove and brought it over. "Cream and sugar?"

"Black, thanks. Wonder where that character got the red hair?"

"That's Terrance O'Rourk Kacharian. That should confound future genealogists."

"Pay a little more attention, please, sir, Mr. Terrance O'Rourk Kacharian," Bonny said severely. "And down it goes. You know, Mr. Garrett, he enjoys eating because it's a social situation."

Carl sipped the coffee. It tasted very good. "Kids are odd. It didn't seem as if we could get enough down my boy, Kip, to keep a fly alive. But his sister Nancy ate like a wolf."

"How old are they?" the doctor asked.

"Fifteen and thirteen. They're off at summer camp. My wife's operation wasn't something that had to be done imme-

diately, so we had Dr. Madden schedule it when the kids
would be away."

"Bernie Madden? Damn good man."

In the silence that followed Carl realized that he had forgotten for a moment the reason why he was in this kitchen
drinking Kacharian's coffee. It made the silence more awkward.

"I . . . I've never been in this kind of a jam before," he
said, and wished he hadn't brought it up. He saw the quick
glance Bonny gave him, and sensed both her contempt for
him and a degree of satisfaction in his predicament, and
knew that her husband had told her what had happened.
And he knew that if he had read about it in the newspaper he
would have dismissed it as a sordid interlude, a typical
scruffy adventure. Betrayed hubby batters wife's lover in
motel rendezvous. Suburban resident, local industrial executive, beaten up when caught with salesman's wife, mother of
two.

"It happens," Kacharian said.

"My wife comes home tomorrow."

"Major operation?"

"Abdominal."

"Hysterectomy?"

"No."

"That's good because she won't be as emotionally disturbed as if she'd had one. But she'll be pretty vulnerable. I
don't want to alarm you, but a mess like this might throw
her into a hell of a depression that she'd be a long time getting over."

"Maybe he should have thought of that," Bonny said
bitterly.

"Hush, girl. We're not sitting in judgment. Garrett, the state
cops won't follow through. There won't be anything in the
papers. What's the chance of keeping it from your wife, at
least for a week or two?"

"I . . . I don't know. The . . . the other couple live
next door. We've been . . . good friends."

Kacharian sipped his coffee, frowning. "I can understand
that the friendship is over, all right. But is there enough
afterglow so you could ask them to . . . well, to play along
with any reasonable excuse you can come up with for your
condition?"

"I can't think of anything reasonable."

"You fell."

Terrance O'Rourk Kacharian shut his mouth implacably against the next offering, and glared at his mother.

"Okay," she said. "The bottomless pit is filled." She wiped off his face, turned the tray back and hoisted him up onto her hip and carried him out of the kitchen.

"Don't be upset about Bonny," Kacharian said. "All wives belong to one big club dedicated to stamping out infidelity."

"You know what's so stupid about this whole thing?" Carl said. "You don't have to try to believe me, of course. But this was the second damn time in seventeen years that I ever stepped out of line."

Kacharian stared at him, and then shook his head in pity. "Good Lord on high! What a streak of luck."

"For the first time in my life I feel as if maybe I ought to see a psychiatrist. I never had a compulsion that got out of control before. I guess the woman and I are equally to blame."

Kacharian took his cup to the sink and rinsed it. "You and the woman and your age bracket and all the curious mores of current western civilization. Something has happened to satisfactions. People don't seem to be getting as much as they deserve out of this fuller, richer life. I like what I'm doing so damn much that I often feel guilty when I treat people for physical ailments that are purely and simply the result of the emotional strain of working year after year at pointless, empty jobs. I beg your pardon. Speechmaking is one of my social afflictions. Bonny's endured this opus many times."

"If there's more, I'd like to hear it."

"Is your job a challenge to you, Mr. Garrett, Carl? Call me Kach, by the way."

"It's all right, I guess. No. I'll do better than that. It's pretty damn dull. And there's a lot of years of it left. And I've even been making it duller than it should be. Masochism, I guess."

"Okay. So how does modern man arrange to rebel against a barren use of his years and his life, rebel against all the wastage of the big dreams he had about himself when he was young? Our civilization is so compartmentalized that the little guy can't see the relationship of his efforts to the whole. So his work is unreal to him, and hence meaningless. The artisan is pretty damn rare. So we get into psychosomatics. A woman spends four years soldering wire A to terminals B and C, and gets an arthritic condition of the hands that gets her out of the trap. Safety engineers put every known safety device on a punch press, but a man will work on it for five years and then manage to get his hand into it, even if he has to push the release with his nose. A meat cutter in a packing house will become an alcoholic. A truck driver will acquire a classic ulcer. But some of them will react in other ways. After eight years of running the same piece of IBM office equipment, the once decent girl will become an after hours pushover. Or the lathe operator will take to beating his wife up. Or killing his entire family and himself. People with the dull little jobs become maniacs on the highway, or turn accident prone in all manner of ways, or just get sick. Or a man like you expresses his rebellion by indulging himself in an affair. I tell you, Carl, nobody will ever be able to measure all the human misery that is the indirect result of the inescapable boredom and sense of purposelessness that derives from a civilization so mechanized and complicated that a man can no longer take pride and satisfaction in the one little fragment that is his part of the whole ball of wax."

Carl tried to smile, but it hurt his mouth. "You give me a nice tidy little rationalization, Kach."

"But it won't be good enough, will it?"

"I don't guess it will."

"You ready to take off?"

"Any time."

"What do I owe you?"

"Let's call it fifty dollars."

"I can mail you a check. I wish I could get my car."

"I think we can fix that. I'll take you to the motel. I'm supposedly the doctor for the motel, and he'll take my check for what he thinks you owe him, and then you can mail that to me too."

After they left the house, Carl said, "Aren't you going the wrong way?"

"I'm a conspirator at heart. I want to show you something." He turned right in the middle of the village and drove out to a small roadside park with picnic tables. He parked and Carl followed him to the edge of a ravine at the rear of the park. There was a narrow footbridge across the ravine and most of the railing had rotted away.

"I treated a kid that fell off that thing a couple of weeks ago. It's only a ten-foot drop, but it's onto rocks. When your wife is well enough to ride around, bring her out and show her the scene of your misadventure. You went for an aimless

ride and parked and, like a damn fool, fell off the bridge.
You'd remembered seeing my sign, so you drove back and I
patched you up."

"You're being very decent, Kach."

"Maybe there's a club of husbands too."

He drove Carl back to the motel. The no-vacancy sign was
lighted. The station wagon was parked in front. Carl remembered that when Bucky had interrupted him, he had left
the key in the ignition. The stately manager took them into
the back office. The itemized bill for damages to lamp, rug,
table, bedding and spread was eighty-five dollars and fifty
cents. He agreed to accept Dr. Kacharian's check, and managed to convey his impression that the doctor was being a
gullible fool. He gave Kacharian a receipt, and put the car
key on the desk where Carl could pick it up rather than hand
it to him.

Carl stood by the car and shook hands with the doctor
and thanked him again for all his trouble, and for the un-
solicited co-operation. It was twenty of seven when he left
the motel and headed west on the turnpike into the sun. He
found that it was difficult to judge distance with only one eye,
and he drove with care.

The quiet efficiency and uncomplicated friendliness of the
young doctor had buoyed him up. But after he had been on
the road ten minutes he slipped into black depression. The
clumsy lie would never work. His marriage could never be
the same. And he could never feel the same about himself. He
was traveling in the outside lane at fifty-five. Fast traffic
churned by him in the inside lane. He thought of a very simple solution. Just one twist of the wheel. Bring the speed up
first, and then merely put the right hand so, at the top of
the wheel, and make a quick half turn. The car would plunge
across the shoulder and down the slope and into the heavy
stand of trees. Insurance in order. A Ballinger pension for
the widow. College education for the kids. And no more
sickly lies to tell.

A fast-moving car cut in on him carelessly, forcing his
right wheels onto the gravel shoulder. He fought it back onto
the road and cursed the fool in the yellow Olds, and knew
then that though he might indulge himself with self-pitiful
and blackly dramatic thoughts of self-imposed oblivion, he
could never actually make the final commitment. And had he
been able to give the wheel that fatal twist, he would have
spent the last three seconds of his life fighting in dreadful

fear and in the sickness of remorse to bring the car under control and thus save himself.

He wondered how many suicides had changed their minds after the irrevocable act that set the chain of death in motion. Did they go out the high windows and, all the way to the pavement, give the great screams of terror and regret? Did they try to crawl toward the phone, panting and fighting against the viscid blackness of the pills?

It was seven-thirty when he reached his home. When he reached for his suitcase he saw that Cindy's was in the car too. He hadn't noticed it when he had gotten into the car at the motel. He took both suitcases into the kitchen, left hers there and took his to the bedroom. He changed his shirt, shaved his tender jaws quickly, and arrived at the hospital at ten of eight.

When he walked into the room he had the feeling that he was crouched and hiding behind the swollen ruin of his face.

Joan sat bolt upright and cried, "Darling! What happened?" Then she clapped a hand over her mouth and glanced toward the other bed where the curtains were still drawn.

He pulled his chair close. "It's a silly story. Did you get the message?"

"Just that you couldn't come. I didn't know what in the world could have . . . I thought maybe it was some sort of unexpected business thing, somebody coming in from New York or something. I told myself that's what it was."

"I got a little drunk last night."

"If you drank any more after I saw you, you certainly were a little drunk. A little more than drunk. Did you get into a fight? I can't imagine you getting into a fight."

"No. I got up late. I felt lousy. I decided to go for a ride. I drove out the pike and turned off and drove through Aldermon. You remember that place."

"Yes. But what happened? Did you wreck the car?"

"No. I stopped at a little roadside park. There is a bridge across a ravine. The railing was rotten. I fell off the damn bridge right onto my face on the rocks."

"Oh, you poor darling! Oh, that must have hurt!"

"When I could move I climbed out and drove back and found a nice young doctor in the village named Kacharian. He sewed up my mouth and set my nose and taped two cracked ribs. I was a mess. So he gave me a pill and it knocked me out and I woke up about five. When you can take rides, I'll drive you out and show you the place. I've never felt so foolish in my life."

"You could have been killed! Wasn't anybody around to help you?"

"Not a soul."

"You must have landed right on your face, poor old honey!"

"All this and a hangover too."

"Are you sure he found all the damage?"

"He took X-rays."

"You'll feel miserable for days. Let me get a closer look at you. It's strange the rocks didn't break the skin, dear. I'd think they'd have split you wide open."

"I broke the fall a little, I guess."

"I'm glad it wasn't worse, darling. Well, there's certainly no need of you hanging around here. I'll bet you feel much worse than I do. You should go right on home and get to bed. You certainly won't try to go to the office tomorrow?"

"I wasn't going to anyway, remember? It's your first day home."

"That's right. Bernie said you should come and get me at about eleven o'clock in the morning. You know, dear, you look just as though you were in a barroom brawl. They're going to kid you something awful down at the office, I know."

"I can't smile. It hurts the stitches."

"You run along. Oh, Carl, is anything wrong with Cindy?"

"Not that I know of."

"She wasn't in yesterday and she hasn't been in today. See if she's all right, will you, dear?"

"All right."

"I think Bucky was supposed to come back today. Have you seen him?"

"Not yet."

"Was it a good party last night?"

"Except that I got clobbered, it was about the same as usual, I guess."

"It isn't like you to drink too much. And . . . fall off bridges."

He touched his swollen lips to her forehead. "See you at eleven, honey."

"Come a little earlier and get the bill stuff straightened out downstairs. Then Miss Calhoun will wheel me down to the front door and out to the car. Park right in front, dear."

SIXTEEN

The intense strain of the ten minutes with Joan had exhausted him. When he was back in the car in the hospital lot he sat behind the wheel for several minutes, too drained to go through the motions of starting the car. The lie had been accepted, but it was only a temporary relief. Too many other things would add up. Eunice Stockland would make certain they added up, in a manner shrill enough to be heard by all of Crescent Ridge.

The last of the summer dusk was gone by the time he drove into the car port. The phone was ringing as he entered the house. He hurried to it but caught it just as the caller hung up. He stood in the dark house with the phone at his ear and felt lost and alone as never before in his life.

He had seen the lights in the Cable house. He turned on the wall light over the phone table, sat down and dialed the Cable number. Though the houses were next door, they were not on the same standard eight-party line.

In the middle of the third ring the phone was lifted and Cindy said, "Hello."

"This is Carl. I've got . . . something of yours. Can I bring it over?"

"I'm alone."

"I'll be right over."

She pushed the screen door open for him and he carried the suitcase into the kitchen and set it down, turned toward her. When she saw his face clearly her lips tightened and her eyes narrowed. She reached out and touched his left cheek very lightly with her fingertips.

"How ugly," she said.

"In every possible way. And I wasn't much opposition."

"Bucky is very powerful. And you were very brave, Carl. You kept getting up and trying. I tried to stop him. I thought he would kill you. I didn't know whether he had or not. So after he left here, I phoned the motel. That manager person was horrid to me, but at least I found out you'd gone off in

172

some doctor's car. Won't you sit down? Would you like a drink?"

"When do you expect Bucky?"

"I don't."

"Oh?"

"He's gone home to his mother, I imagine."

"If coffee wouldn't be too much trouble," he said, and sat at the breakfast booth.

"Is instant all right?"

"Fine."

"It will only take a minute."

"What happened to you after . . . I was out of the picture?"

"I shall never in my whole life spend a fifteen minutes in more terror and humiliation than that time I spent under the bed. It was so damn grotesque. After he got you against the wall and kept hitting you, I was screaming and somebody was hammering at the door and I caught his arm and pulled him away. You slipped down in a heap and you didn't move. Bucky looked at you for a few seconds, then he grabbed me by the wrist and pulled me out of there. There was a man at the door and he pushed him out of the way. Bucky was almost running, and I was stumbling along behind him trying to stay on my feet all the way down the road. He practically threw me into the car. The only time he spoke all the way back was when I would try to say something. Then he would shut me up by calling me a foul word. I was blubbering by the time we got here. He told me to go into the bedroom. I didn't know whether he was going to kill me. He acted like a crazy man. I didn't much care."

The pot began to steam. She filled the cup, stirred in the powdered coffee and brought it to him. "I'm sorry I won't be able to sit down with you."

"What do you mean?"

"I can stand. And I can lie down on my side or my tummy, but I won't be doing any sitting for a while."

"I don't . . ."

"I went into the bedroom. He came in in a few minutes and he had a putter in his hand, his old one that was out in the closet in the car port with his fish poles and the croquet set. He had hold of it by the end you putt with. He told me to take off my clothes. I didn't think he was serious, that he could be serious. I told him that I certainly wasn't going to let him whip me. Then he caught me by the waist and ripped my good skirt right off. So I decided I would play his stupid game and if I didn't make a sound he'd stop when he began feeling silly. So I took everything off and asked him if there was any special position he favored. He grabbed my wrist and turned me sideways and whacked me across the bottom with the steel shaft of that putter. He swung it so hard it whistled, and it made a horrible cracking sound when it hit me. I had no idea it was going to hurt that badly. I was able to stand still and make no sound for about three whacks. And then I couldn't stop myself from dancing around, trying to get away from it. And that made it worse because it made his aim bad and sometimes he'd hit me way up near the small of the back and sometimes as far down as the backs of my knees. And pretty soon I started howling and yelping and bellowing. It . . . it took away every scrap and atom of dignity I've been able to acquire in my whole life. I'll never get it all back. I'll always have that memory with me—of leaping around, blubbering and begging, trying to get away from that horrible hurting, going around and around in a crazy dance, blinded by my tears, hooting and shrilling like a soul in hell. Finally—I guess his arm got tired—he let me go and I staggered to the bed and fell across it and bit the pillow. I felt as if my backside from my waist to my knees was afire. I heard him breathing heavily and I knew he was standing beside the bed looking down at me. I think he got some twisted kind of sexual satisfaction out of it. Then he went away and closed the bedroom door behind him. And I began to cry a different kind of tears. Humiliation and shame."

She smiled in a way that turned the corners of her wide mouth down, and said, "Don't you think it has a sort of delightful T. S. Eliot touch? The errant wife beaten with a putter. It sort of goes with that thousand lost golf balls thing in *The Wasteland.* For a Victorian motif the man could use a buggy whip or a piece of kindling. But this made it very modrun, don't you think?"

"I'm sorry, Cindy. I'm terribly sorry about . . . the way it all came out."

"I'm a mess," she said. "I'm all swollen and streaky and bruised. I've got as many colors as those funny kind of monkeys. I do wish I could sit down, dammit. Anyway, I didn't finish. After the tears were sort of dwindling away and I was having those funny sobs like hiccups, I heard his voice but I couldn't hear what he was saying. I thought somebody had stopped by, but I could only hear his voice. Then I picked up the bedside phone. He was talking to his mother, and it was all very gooey. They were both crying. It was very emotional. I knew right away he'd told her he'd caught me in flagrante delicto. She said, over and over, 'My poor boy, my poor boy. Your father and I could have told you that something like this would happen sooner or later. No normal wife and mother sends her darling little babies away for the whole summer. I could have told you she was no good, but you wouldn't have listened. And now you know. But I'm sorry it had to happen this way.'

"Then I heard him tell her his plans. Pack and move out. He said he had some appointments next week, but he'd get out to their place by Thursday to talk to them and see the kids. He said it was remotely possible I might come after the kids. Don't turn them over to me. He would be seeing a lawyer at the first opportunity, and it was pretty damn certain that I wouldn't contest it and neither would I get any rights at all in the children. He said, actually said, that I didn't have a leg to stand on. I hung up but he kept on talking to her for a long time.

"Then he came to the bedroom and packed. I'd covered myself up and I kept my face to the wall. It didn't take him very long. He stood by the bed and said, 'I'm leaving.' I didn't answer him. 'For good.' I still didn't answer. So he slammed the door hard and a little while later I heard the car drive out, with him gunning it like a hot-rod kid."

"I'm sorry, Cindy."

"Don't try to take it on yourself. I was the one who made the final fatal move that got us into this. How was your delightful day?"

He told her about Kacharian and the officers and the bill for damages and the lie he had told Joan. And he told her what Kacharian had said about Joan and what this might do to her, and told her he had come over to plead with Bucky to keep up the pretense of friendship for a couple of weeks just for Joan's sake. And he told her that Joan wondered why she hadn't come in the last two days.

"I'll come over tomorrow and be there when you bring her home, Carl. I'll have to wear slacks because he got me a couple of mean ones across the right calf. See?" She half turned and pulled up the skirt of her long yellow robe. There were two raised welts, of a dark and painful red, the adjacent area blue as a result of the bruising.

"We're a great pair," he said.

"The uncalculated risks of adultery. Let's not go on this way, because if I ever start to laugh it's going to turn into the most God-awful case of hysterics ever seen by man. More coffee?"

"No, thanks."

She walked him to the rear door and out into the sultry night. He felt it curious that there was no strain or tension between them. They were like enemies who, after being wounded in the same battle, feel more of kinship than animosity.

"What are you going to do?" he asked her.

"I don't know. Just wait."

"What do you think you want to do?"

"Oh, Carl, I know what I want to do. I know what I want so badly it makes me feel all empty and aching. What I want more than anything in the world is to be here in my house with my husband and my kids. That's what I want."

"If you want that badly enough . . ."

"Please skip the homely philosophies, Carl. Do me that favor. Now that it's gone for good, I learn, with my usual discernment, how good it was for me. Now I find out I was putting on a big act. I love the guy. But because I'm exactly what he labeled me, a bitch, I got all petulant and discontented and reckless. And plowed up the pretty pea patch. And sowed it with salt. It isn't your fault. I fell into your lap. And right now I feel honest enough to take you all the way off the hook. Honest enough and generous enough."

"What do you mean?"

"That first night, the ankle was uninjured. I just wanted your arm around me. And when I came over to your house the next day, I told myself I was being sensible, but all along I knew I was coming over to be kissed again."

"Cindy, I . . ."

"Hush, now. Just trot on home. Let's stop thinking about what a pair of damn fools we are and start thinking about Joan for a change. Good night, Carl." She kissed him on the cheek. Her lips were cool. It was the kiss of affection of a sister. "If somebody has to be messed up, I hope it's just one of us, my dear."

On Monday morning, after he had paid his portion of the bill and received his hospitalization policy back, he went up to give the patient release form to the floor nurse. After his breakfast he had purchased a pair of very large and very darkly tinted sun glasses, and had covered the white tape across his nose with flesh-colored adhesive tape. His lips were down almost to normal dimension, but he ached in every joint and muscle, and every movement brought a twinge of pain. He told himself that he had merely been knocked around a little. He felt as if he had fallen down forty flights of concrete stairs.

Joan was dressed and radiantly ready to be taken home. Her suitcase was packed and the nurse had made a package of the books and cards. Joan rode in the wheel chair with the package on her lap. The nurse pushed the chair and carried the suitcase. Carl carried two potted plants.

"I feel like I was graduating or something," Joan said. "You really look much less terrifying than you did yesterday, darling. Is the car right out in front? Have you paid the bill and everything? Is Marie alerted to start tomorrow working full time for us?"

"Everything is under control."

She got from the chair into the car with more agility than he anticipated. They said good-by to the nurse. He drove away from the hospital.

"Go real slow, darling, because I want to look at every single thing. I feel as if I'd been shut up for years. And please don't hit any bumps because I feel as if the incision would pop open. I mean I don't feel bad, but just sort of . . . skeptical, you know. Are the plants where they won't fall over? Darn it, listen to me! Jabber, jabber, jabber. I guess I'm excited."

"There's going to be a storm, I think."

"I saw those clouds. When they get that funny brassy look it means trouble. Did you leave windows open?"

"We'll be home hours before it hits, girl."

When they turned onto Barrow Lane she quite suddenly stopped talking and sat with her hands folded in her lap like an awed child at school. He took the driveway bump very carefully and stopped short of the car port.

"It's lovely," she said. "Just lovely."

He went around and opened her door and helped her out. "I wouldn't *really* have to lean on you," she said, "but I guess I should."

He took her slowly to the front door, took on most of her weight when he helped her up the steps. Cindy came from inside the house, beaming, and held the screen door open and said, "Welcome home, Joanie."

The two women kissed, and Joan snuffled and said, "I'll be darned if I'm going to cry."

Joan stopped and looked around the living room. "It's hardly messed up at all. You didn't even take the wrappers off all the magazines, Carl. You couldn't have spent much time here at all."

"Off to bed, you," Cindy said firmly. Carl looked at her. She wore wine slacks and a white halter top. Her hair was tied back in a pony tail with a piece of wine yarn. Her smile was bright, but her eyes looked sunken, with dark patches under them.

As they walked to the bedroom Joan said, "Where were you Saturday and Sunday, Cindy?"

"I had a germ. I didn't think I should take it to the hospital."

"You don't look too well. How do you feel now?"

"Better."

Cindy had turned the freshly made bed down and had put a vase of cut flowers on Joan's dressing table in front of the mirror. Carl went out to the kitchen and opened a can of beer while Cindy helped Joan get into bed. When he went back in with his beer, Joan was in her bed jacket and propped up on two pillows.

Joan smiled at him and said, "What do you think of my clumsy husband, Cindy, falling on his face?"

"It gives him a nice dissolute look, don't you think? Like a movie villain."

"Is Bucky home?"

"He came and went again. He sends his love, Joanie."

"You might almost as well be married to a sailor, Cindy. Why don't you sit down, dear? You look as if you were itching to get away."

"Really, I should . . ."

"Carl is going to go out soon and bring us both back some lunch. Why don't we have lunch for three, right here?"

"I'm sorry, Joan, but I've got a lunch date."

"The least you can do is sit down for a minute, Cindy. Besides, I want to tell you about that Eunice Stockland."

"And her vivid imagination?" Cindy said.

"Do sit down, honey. Please."

Carl saw the quick helpless look Cindy gave him. She went to the dressing table bench and sat down. Her face turned yellowish under her tan and for a moment there was agony in her eyes. Slowly her color returned to normal, but Carl could see how white her knuckles were where she clenched the edge of the bench.

Joan relayed Eunice's poison. Cindy said with proper casualness that she had been driving up to the lake and sleeping in the Jessups' camp because it was so much cooler there than in the city.

Cindy left a little while later, promising to come back as soon as she could. After Carl was assured by Joan that she was comfortable and had everything she needed, he went out and bought lunch at a popular local restaurant which had a catering service on the side.

When he drove back into the car port he realized that the house had a different look to him. It had come alive. It moved and breathed again because she was home. It seemed to him that he had gone through a little time of death, and had now emerged on the other side, miraculously unscathed. He told himself that Joan would find out, sooner or later, but for now, for this day, he permitted himself the luxury of the hope that she would never learn about it.

Marie arrived for work on Tuesday before he left for the office and, after greeting Joan, began to fix her breakfast. Carl had breakfast on the way to the office. All day he endured the gibes of the rest of the staff. How'd the other guy look, Carl? You run into a door or something, Mr. Garrett? Maybe he run into a swinging door, huh? Naw, he picks up a couple of bucks weekends fighting semi-pro only this time he was out of his class. Honest, fella, what the hell happened?

I fell.

Fell?

Fell.

And they'd shrug and smirk and walk off. It was a long day. And the worst of it came right at the end. Jim Hardy called him to his office. Ray Walsh and some other staff members were there. Ray had a look of heavy satisfaction.

Jim Hardy stared at Carl as he sat down. "Somebody said you were a little banged up, but I didn't know you looked this bad. What the hell happened, Carl?"

"Like a clumsy damn fool I fell off a foot bridge into a mess of rocks. The hand rail was rotten."

Hardy stared at him with a certain skepticism for a few

seconds and then said, "Well, let's get down to it. Ray has come up with an idea for reorganizing the staff, and it looks to me like it might clarify the lines of authority and responsibility, and it looks to me like the sort of thing New York might go for in a minute. But I don't want to bring up all my artillery and then find out I haven't got enough ammunition. So I had this idea of Ray's duplicated to save time, along with a simplified organization chart. Nearly everybody directly affected by the proposed change is right here, so suppose we take a couple of minutes and go over it. And I want you to give it some real thought."

Carl, as he read the page and a half of explanation and looked at the chart, managed to conceal his shock and chagrin at how quickly and boldly and cleverly Ray Walsh had moved against him. Most of the proposed changes were minor. The single major change involved Carl's section. Beneath the sheen of such words as efficiency, logical flow, focus of attention on critical factors, was the proposal to remove from Carl's section a full half of his designated and implied authority and responsibility, and leave him with only the function of precisely measuring factory unit costs. It left him with a function so automatic and so clerical that, if it was accepted, it would not be long before New York would begin to wonder why a man should be paid so much for such a circumscribed function. He would no longer be required to follow up on those situations where unit costs slipped out of line. He would merely turn his findings over to a new section called Factory Co-ordination, headed by Ray Walsh. And it was suggested that Will Sherban be released by Carl and transferred to the new section.

He realized that the others had all finished and that he was still staring rather blankly at the mimeographed organization chart, and they were waiting politely for him to finish.

He pushed it from him so violently that it slid over to Ray Walsh. Walsh pushed it back to the middle of the small conference table.

"What's the verdict, men?" Jim Hardy asked heartily.

"I . . . I seem to be the one most directly affected, Jim," Carl said, groping for the right way to phrase what he was thinking.

"Then let's get your slant first. You take the first turn on the firing range."

Carl pushed his chair back and stood up and walked over

toward the windows. He turned and said, "It takes a specific function out of my hands and turns it over to a new section. That might make sense if it weren't being properly handled. But, as you must know, Jim, every time unit costs jump, my section follows it up immediately, finds the reason and, jointly with the department concerned, recommends the necessary action. It works smoothly and I see no reason why it shouldn't continue to work smoothly. So it seems a little nonsensical to place that responsibility with a . . . what's that name again?"

"Factory Co-ordination Section," Ray Walsh said. "I see your point, Carl. But I look at it this way. No offense intended, but your boys have been handling it as routine. You find a hole and you slap a bandage on it. The F.C. Section could operate a public health program, so to speak. Keep the holes from showing up. Work more closely with the production areas and, while doing so, find more opportunities to shave costs on other items."

"Isn't it everybody's responsibility to keep . . . a sort of creative eye on factory costs, Ray?" Carl asked.

"Some of us take the responsibility more seriously than others, Carl," Ray said gently.

"What does that mean?"

"No offense, Carl. We've got a lot of bright young men around this shop. Take that Will Sherban of yours. Yesterday, when you weren't in, I had to go to Will about something that came up. We got to talking and he showed me a memo of an idea he had over six months ago. I checked it out with Purchasing and they fell for it like a ton of bricks. If we'd been sharp enough to put that idea to work six months ago, Purchasing estimates it would have caused an overall saving in the neighborhood of twelve thousand dollars. With a Factory Co-ordination Section, Carl, ideas like that wouldn't die in the files. They'd get action promptly."

"Why be so civilized, Ray? Bring up the point that my initials were on the file copy, why don't you?"

"Boys, I think we're getting more heat than light here," Jim Hardy said. "We're in the field of ideas, not personalities."

And Carl saw how completely and thoroughly he had been defeated. Ray had all the ammunition he needed. But Carl knew that the proposed scheme was invalid. It would complicate the staff, increase paperwork and complicate interdepartmental co-ordination rather than improve it.

With faint hope and too much recklessness he turned to Jim and said, "Beg to differ. This is personalities."

"I don't think I like that attitude, Carl."

"I don't think I bear any special malice toward Ray Walsh, Jim. He's a shrewd and a very ambitious man. Too many people around here are a little scared of Ray because they suspect they may be working for him some day."

"I can't permit this to . . ." Jim said.

Ray interrupted. "Let's listen to him hang himself, Jim."

Carl felt the sweat on his palms. "Ray and I had a little tiff the other day. It got pretty ugly. I said some things I regret, and I dare to hope that Ray regrets some of the things he said. I had a strong hunch that Ray, who has a streak of vindictiveness that he will have to outgrow before he can reach full operating efficiency, would find some way to cut my throat. Please don't interrupt me, Jim. Ray did me a favor the other day. He brought me up short and he gave me a very candid look at myself. I'm grateful to him for that. A man can get into a rut. He can organize his work so that it becomes too undemanding. Jim, I haven't been hauling my weight around here lately, have I?"

Hardy looked embarrassed. "Well . . . you haven't been catching any crabs, but you haven't had your back in the stroke all the time."

"Ray woke me up, and after he left my office I made the first step in setting up a definitive program so that ideas like Will Sherban's won't get lost in the shuffle." He now knew, suddenly, where he was going, and he felt an unexpected confidence and eloquence. And even sincerity.

"Because it can truthfully be said, gentlemen, that I haven't been doing as well as possible with some of the non-clerical aspects of my job, I find myself without ammunition to oppose a reorganization scheme that I think is faulty and topheavy." He leaned on the back of his chair and looked directly at Walsh. "Ray, I think you're honest enough to admit that in your heart you know this plan will be awkward organizationally and administratively speaking."

"Do you want me to answer? When you can't get something done one way, you try another, even if it is a little awkward."

"Thanks for your honesty, Ray. So long as I have bared my soul, maybe I've earned the right to make a counter suggestion." He looked at Jim Hardy who nodded, his expression troubled. He was a man who was made uneasy by dissension.

"I would like to propose this. There are certain elements in Ray's plan that seem to be of value. Rather than create a new section, I would like to see that section set up as a sub-section of my department. I feel that that is where it logically belongs."

"Now just . . ." Ray tried to interrupt.

"That's where it belongs, and I would like Ray Walsh transferred over to run it. Will Sherban can be his second in command. Will is a very able boy. I will give Ray as free a hand as I can while at the same time exerting the normal authority of the department head who must take the responsibility for all actions performed and contemplated by his department. Ray and I can devise the most sensible and logical setup and working methods. I don't think our little hassle will prevent our working together efficiently. And calmly. It can be a big job, and I think it needs a man of Ray's varied talents. In that way we won't be unduly complicating our structure." He paused and smiled as widely as his sewn mouth would permit. "Also, Jim, it certainly ought to keep me on my toes. If I goof, Ray will have my job before I can turn around. But I don't intend to goof."

He walked around his chair in the heavy silence and sat down again. He glanced at Ray. Ray's face was red, his mouth bitter. Jim Hardy coughed and sighed and tapped a pencil on the edge of the table and said, "Any rebuttal, Ray?"

Carl knew Ray was flanked. "I suppose we could . . . give it a trial run."

"You've no objection to working for Carl?"

"Oh, no! None whatsoever. I'll do my job wherever I am."

"Carl, thanks for being so exceptionally frank," Jim said. "No other comments from anybody. Okay. Carl, you redraft the proposal for New York. You and Ray get together on this and work it out and put it in shape to send in over my signature. That's all, boys."

Ray Walsh was silent until they were in Carl's office with the door shut. Then he looked bleakly at Carl. "How did you get to be so damn fast on your feet?"

"Necessity, maybe. That was a good knife job. With Will Sherban's help, of course."

"So where do we stand, boss man?"

"Sit down, Ray. I'll lay it out for you. You will work for me. I'm not a nit-picker. I'll give you all the elbow room you need. But I'm not going to let you run with the ball unless I get a look at the signals first. When and if you fluff something, I'll take the blame. When you shine, I'll take some of the credit and make damn sure you get your share. I'll fight for you when it seems advisable, and yank on the check rein when I think you're wrong—and always give you the chance to argue your point. You're bright and you've got a lot of energy, and maybe this is the time and place when you start to really grow up. If I find you trying to undercut me or backbite or knife or somehow arranging things so I look bad, I'll do every damn thing in my power to get you booted out of the organization. I might not succeed, but I'll put some marks on your master record that won't ever come off. So, for God's sake, drop your guard and let's see if we can make this thing run."

Ray Walsh had the look of a man who reaches into a familiar drawer and feels something close around his wrist.

"What happened to amiable Carl Garrett, the happy joke-ster?"

"All kinds of ridiculous people are growing up these days."

"Overconfident Ray Walsh."

"Well, what do you think? I know I've suckered you into having to make a try at this thing. But I'd like to suspect there could be a little willingness along with it."

Ray clenched his right fist, inspected the knuckles, and then held his hand out suddenly. They shook hands.

"You're the boss man, Carl. Let's go to work."

SEVENTEEN

Marie left after serving their dinner on trays in the bedroom, leaving Carl to clean up. Joan said she'd slept most of the afternoon, that some visitors had stopped by while she was sleeping, but Marie had turned them away. After they ate she decided she'd like to sit out on the terrace through what was left of the daylight.

She sat in the lounge chair, and after he had done the dishes, he sat on the low wall. He tried to feel comfortable with her, but he could not. He knew that he would never again be able to feel completely at ease in her presence.

He told her the Ray Walsh story, without letting her know that it had been a most critical point in his career. It had been that poised moment wherein it was decided whether he would go up or down. It seemed shocking to him that the adverse decision could have been made in such a quick and casual way. And he felt slightly sweaty when he thought of how it would have come out had he not been able to improvise a counter proposal that made sense.

And deep within himself he felt a tiny, unfamiliar quiver of excitement when he realized that, should the expanded department work out the way he wanted it to, whoever headed it up—one Carl Garrett—might be the most logical man to consider when Jim Hardy stepped out. It had been a long time since he had felt the stirrings of ambition. Yet it was not unwelcome. Maybe now, at last, he could make the full commitment of his energies and abilities. Maybe he could find it within him to take the destinies of Ballinger with deadly seriousness, become a company man, age forty-two. In thirteen years he would be fifty-five. What could thirteen years of concentrated effort bring? Something better than boredom, perhaps. Much better than the Cindys of the world. Much better than a gray vista ahead, filled with the sterile amplitude of Mrs. Brisbie.

They were both asleep at midnight when the bedroom phone awakened them. Joan picked up the phone as he was reaching for it.

"Hello? Oh, yes, Cindy. What's the matter? All right. Here he is."

He turned on the bed lamp and took the phone from her.

"It's Cindy. She sounds terribly upset."

"Hello, Cindy."

"Carl. Oh, Carl, could you come over, please? Just come over here. Put on a robe and come over, please."

"What's the matter? Cindy? Cindy?" He replaced the phone. "She wants me to come over."

"What could it be?" Joan asked, wide-eyed. "Bucky?"

"It could be."

"Oh, I hope not. I think I could walk over there all right. Should I come?"

"No, honey. You stay right where you are. I'll come back and tell you just as soon as I find out."

But, on the way across the dark lawn in robe and slippers, he knew that it was Bucky. It was inevitable that it should be Bucky. It was the final and irrevocable irony, smelling of a chance fate could not afford to miss.

He tapped on the screen door, pulled it open and walked into the empty lighted kitchen. He heard her quick steps and she came quickly, silently to him, her face a mask that broke apart in her last two steps and then was convulsively hidden in the pocket of his throat and shoulder and jaw. He held her throughout the spasmed sobbing, feeling pity and tenderness, and also an awkwardness. The awkwardness made him feel detached, a bit apart from this woman who, in tragicomic abandon, articulated her great sobs, crying haw haw haw against him, and grinding her round forehead against the angle of his jaw.

When the worst of it was over she whirled away from him and walked into the dark living room, and he followed her. She blew her nose, then stretched out on her side on the couch. He hesitated, then sat on the floor and took hold of her hand.

"Sorry," she said. It was a cold and lost and lonely word.

"Bucky?"

"They called a little while ago. I didn't want him to fly at night. They said he hit power lines. They said . . . it was quick. I . . . did it to him, of course."

"You shouldn't think that way."

"Don't be tiresome, Carl. There's absolutely no rationalization that can keep me from thinking I did it."

"Then say we did it."

She gave a great sigh and her hand flexed in his and then was still again. "We played a nasty little game, didn't we? Compared to this . . . that's all it was. A selfish, diseased little charade. It wasn't even real. But this is real, Carl. This is so very damn real. It's so big and so real I can't even fit my mind around it. I know him so. His hands and his grin, and how noisy he was brushing his teeth, and not being able to take a shower without getting the bathroom awash. Oh, Christ, Carl! What is going to become of me? I'm so damned empty. What's wrong with us? Other people can be silly and naughty without their world going to smash. Why is my luck like this? I loved him and I was just too shallow and silly to be able to keep . . . to be a good guardian of what was his."

"Cindy. Dear Cindy."

"Yes, of course. Dear Cindy. Model wife."

"Don't do that to yourself."

"But where do I go from here? Just where? Where is there any place for me where this didn't happen?"

"I'll have to go over and tell Joan. She's over there worrying about it."

"Of course."

"I'll be right back."

"Don't bother, please."

"Where did it happen?"

"The phone call came from Wichita. It happened near there, in a thunderstorm."

"Who's your lawyer?"

"Lawyer? Bob Eldon. Why?"

"I'll be right back."

He went and sat on Joan's bed and said in a dull tone, "It was Bucky. Flew into a power line near Wichita."

Joan looked stricken. Her eyes filled with tears. She turned away from him and began to cry. He picked up the book and found Bernie Madden's number and phoned him.

Bernie's sleepy and irritable voice answered the phone and became immediately alert when he had identified Carl. "Something wrong with Joan?"

"No, not Joan, Bernie. Cindy Cable. She got word a little while ago that Bucky got killed in his plane. She's pretty ragged. I thought maybe a shot or someth . . ."

"I'll be there in twenty minutes. Line up somebody who'll stay with her, Carl. Don't let Joan try to do it. She isn't up to it."

Carl hung up. "Joan? Bernie says somebody should stay with her. Not you. Who do you think?"

"Wouldn't . . . Molly be good?"

He decided that Molly would be very good. The phone rang a long time at the Raedeks' before Molly answered. She agreed, without hesitation or reservation, to come at once. There was no need for Carl to pick her up. She'd drive herself over.

When he went back over, Cindy was still on the couch. He stood over her and said, "Bernie Madden's coming by to give you something. And Molly Raedek will stay with you."

"How competent and orderly," she said in a small chill voice.

"How about his people? Do they know yet?"

"I don't know. No. I didn't call them."

"I'll do it. Do you have the number?"

"It's on the front of the phone pad. Carl!"

He turned back. "What?"

"Don't tell them your name."

"Why not?"

"Bucky told them your name."

The call went through without difficulty. He placed it person to person to Mr. Cable. He didn't identify himself. Mr. Cable had a deep brassy voice. "I'm sorry to have to tell you in this way, Mr. Cable, but your son has been . . . has had an accident."

"With the airplane?"

"Yes."

"And he's dead."

"Uh . . . yes, sir."

There was a long pause. The connection was so clear that he could hear the man's slow and heavy breathing.

"Where did it happen and who do I contact to make arrangements about the body?"

"It happened near Wichita apparently. Perhaps if you phoned the Wichita police . . ."

"Who are you?"

"Just a neighbor. Cindy isn't . . . wasn't able to make the call."

The brass voice became deeper and stronger, slow and oratorical. "That adulterous woman would not have dared to telephone this house. She broke my son's heart and she killed him." Between his slow words Carl could hear a woman's voice in the background, high and shrill with an unbearable grief. "It may be of no importance to her, but you may tell her that Gilbert telephoned his mother on Sunday and told her what he had learned about his wife. And you may tell her that I will spare no expense in a legal fight to retain custody of Gilbert's children. She is not fit to have them, and should she undertake to oppose me, I shall prove in a court of law that she is a loose woman of bad reputation. Please give her that message. Tell her my son will be buried here. Tell her I cannot prevent her from attending the services, but she will not be made welcome and she will not be permitted to see the children."

The line went dead. Carl hung up and went to the front door and let Molly in. Molly took Cindy into the bedroom. Cindy had become apathetic, spiritless. When Bernie arrived, Carl let him in and pointed out the bedroom. He turned on a floor lamp and sat in an armchair and turned the meaningless pages of a magazine until Bernie came back out.

Bernie came over and sat on the low coffee table. "I loaded her up with happy juice. She's out now. No matter how bad a deal is, if you can pile some sleep on top of it, it takes some of the edge off. Molly has some pills to feed her when she comes out of it. But there's something else. Do you happen to know of any special trouble between Cindy and Bucky?"

"Why?"

"Molly spotted something when she helped Cindy into bed. After she was passed out, Molly told me to take a look. That girl has had the living bejaysus beat out of her, and recently. It would take a special kind of mind or a special provocation to do that much damage to the tender parts of a cutie like Cindy. You have the look of a man with information."

"Bucky did it. With a putter. And then left her for good."

Bernie's smile was ironic. "Maybe he didn't really mean it to be for good. But it sure as hell is now. The usual provocation?"

"Yes."

"Hard to believe it of Cindy. I always cased her for the type that might look available, but definitely isn't. This is going to be bad, Carl. Real bad."

"What do you mean?"

"The death itself would be bad enough. But on top of it she's got a load of guilt that may be a little too heavy for anybody as sensitive as Cindy to carry around. And when the load is too heavy, you escape from it. When existence becomes untenable, you build a new place to live in. A fantasy."

"There's . . . something else too. Bucky told his parents about . . . the provocation and why he was leaving her. The kids are staying with them. I told Bucky's people the news just before you arrived. His father told me they will go to court to retain custody of the kids."

"Brother!" Bernie said. "With the responsibility of the kids she might be gutsy enough to hold herself together." He took off his glasses and began to polish the lenses on his handkerchief. "Got any idea of who the villain of the piece is?"

Carl could not make a sound. He felt as though his throat had closed. Bernie looked at him somewhat crossly. "Well?" And still Carl could not answer. Then Bernie's expression changed. He looked at Carl with growing pity and contempt.

"How can I be so stupid?" he said. "Bucky left his marks on both of you. Joan was out of the way. A golden chance. And you were both stupid enough to get caught." He had lowered his voice so that Molly could not overhear. "Where did he catch you? Right here?"

Carl swallowed the coarse lump in his throat. "In a motel."

"Real juicy. Tabloid material. I wouldn't say you didn't surrender to one very normal impulse, Carl. But I will tell you that I wouldn't want to be in your shoes. What happened to Bucky may be a piece of luck for you. It may mean you can successfully keep Joan from finding out. As her doctor, I wouldn't want her to find out too soon anyway. I've had my foolish moments, but thank God I never ended up with the weight you've got hanging around your neck. If you were a nice normal son of a bitch, it would roll right off you. But I know you well enough to know how hard you take things. Cindy is right in your lap and you know it. And I don't know what the hell you can do. I know what I'm going to do. I'm going to move Cindy to a rest home tomorrow, a nice quiet country-type place where there'll be some canny pros to keep an eye on her until we can know which way she's going to go."

He held his glasses up to the light, then slipped them on, stood up. He looked at Carl and said, "What a hell of a simple world it would be if you and I didn't have that streak of the goat in us."

After Bernie left, Molly came out of the bedroom. "She hasn't moved a muscle since she went under," she said. "I never saw anything happen so fast. Does this joint serve beer?"

They went into the kitchen. Carl took two beers out of the refrigerator and they drank them in the breakfast booth.

"Bernie ask you about the ghastly condition of her little sit-down?"

"Yes. I . . . don't know anything about it."

"I wouldn't call Cindy the type wife that needs to be beaten. I've heard it does improve some of them. I could make a list. I wouldn't have put Cindy on it. Unless, of course, our Eunice came up with the incriminating facts and handed them to Bucky."

"I suppose."

"Wouldn't it be hell, Carl, if Bucky had caught her out of line, beaten her, and then flown off and clobbered himself? What a fine terminal memory for what appeared to be a pretty good marriage, as marriages go around the Crescent Ridge section."

"It would be a bad thing."

"All right," she said. "I could sit here all night and try to pump you and never get a thing. I brought a nightie and I'm going to crawl into the adjoining bed. Give my love to your Joan and tell her I'll pop over as soon as I get a chance. The last time I saw you, pet, you were very drunk, and your face was in better condition."

"I fell."

"Pet, did you fall heavily against Bucky's right fist?"

He slowly poured the last of his beer into the glass and watched the head form itself. "Molly, I don't want to be rude. I don't want to accuse you of anything you have no idea of doing. But one very important thing right now is that Joan should not be disturbed or upset by having . . . odd coincidences called to her attention."

She was very still, and then she put her hand on his. "You poor guy! I was afraid it was true. I was hoping it wasn't."

"It's beginning to look as if I should have hired one of those skywriting outfits and published a running account at about ten thousand feet."

"You aren't the type for intrigue, pet. Neither is Cindy. You were silly clumsy lambs. And you've done a hell of a lot of damage."

"But Joan . . ."

"Don't fret about that. She won't get a clue from me. I'll alert Marie in the morning to brush off the Stockland woman firmly if she tries to show." The phone rang. He hurried in and answered it.

It was from the news room of a Hillton paper. The man on the line was persistent. Carl gave him as much information about Bucky as he could, and when the reporter wanted to talk to the widow, Carl told him that was impossible.

He said, "Mrs. Cable wasn't given any details of the accident. Do you have any more?"

"Just what we got on the wire. He took off into bad weather last night, and he couldn't climb over a storm front, apparently, so he tried to sneak under it into Wichita before it closed down on him. He could have been hedgehopping and didn't see the power line, or a downdraft could have pushed him into it. When he hit, he went off like a torch."

"Will that be in the paper, the part about burning?"

"Not like I said it, but it will be in."

"Thanks. I wouldn't want Mrs. Cable to see that."

"It won't get any big spread. It'll be a small page one box maybe, but probably page one of the second section. We got a cut of him here from back when he won some kind of sales award."

Carl said good night to Molly and crossed the back yards. He paused near the red maple and touched the bark with his hand, and had a sudden furious and ridiculous impulse to get the hatchet from the garage and cut it down.

Joan was asleep with the light on when he walked into the bedroom, but she awoke immediately. He went and brushed his teeth again, and when he was in bed with the light out he told her how it had been, and what had been done.

He was awake long after she had gone back to sleep, unable to relax, unable to steer his mind away from Cindy. It was impossible to avoid thinking of it all as punishment for evil, to avoid the superstitious feeling that some implacable fate had meted out this penalty for evil. Yet the penalty seemed out of proportion to the sin. Death and the lost children and the threat of madness. Just as he was finally drifting into sleep he remembered his forgotten promise to call the kids and tell them their mother was home and doing well. And that kept him awake for another half hour, thinking of the effect on the kids should Joan learn of his affair with Cindy. He did not imagine they would separate. But the warmth and closeness and the trust would be gone. They could go through the motions, but the children would not be deceived. It would be a different kind of house, a different kind of family. Had it been a quick and careless thing involving an unknown woman in a far place, it might have made a flaw in the marriage that in time would become imperceptible. But this was too close. And, from Joan's viewpoint, too humiliating. She would remember both of them visiting her in the hospital, and she would feel that they had made a fool of her. She would remember Cindy welcoming her home, Cindy looking so radiant, his lie about the fall, his lie about Gil Sullivan. All his lies. And she could never really believe any statement, no matter how vehement, that she had not been betrayed right here in this house, in this place upon which she had expended so much care and thought and love. It would be soiled for her. Beyond repair. With the empathy that can be attained in darkness, he put himself in her mind—and found how easily he could despise Carl Garrett.

He checked with Molly before he went to work on Wednesday morning. Cindy had awakened at six. She had acted so remote and listless that it had made Molly uncomfortable. She had given Cindy two of the pills and she was sleeping again. She seemed sound enough asleep so that Molly came over to the house with him to see Joan for a few minutes and quietly instruct Marie about what visitors should be permitted. Carl reminded Molly about disposing of the morning paper. He had read the short item in a page one box at breakfast: "Gilbert Cable, aged 32, local resident and sales executive, met flaming death at eleven-forty last night when his private single-engine aircraft struck high tension lines fifteen miles northeast of Wichita, Kansas, on the outskirts of the village of Potwin, and threw half of Butler County into darkness. A scorched briefcase thrown clear of the crash provided provisional identification until, through the registration numbers of the airplane, it was found that he had obtained flight clearance at the Hillton Airport at seven-thirty yesterday evening. Mr. Cable was traveling alone on a routine business trip in the private aircraft he used to cover his large territory, and it is believed that bad weather conditions were a contributing factor. He is survived by . . ."

EIGHTEEN

Dr. Madden moved Cindy Cable to the Proctor Rest Home in the pleasant hilly country twelve miles west of Hillton on Wednesday afternoon. Molly Raedek closed the Cable house at 12 Barrow Lane, and left the keys with Joan.

On Wednesday Carl Garrett was able to work with a concentrated attention that he would not have thought possible. But he took little satisfaction in being able to do so, as he realized that it was a way in which he could avoid any thought about anything but the work at hand, and thus became a desirable type of oblivion. And he suspected that such intensity might well become habitual with him from now on.

At four in the afternoon he phoned Bob Eldon at his downtown office in Hillton and made an appointment for five-thirty. Bob said, "It's a damn shame about Bucky. He was one of those guys you think of as indestructible. I've been trying to get in touch with Cindy but without luck so far."

"Dr. Madden put her in the Proctor Rest Home. She isn't in very good shape."

"That's a damn shame. Bucky's affairs are in pretty good order. It won't be much of a chore to wind up the estate. The Hillton Bank and Trust is named in the will as executor, and there's nothing that should present any problem to the probate court. There really isn't much to be gained by an appointment at this stage, Carl."

"There's something you don't know about."

"Oh. Well, then, I'll be right here at five-thirty."

Carl phoned Joan and told her he would be late, and arrived at Eldon's office on time. It was a large law firm and most of the offices had emptied out by that time. The receptionist was just leaving as Carl arrived. She told him to go on back, the third door on the left. Mr. Eldon was expecting him.

Bob Eldon, the Eldon of Conway, Bright, Carey and Eldon, was a man who managed to look much closer to thirty than to his actual age of forty-four. He was lean and elegant and blond, with a small blond mustache and weak blue eyes, and a wispy off-hand manner that was in sharp contrast to the quickness of the hidden mind. He came around his desk and shook hands with Carl and seated him in a leather chair beside the desk.

"Hell of a note," he said.

"I know. Can you tell me how well fixed he left Cindy without violating any confidences?"

"She won't be hurting. Bucky made good money and he was a shrewd man with a buck. His insurance program was sound and he's covered for the kind of accident he had. He made a new will recently, and it's set up to allow a minimum tax bite. I know he recently set up educational policies for the kids. I don't know how much stock he has, but I know he was buying it carefully. She should come out of it, all things considered, somewhere in the neighborhood of six thousand a year, which is pretty damn good for a man of thirty-two to leave her. The bulk of it will be from his heavy insurance program. She'll have enough to raise the kids and see them through school. And I wouldn't make any bets about her not marrying again. Now what is this I don't know about?"

Carl hesitated, and said, "It's . . . pretty personal. And unpleasant."

"And a privileged communication. So don't sweat."

He told the story. He told it haltingly at first, trying to be utterly factual, making no attempt to color it in order to be less hard on himself. When he stood up and went to the window and talked while he watched the traffic three stories below, he found the words came easier. He repeated as accurately as possible Bucky's father's pronouncement, and Bernie Madden's pessimistic appraisal of Cindy's potential condition. He was glad when it was over. He sat in the chair again. He avoided Bob Eldon's eyes. His face felt hot.

"A very gaudy little tale, Carl. You both seem a little miscast somehow. What's your problem?"

"Can she get her kids away from them?"

"Some of that will depend on how shrewd Mr. Cable's lawyer is, and how much detail Bucky told them over the phone, and how much they remember of it."

"What do you mean?"

"It sounds as if Bucky was crucifying himself by giving the gory details of how he came to be wearing the horns. Suppose he mentioned the name of the motel. If I happened to be working for Mr. Cable, I would employ a reliable investigation firm to get the facts, the motel registration, a statement from the manager, a statement from the state cops who took down your name and address, a statement from that doctor. I'd want a transcript of telephone company records to show exactly when Bucky called his parents. Through the statements of witnesses, I'd get a positive identification of Cindy as the woman in the picture. Then, with all my ammunition in hand, I'd pay a call on Cindy. I'd tell her that if she wants to avoid a stink, she can sign this harmless little paper that relinquishes her children to their grandparents. If she doesn't want to sign, we will petition the court for custody of the children, claiming their mother is an immoral influence, and make a stench that will kill shrubbery for miles around."

"And would they get the kids?"

"They might. And they might not. It would depend on the judge. In such cases there are many judges who feel that small children are better off with their natural mother, particularly if it can be shown, as Cindy can show, that she can support them adequately. Also, the attitude of the children is considered. But on the other hand the judge might be one of those self-styled men of unbending honor who justify a cruel and inequitable decision on the basis of moral righteousness. However, the chances of her keeping them will be very slight indeed if Bucky confirmed his telephone conversation by a letter to them. The court would be inclined to listen to the wishes of the dead betrayed father rather than to the wishes of the woman who betrayed him. We can hope such a letter wasn't written."

"Do you think . . . Cindy should have them?"

"Of course."

"Is it possible that they could dig up any other blemishes on Cindy's record?"

"I . . . I don't know. She had an affair before she was married. I believe she lived with the man for a time. In New York."

"But nothing since her marriage that you know of. Except this situation."

"I would swear there hadn't been anything else."

"If, through the load of guilt Dr. Madden mentioned, Cindy should go off her rocker, it could blow up her chance of getting her kids back."

"Bob, will you . . . see what you can do?"

"I've already started."

"What is there that . . . I could do?"

Eldon studied him for a few moments. "Nothing that you'd care to do, I'm afraid. Nothing that you should be asked to do."

"What do you mean?"

"Suppose it gets to the point of a hearing. With luck it might be a private hearing in the judge's chambers, but we can't count on that. It occurred to me that I could pull something real wild. I might be able to introduce you as a character witness for Cindy. When you told me your little story, you came through strongly as a decent and troubled and penitent man. You are certainly no wolf. You might make exactly the right impression that would swing it her way. But you say your wife doesn't know, and it's possible she may never find out. Suppose it was an open hearing. She'd have to know. It would clobber her, and maybe clobber you in your job. You can't tell when a corporation will turn righteous. But I won't ask you to do that, Carl. It's too damn much to ask of any man."

"What will you do next?"

"Talk to Cindy and get her okay to go ahead. Then look up the law and find out how other decisions went. Get the actual machinery clear in my mind. Maybe we should attack, and petition for the immediate return of the children to their rightful mother. I'll decide that after I do the research. This custody of minor children is a poorly defined and unpleasant area of the law. It could be that such an action on our part might result in the children being turned over to a public institution until such time as the question of custody can be determined. And if it dragged on too long, it might put quite a deep mark on those kids. But, on the other hand, maybe the old boy will reconsider."

"If you'd heard him, you'd know that will never happen."

Eldon took his hat, closed his office door and walked down the hallway with Carl and went down in the elevator with him. They paused for a moment on the sidewalk. Eldon punched him lightly on the biceps and said, "It isn't the end of the world, Carl. I admit this has its seamy side, but compared to another case I'm on, this one is as remarkable as a garden party, believe me."

"I want to be the client in this thing, Bob. I mean I want to pay for it."

"You're not a party with a direct interest. She'll be my client. But I'll let you pay if you feel you need that sort of a gesture."

After Carl and Joan had dinner, Carl phoned Bernie Madden and asked him how Cindy was and when he could see her.

"I wouldn't advise it right now. She's pretty withdrawn. I'll be in touch and I'll phone you."

"Bob Eldon wants to see her about some legal problems."

"They'll have to wait. She's my patient and I'll decide whom she can see and when."

Bucky was buried in a family plot in Battle Creek on Friday morning. Joan found the small announcement in the Hillton paper, requesting that flowers be omitted.

Joan was gaining in strength each day. She had begun to talk about how soon she could let Marie go so they could have the house to themselves. She worried constantly about Cindy, and wrote long and careful letters to the kids telling them of Bucky's death.

On Saturday morning, while Carl was clipping the hedge, Bernie Madden phoned and said, "Our new miracle drugs for the mentally disturbed don't seem to be performing any miracles. I just came back from Proctor. Bill Suthern out there is a hell of a good man. He can still reach her, and get limited responses, but he has the feeling she's getting away from him. He knows all the facts. He had to be told, of course. We think you should take a run out there this afternoon. It's a calculated risk. It may do some harm, but Bill thinks it's a chance worth taking."

"What do I do?"

"Talk to Dr. Suthern when you get there."

He told Joan what Bernie wanted him to do.

"But why you, Carl? I mean we're good friends and all, but I'd think that Molly or me would be better."

"It's Bernie's idea."

"It's funny he should think you might reach her. Gee, the poor thing. But I guess if anything happened to you, I wouldn't be much better off."

Dr. Suthern was young and brisk and professional. He led Carl across the grounds and pointed at a bench under a shade tree a hundred yards away. Cindy sat on the bench. A woman in white sat beside her, reading a magazine.

"The attendant is instructed to leave you alone with her, Mr. Garrett. Try to get any response you can. Anger her if you can. Think of her as somebody slowly drowning who refuses to take the first stroke toward shore. If she should become violent, and I consider that most unlikely, the attendant will be observing you from a distance."

As he approached the bench he was shocked at Cindy's appearance. Her features had an uncharacteristic heaviness about them. She sat perfectly still, hands in her lap, looking with dull unfocused eyes at the grass fifteen feet in front of the bench. Her lips were parted and when he came close enough to see the string of saliva at the corner of her mouth, he felt as though his heart had turned over.

The gray-haired attendant stood up and said, as though speaking to the deaf, "There's a visitor for you, dear. A nice man has come to see you. Isn't that nice, dearie?"

Cindy made no response. The attendant took out a handkerchief and dabbed the spittle from the corner of Cindy's mouth, shrugged expressively at Carl and walked away. He sat beside her, turned toward her, looked at her wooden profile and did not know what to say.

"Cindy. Cindy, this is Carl." She did not respond. He sat on his heels in front of her so that she was looking into his face. He thought he saw a tiny shift of expression in her eyes, but then they were as dead as before.

"You can hear me," he said. "You're hiding, but you can hear me. Don't keep on hiding, Cindy. If you keep on hiding, they will take Bobby and Bitsy away from you forever. They'll take them away while you're hiding down in there, and you'll never see them again. You'll never see Bobby and Bitsy again."

He waited but there was no response.

"You have to wake up and fight, or you'll never see them again."

And he saw a tightness around her eyes. The dulled lips moved and she said in a whisper that was as faint as a sigh, "Please."

"They're your kids, Cindy. What a lousy life for them, living with old people who will teach them to hate their mother."

"No," she said, with more strength.

"But you'd rather hide and feel sorry for yourself. You'd rather be gutless. It's easier for you. You don't want to fight to keep them."

The heavy-featured look disappeared slowly. And her eyes became intent and aware and fully awake. "I want them!" she said with passionate conviction. "They can't have them!"

"Then wake up and start fighting."

She stood up so abruptly and started away so quickly that she caught him unaware. He caught up with her at the same time the attendant did. Cindy stopped and said to the attendant, "Let go of me. You're hurting my arm. What do you want?"

"Now where were you going, dearie?"

Cindy looked around at the lawns and the brick buildings and said, "I'm going after my kids. I can't stay here any more. I've got to go find my babies."

"Now you come on along with Clara, dearie, and we'll get you all fixed up and packed and everything so we can let you go find your children."

Carl waited twenty minutes in the waiting room before Dr. Suthern returned from examining Cindy. He looked coldly pleased.

"It worked the way Dr. Madden and I hoped it would. I was hesitant to attempt electro-shock at this stage. We don't know where she had withdrawn to but I suppose that in one sense she was mending while she was away from . . . our too real world. If it is convenient, I would like to have you visit her tomorrow. At about two?"

"I'll be here, Doctor."

Cindy was composed and rational on Sunday. She acted very tired, but her mind was clear. She made no reference to any feeling of guilt or blame for what had happened. She wanted to know what Bob Eldon had said, and what would happen next, and when she could bring Bobby and Bitsy home.

"Once Bob fixes it up, I can go get them in the car. Where is the car?"

"He'd left the key at the air terminal. The airport people brought it back to the house last Thursday."

"And today is Sunday. I have to remember that. Sunday the day . . . twenty-eighth. They're being stupid here. They won't let me out until Tuesday, they say. I'm perfectly all right and I keep telling them so. Tell Bob to come and see me, please."

Cindy Cable came home on Tuesday. On Wednesday Joan felt well enough to cut Marie to two days a week to do the heavier work around the house. By Thursday Carl was certain that the arrangement with Ray Walsh was going to work smoothly, efficiently and well.

It was on Thursday evening, after dinner, that Joan said, "Put your paper down a minute, dear."

"Yes?"

She had put her sewing aside. "Cindy has put their house on the market."

"She has?"

"She doesn't seem to have very definite plans of where she'll go. All she can think of is getting the children back. She can't seem to think beyond that point. And I certainly can't understand why Bucky's parents should try to keep her own children away from her. It's absolutely ridiculous. Cindy is odd, of course, but she's been awfully good with those kids. Can you understand why they're making such a fuss?"

"No, dear."

"Cindy doesn't come over here at all during the day like she used to. And I'm beginning to feel uncomfortable about going over there. It isn't that she's unfriendly. She's just sort of . . . polite to me when I stop over. It isn't casual any more. It makes me uncomfortable."

"I guess she's under a strain."

"I keep having the feeling that she's keeping something from me. I think it has something to do with the children. I've sort of hinted, but nothing happens. If she's in some kind of trouble she should tell her friends, so they can help her."

"I guess it's just that Bucky's folks never approved of her."

"I think they're very stuffy people. Cindy is a fine person."

"She certainly is."

"Even though they're making all this trouble about the children, Cindy packed a box with a lot of things of his, some of his boyhood things, you know, and shipped it to them because she thought they might like to have them."

"That was nice of her."

"She's been going through everything, deciding what to keep. She gave me a pipe to give you."

"What?"

Joan went and got the pipe and brought it to him. It was a dark briar in a fitted box. It had a wide silver band around the stem. It was obviously expensive, and brand new.

"It's nice, but . . ."

"His birthday would have been in August and she got it a month or so ago, she said. She wondered if you'd have any use for it and I said I thought you would. I think it was very expensive, that's such a nice case for it. And you never smoke a pipe any more. It would be better for you, darling, than all those cigarettes. I wish you'd try to switch over to a pipe. I like to see you smoke a pipe. And I like the smell."

"I might give it a try."

"She was going to have his initials put on the band, but she hadn't gotten around to it. She said you might want to come over and look at his fishing tackle and see if there's anything you could use. I told her you never were much of a fisherman. Do you think you might want any of it?"

"I guess not."

"I'll tell her, then. She thinks she'll give it to Ted Raedek, probably. Carl, what's wrong with you?"

"What do you mean?"

"You seem . . . so far away, I can't seem to get anywhere near you. Ever since I got back from the hospital, you've been . . . sort of gloomy and remote. It's almost as if you're being . . . polite the way Cindy is."

"I've been working pretty hard on the new lineup in the office."

"I know you have."

"I'm sorry I'm not more company."

"It's almost like . . . being alone in the house." Her voice trembled slightly.

"You're not alone. I'll . . . try to do better."

"I don't want to be something you have to do something better about. I'm not an object or a problem in endurance or something, am I? I'm beginning to feel better than I've felt in two years . . . and there doesn't seem to be anybody to enjoy it with. I wish the kids were home."

"It won't be long now."

"Please pick up your paper and start reading again. That would be much better than having you sit there and look at me with all that patience."

She left the room. He thought of going after her, then picked the paper up and began to read again.

Bob Eldon phoned him Friday afternoon when he was in conference. He phoned Eldon back at four o'clock and asked him if he could stop by the office at five-thirty.

Bob's manner was less languid than usual. He was direct, intent and very serious.

"We've got the hearing set up, Carl. For Wednesday next at ten in the morning, before a Judge Howard."

"Here?"

"No. Battle Creek. A man named Quickling has been handling our side of the case from there. I'll drive Cindy over on Tuesday and we'll have a conference with Quickling and stay over for the hearing. The Cables will appear with their legal counsel and the kids."

"How does it look?"

"From what we can find out, not good. They'll appear prepared to show proof that Cindy spent four consecutive nights in a motel with a man who was not her husband and who had registered them as man and wife under an assumed name. All we've got to depend on is the attitude of the kids, our proof that Cindy can support them, and the impression Cindy will make."

"Will it be a private hearing?"

"Yes. Judge Howard isn't the sort of man to yearn for that kind of publicity. If it goes the way the Cables want it to go, nothing will be heard of it. But if Cindy wins, there's nothing to keep Cable from announcing his wish to appeal the decision to the press. It would appear that Bucky wrote no letter to them. They will try to claim that it was Bucky's wish that they had the children. That statement, of course, is unsubstantiated and under more formal circumstances could not be admitted as evidence. But in an informal hearing such as this, the judge will want to listen to it even if it is hearsay."

"You're not very optimistic."

"No, I am not. The Cables have sufficient money, a nice home, a full-time servant. Cindy is a woman alone. If she had possession of the children I would be more optimistic in being able to prevent them being taken from her. But it will be considered that she turned them over to the Cables for practically the whole summer. Thus it can be implied that she considered the Cable home a suitable place for them to be for quite an extensive time."

"I asked you before and I'll ask you again. Can I be of help?"

"I've talked to Dr. Madden and a Dr. Suthern about Cindy. It alarmed me that she should be so completely and utterly confident that the children will be turned over to her. She can't imagine anything else happening. To use Dr. Suthern's word for it, her conviction is obsessional. Both doctors assure me that if the children are given into her custody as their natural mother, she will handle them well, and be a perfectly balanced person. But they say that if it should go the other way, there might be a most unfavorable prognosis. They think she'll go back over the edge, and go so far they won't be able to reach her."

"What do I have to do?"

"I won't ask you to go over there with us. I won't ask a man to turn himself into a martyr. I refuse to work on your sense of guilt. I told Dr. Madden that and he agreed with me. If we should be unlucky and Mr. Cable should be indiscreet enough, a wire service could pick this up. It has all the elements of a story that could make this whole situation notorious. You must bear in mind your responsibilities to your wife and your own children. Also you must know that my little device might fall flat and do Cindy more harm than good."

"But it looks bad enough so that you'd like to take that chance."

"I'd like to hope that Judge Howard is sufficiently human to understand how proximity and accident and opportunity entered into this, and how it became a very human lapse more easy to understand than forgive."

"Does Cindy know about your idea?"

"I brought it up. She flatly refused to permit it. She told me I should not make such a proposal to you. She said it wasn't necessary anyway. Who ever heard of taking children away from their own mother?"

"Bob, I . . ."

"Don't say anything. Right now you're under pressure. Don't give me any kind of an answer. If you feel you have to do it to . . . get right with yourself, phone me Monday. If I don't hear from you I will understand perfectly, and believe me, nobody will condemn you. It would be one of the most difficult things imaginable. I would try to give you every chance to run through the whole thing. I can't prevent your being questioned, however. And that would be rougher than you can imagine. Think it over over the weekend, Carl. Try to be impartial with yourself. Think of where your true duties lie."

On Saturday they drove to the camp and saw the kids.

He slept very little on Saturday night. Eldon had made it so easy. Just don't phone. And Cindy would be moving away. He could put it all out of his mind. Bobby and Bitsy would have a good home with Bucky's people. And, if Cindy was in any danger of losing her mind, did that indicate she would be a reliable mother? Think of the stink that could occur. Lover of adulterous wife appears as character witness for her in child custody case. Husband thrashes lover and wife and is killed in plane crash. Deluxe motel scene of infidelities. Wife of executive who today gave testimony was in hospital at time of four-night affair. Unfaithful wife beaten with putter by husky sales executive.

But there might not be a stink at all. It might not be peddled in the streets to give a nation a knowing smirk.

But wouldn't a man be a fool to risk everything in order to satisfy what most men would consider to be a quaint sense of honor?

And hadn't Bob Eldon maneuvered him most cleverly!

Joan sighed in her sleep and turned over. He went silently out and sat in the dark living room, smoking. Somewhere a puppy was yapping dolefully to be let in. There was a faraway hum of a high airliner. A quick wind rattled the maple leaves and died away.

My house, my wife, my kingdom.

And Cindy sleeps approximately sixty feet away from me, and she would not permit Eldon to call on me for help.

I can't even be sure it would be of any help,

It might be a stupid and unnecessary sacrifice.

By Sunday afternoon he had not been able to decide. He suspected the quixotic impulse. He did not know what he would do.

"I would like to be taken for a ride," Joan said. "It's a lovely day, honey."

"Okay, where would you like to go?"

"Anywhere. I'm just tired of watching you pace around here like a bear with a sore tail."

"How soon?"

"Right now. Why don't you take me out and show me where it was that you fell and hurt yourself?"

He stood frozen for a moment and then said, "Sure. My favorite little bridge."

He did not want to talk on the way out. He did not know what to say to her. He could not imagine ever having anything in particular to say to her. He found a ball game on the car radio. She seemed content to sit and look at the countryside.

He drove through Aldermon and found the turn to the right and found the little park, turned in and turned off the

motor. A family with three small children had apparently just
finished a picnic and were getting ready to leave. They were
burning papers and loading equipment back into an elderly
sedan. They smiled in casual friendliness at Carl and Joan.

"Over this way," he said.

She walked down the path beside him and he stopped
when they reached the bridge.

Joan stared at it and said, indignantly, "Why, it's criminal
practically to have a thing like that around. They ought to
fix it or tear it down."

"I most heartily agree."

She moved closer to it. "Where did you fall, exactly?"

This would do it, he knew. This would make it all visual
to her, and he would be forever safe.

"I walked out to where . . ." And he stopped.

"What, darling? How far?" She turned and looked up at
him. "You look so strange! Are you sick?"

"No."

"How far did you walk out?"

"Joan. Joan, I can't. God help me, I can't."

"You're as pale as death! And I don't understand."

"Come back where we can sit down."

The elderly sedan was gone. They were alone in the raggedy little park with its three defeated picnic tables, the
smoking fireplace with rusted grill. They sat at one table, on
the attached benches facing each other. He held her hands
and looked at her and did not realize how tightly he was
holding until he saw the pain change the shape of her mouth.
He loosened his hold. He saw a changed expression in her
eyes, a look of awareness.

"It's about time, isn't it?" she said.

"What do you mean?"

"I can't think things the way you do. I can only feel them.
I don't know what you want to tell me. But I think it's going
to hurt, and I think it's about time. I'm tired of . . . being
alone."

"It will hurt. I hope I can keep from begging."

"I might not mind begging."

"I love you. I hope that's a good way to start. Try to keep
hanging onto that, if it will do any good."

"You're really talking to me, aren't you? To me. To Joan."

"There's something I have to do. Something difficult and
unpleasant and . . . possibly disastrous. I didn't know I had
to do it, that there was no way to get out of it, until I tried

to follow through on the lie about the bridge, and I couldn't. The words stuck. I have to go away for a day and do this bad thing that I brought on myself, and then come back if you want me. But before I go away I have to tell you how it all was, and try to explain what can't be explained."

"The lie about the bridge?"

"And a hundred other cheap, stupid, insulting lies."

And he began to tell her, starting at the beginning, restraining her when she tried to pull her hands away from his. And it was not long before she had lowered her head so that he was talking directly at the top of her brown hair, and he hoped she would keep her head that way because it made it just a little bit easier. His voice was quiet in the park, and a sun-made coin crept across the weathered wood. He saw her first tear fall and soak into the silvery gray of the wood, next to a carved heart that encircled two sets of initials. He stopped for a moment when the tear fell and then went on, and saw the others fall and did not pause.

And after an endless time it was over, and he had told her everything, and why he had to go away. "I love you," he said, and then listened to the long silence.

He knew that soon she would raise her head and look at him. And he did not know what he would read in her eyes. He knew it could be complete rejection. Or he might see something that could give him cause to hope. Though he knew that it was one of the most important moments of his life, he waited without tension. He felt almost at peace with himself. And very soon he would know.

Carl Garrett sat in the little unkempt park and held his wife's two hands in his.

And after a little while she raised her head slowly and looked into his eyes.